THE SKIES WILL NEVER BE THE SAME...

continued . . .

DEBT OF HONOR

It begins with the murder of an American woman
in the backstreets of Tokyo. It ends in war . . .

"A SHOCKER."   —*Entertainment Weekly*

THE HUNT FOR RED OCTOBER

The smash bestseller that launched Clancy's career—
the incredible search for a Soviet defector
and the nuclear submarine he commands . . .

"BREATHLESSLY EXCITING."   —*The Washington Post*

RED STORM RISING

The ultimate scenario for World War III—
the final battle for global control . . .

"THE ULTIMATE WAR GAME . . . BRILLIANT."
                               —*Newsweek*

PATRIOT GAMES

CIA analyst Jack Ryan stops an assassination—
and incurs the wrath of Irish terrorists . . .

"A HIGH PITCH OF EXCITEMENT."
                               —*The Wall Street Journal*

TOM CLANCY'S

H·A·W·X

WRITTEN BY

DAVID MICHAELS

BERKLEY BOOKS, NEW YORK

THE BERKLEY PUBLISHING GROUP
Published by the Penguin Group
Penguin Group (USA) Inc.
375 Hudson Street, New York, New York 10014, USA
Penguin Group (Canada), 90 Eglinton Avenue East, Suite 700, Toronto, Ontario M4P 2Y3, Canada
(a division of Pearson Penguin Canada Inc.)
Penguin Books Ltd., 80 Strand, London WC2R 0RL, England
Penguin Group Ireland, 25 St. Stephen's Green, Dublin 2, Ireland (a division of Penguin Books Ltd.)
Penguin Group (Australia), 250 Camberwell Road, Camberwell, Victoria 3124, Australia
(a division of Pearson Australia Group Pty. Ltd.)
Penguin Books India Pvt. Ltd., 11 Community Centre, Panchsheel Park, New Delhi—110 017, India
Penguin Group (NZ), 67 Apollo Drive, Rosedale, North Shore 0632, New Zealand
(a division of Pearson New Zealand Ltd.)
Penguin Books (South Africa) (Pty.) Ltd., 24 Sturdee Avenue, Rosebank, Johannesburg 2196,
South Africa

Penguin Books Ltd., Registered Offices: 80 Strand, London WC2R 0RL, England

This is a work of fiction. Names, characters, places, and incidents either are the product of the author's imagination or are used fictitiously, and any resemblance to actual persons, living or dead, business establishments, events, or locales is entirely coincidental. The publisher does not have any control over and does not assume any responsibility for author or third-party websites or their content.

TOM CLANCY'S HAWX

A Berkley Book / published by arrangement with Ubisoft, Ltd.

PRINTING HISTORY
Berkley premium edition / January 2010

ISBN: 978-0-425-23319-1

BERKLEY®
Berkley Books are published by The Berkley Publishing Group,
a division of Penguin Group (USA) Inc.,
375 Hudson Street, New York, New York 10014.
BERKLEY® is a registered trademark of Penguin Group (USA) Inc.
The "B" design is a trademark of Penguin Group (USA) Inc.

PRINTED IN THE UNITED STATES OF AMERICA

10 9 8 7 6 5 4 3 2 1

"FALCON THREE . . . LOENSCH . . . DO YOU HAVE A shot?" Jenna Munrough shouted as she banked her F-16 away from the target. With jammed guns and both of her air-to-air missiles expended, she was out of action. Everything now depended on her wingman.

"Gotta get a lock-on," Troy Loensch said, gritting his teeth. Hitting the Raven was like trying to hit a mouse with a hammer in a dark room. Like most recent jet fighters, the Raven had suppression systems that physically masked the heat signature of the engines. The only way to achieve the radar lock-on necessary to launch heat-seeking missiles against the stealthy aircraft was to get in directly behind it.

As a HAWX Program bird, the Raven was fast—

probably capable of something north of Mach 3—but he knew that his quarry had to slow down to below Mach 1 to deliver his deadly payload against his highest of high-value targets.

Troy could *not* let this happen.

There was no way in hell he could let this happen.

How had it all come to this? After flying, fighting, and proving himself in four brush-fire wars, Troy had joined the HAWX Program to fly the fastest and highest-flying combat aircraft in the world. Now it had come down to his chasing and trying to kill the single fastest and highest-flying aircraft in the HAWX arsenal.

It was the mother of all ironies, but Troy had no time to ponder the sick paradox in which he found himself. He had to kill the damned Raven.

Troy could *not* let the Raven get to its target.

There was no way in hell he could let this happen.

As the two aircraft scissored across the Maryland landscape, Troy knew that if he could coax the other guy into maintaining his defensive turn, rather than reversing and turning the other way, he would have the opening that he sought. But this wasn't working. The other pilot could not be coaxed.

Again and again, Troy turned and watched the other aircraft slip away.

Gotta try something, Troy thought.

As he got behind the other aircraft, and just before the guy reversed his turn, Troy throttled back, allowing him to stem their lateral separation and turn with the Raven.

The two aircraft rocked and rolled, the Raven staying just a split second and a couple of degrees out of the bull's-eye in Troy's heads-up sight. He had to find that opening, that opening to a no-miss shot!

"Lock on now!" Jenna urged. She was barely two miles away, also on afterburner and following Troy into battle.

"Fuck it," Troy shouted. "This is it. Missiles hot!"

"Roger, Falcon Three," Jenna confirmed, angrily wishing that her two Sidewinders had not been eluded by the Raven. "You are a go with missiles hot."

The Sidewinder air-to-air missile had an effective range of around ten miles, but to take a no-miss shot, Troy would have to be a lot closer.

The bad guy still had the advantage. His maneuverability options increased proportionally to his slower speed. Because he had only one vulnerable spot—straight back—any evasive action, no matter how slight, was potentially effective. He could remain on course to his target, weaving slightly, and still interrupt the F-16's lock-on.

Troy watched his lock-on stop and start, flicker and hiccup, like a bad connection on his iPod jack.

There was nothing he could do but put the pedal to the metal and get closer to the Raven.

Seven miles separated the two aircraft.

Rocking and rolling, the Raven raced onward as Troy screamed forward on full afterburner, gaining on him.

Five miles.

When? Troy sweated the decision to shoot. He was almost there. He could ride the lock-on all the way.

Three miles.

Okay, dammit, this is it.

"Fox Two!" Troy shouted.

He felt a slight wobble as the Sidewinder left the rail.

He watched as the Raven banked hard to the left and saw the fast-moving contrail of the Sidewinder arc left.

CHAPTER 1

Northridge, California

"I'LL GIVE YOU *THREE* GOOD REASONS WHY THIS IS A
bad idea!" Carl Loensch growled angrily, holding up his
left hand. "Count 'em."

Of course, Troy could *not* count them.

They weren't there.

His father had left those three fingers in the sands of
Kuwait a quarter century ago on the same day that Troy
was born.

Through the years that Troy was growing up, his
father had almost never mentioned that day when he was
with the 3rd Battalion of the 3rd Marines during the
liberation of Kuwait, or the split second of cartwheeling shrapnel that maimed Carl's hand and killed his best
friend.

During those years, he knew that his father was different, but he was no less a man, no less a father for having just a single finger and thumb on that hand. It was something that was never mentioned, because there was nothing to be said. It just was what it was.

For all those years, his father had never let his disability interfere with his life, nor with his successful career in sales with a major Southern California office supply chain—nor with the time that he spent tossing the football with Troy.

"Count 'em!" Carl demanded.

Troy had rarely heard his father make even a passing reference to his disability. He had never heard his father speak so angrily about it. Carl's stoicism through those years was in such stark contrast to this moment that Troy now felt his body trembling. The star wide receiver for the UCLA Bruins had never felt so caught off guard.

"I've lived the better part of my life knowing that I went through hell on earth in that goddamn desert so my son wouldn't have to . . . *ever* have to . . . put on a uniform and go into a war."

Troy could see tears streaming down his mother's face.

For Barbara Loensch, this was one of the most awful moments of her life. It was certainly one of the worst since those terrible months just after Carl came home. She had been with Carl as he worked through his anger and pain, and she had watched him bottle it up and contain it as their baby grew into a boy. She had watched

Carl reinvent himself as a good father and a better-than-average husband. Now, it was as though it were all coming apart.

"Dad, I really have run out of options here," Troy tried to explain. "My life is kinda coming apart, y'know."

"What the hell do you know about your life coming apart?" Carl shouted. "It's only a friggin' *game!*"

Barbara knew that football was more than just a game to Troy. Ever since he was a little kid, tossing the ball around with his dad, you could tell there was something special. From the moment that he lettered as a freshman in high school, it seemed that everyone realized something special was about to happen when Troy Loensch stepped onto the field.

"Well, Dad, that *friggin' game* was my whole life," Troy shouted. "For the past eight years, my whole life was built around that *friggin' game.*"

After he had gone to UCLA on a scholarship, there had been plenty of talk about Troy's NFL prospects. Last fall, there had been the visits from the scouts. The people from the Atlanta Falcons had taken the whole family to dinner at the Biltmore. The Eagles flew in to woo Barbara's only son. The Broncos came and talked about the wonders of playing in Denver, and the San Diego Chargers visited the modest Loensch home in Northridge *twice*.

It seemed as though a pro career for Troy was just a matter of waiting for the formalities of the NFL draft in April.

Then, in the blink of an eye, things changed.

"Everything I did for those past eight *friggin'* years, built around that *friggin' game*. Now I don't have that *friggin' game*. The whole course of my life has changed."

"Whose fault is that?" Carl asked angrily.

They both knew.

The way the course of Carl Loensch's life was irrevocably altered in Kuwait was out of his control, but Troy had done this to himself.

If he could take it back, he would.

In retrospect, it was an inconsequential remark, but it pissed Troy off big-time.

Lots of punches get thrown in locker rooms. Lots of punches get thrown in locker rooms with minimal consequences. The coaches rant, but hands are reluctantly shaken and incidents are forgotten. This time, however, there was a dislocated jaw and permanent nerve damage.

No amount of anger management counseling could take back the punch that Troy wished he had never thrown.

No charges were filed, and nothing hit the papers about the star wide receiver's indiscretion, but the word got around. The NFL scouts never said anything, but that is the point. They said *nothing*. They stopped calling. The draft came and went.

"You had that one offer . . ." Barbara said, her voice shaking a little.

"The *CFL*?" Troy replied as though his mother had just cursed at him. The goddamn CFL?"

The Saskatchewan Roughriders of the Canadian Football League called, but Troy refused even to consider the humiliation of playing in a second-tier league.

"So you're too good for Canada, and you go out and throw your life away by goin' into the military?" Carl said disgustedly.

Troy almost reminded his father that he himself had once made this same life choice over *his* father's objections. Once Carl had made the decision to become part of the toughest of the tough and join the Marines, there was nothing that his father could say.

Troy almost mentioned this, but he knew that it need not be said.

"Why don't you just get a regular job?" Carl asked.

"It's the Air Force, Dad. It's *Officer* Training School. It's not like I'm joining the Army to be cannon fodder somewhere. This is something that when I get out, y'know, my job prospects are a whole lot better after being an officer . . . you know that . . . you always say that the best hires you've ever made were former officers."

"Yeah, I know," Carl said reluctantly.

The whole family just stood in silence. The venting was over. There was nothing more that could be said.

CHAPTER 2

Pacific Coast Highway, Seal Beach, California

"MAYBE WE SHOULD JUST . . . Y'KNOW . . . GET MARried," Troy Loensch suggested.

"That was the lamest proposal I could ever imagine!" Cassie Kilmer said with mock disgust that hid the real disappointment.

It was a warm Southern California afternoon, and neither of them had any classes. Cassie had suggested that they just go take a long drive down the coast and jump into the surf for a while.

"We've been talking about it since before—" Troy began.

"We've been talking about it since before you decided that you were going to take off and leave me for four years." Cassie laughed, finishing his sentence.

"You're the only one who supported my decision at all."

"I supported your decision, big guy, because I thought it was the right thing for *you* at this point in your life."

"So, does that mean you don't *wanna* get married?"

"No, it just means that I don't wanna get married before you go off for four years to fly jets or whatever you do in the Air Force."

"I thought you've been saying that you thought this was the right thing for me to do with my life?"

"Yeah," Cassie said. "I think it's the right thing for *you* to do at this place in *your* life, but it isn't the right thing for *our* lives . . . right now."

Cassie and Troy were at a crossroads in their intertwined lives. In a matter of weeks, they would both graduate from UCLA and step into a distinctly different phase in which their lives would no longer be intertwined. They had long since considered themselves a couple, and with that, there had been a comfortableness and talk of commitment, of permanence and of marriage. Yet, as much as these things were a topic of many conversations, they remained just that. Each knew that with graduation, their lives would change, and both of them wondered whether there would be a place in those changed lives for the comfortableness they had enjoyed, and the permanence they had once craved.

"Does that mean . . . ?" Troy asked as he stopped at a red light, pushed up his sunglasses, and looked at Cassie.

"That you wanna, y'know . . . does this mean you wanna break up?"

"No, big guy, I don't wanna break up with you . . . It's just that I want to marry a guy and be with a guy . . . I want to not have you gone or out of town for the first four years I'm married to you. We talked about getting married when we both thought you'd sign with some franchise or other . . . y'know . . . and we'd be together somewhere."

"Lotsa guys in the Air Force are married—"

"I *sure* as hell don't wanna be living in some barracks somewhere."

"We shoulda talked about this before you talked me into joining up."

"I didn't talk you into joining up," Cassie said crossly. "*You* talked you into it. You wanted to have some purpose in life, some big way for you to shine like the star you've always been . . . I just agreed with you."

Troy pulled the car into the parking lot at Huntington State Beach, and they both got out. He looked at Cassie as she took off her sunglasses and marveled at the way her tan torso slithered out of her T-shirt.

"What are you staring at, big guy," Cassie asked as Troy admired her body in the skimpy, coral-colored two-piece. Even after knowing her for nearly three years and sleeping with her for almost as long, he just couldn't keep his eyes off that body.

"You're really awesome." He smiled.

"Don't you forget it, big guy." She winked, playfully snapping at him with her beach towel.

She allowed him to grab her and relished the feel of those wide receiver arms as he wide-received her.

As she rewarded his bear hug with a wet and passionate kiss, she thought about how much she would miss him. She resented not having tried harder to talk him out of joining the Air Force, but she realized that it would have been impossible. She knew, as he did, that it was a decision toward which the momentum of his life had propelled him. She also admitted to herself that it was something that could not be altered without a change in his essence that neither of them could accept.

She wondered—as she imagined that he was wondering too—how the relationship they shared would look as it emerged from those four years.

She gently touched his cheek and saw him start to relax. For now, though, there was only *now*.

CHAPTER 3

Colville National Forest

LIEUTENANT TROY LOENSCH WAS IN THE MIDDLE OF the wilderness, seventy miles north of Spokane, Washington, and running for his life.

Over the dozen months since he'd put his future with Cassie Kilmer on hold, his life had gone through so many twists and turns that he found it hard to remember the long-ago simpler days.

Not that he had time to think about it. At the moment, there was no opportunity for reflection. Troy was on a slippery mountainside with a sprained wrist, a complaining companion, and an unknown number of bad guys on his trail. He was wet, cold, and hungry. During four years of football, his body had been tested and he had triumphed. But out here, there were no time-outs, no locker room, no ice chests full of Gatorade, and no steak dinner at the end of a couple of hours of exertion.

"Man, this is awful," grumbled Lieutenant Halbert Coughlin as he stumbled up the hillside. "How far you suppose we've come?"

Walking up a forty percent grade on wet rock and mud was bad enough, but with the tangle of brush, half the time you couldn't see where you were stepping. It seemed like there was as much slipping and falling as stepping.

"Not far enough," Troy replied. "We gotta make the top of the ridge before dark."

"Shit, man," Coughlin replied, looking up the slope. "I don't see how . . ."

"We made it this far, Hal," Troy said, taking a deep breath and looking back into the spruce-choked chasm from which they had been climbing all day. "At least it's not a hot day."

As far as the eye could see, it was a vast landscape of heavily wooded hillsides, with fog nesting in the valleys and a light drizzle blurring the more distant, higher mountains of the Kettle River Range.

Over the past year, Troy had aced the Air Force Officer Qualifying Test (AFOQT), and despite being a C-plus student at UCLA, he had come through the more than three months of Officer Training School (OTS) near the top of his class—a class in which four out of five who started didn't make it out at all.

Flight training at Laughlin AFB in Texas had gone well for Troy, who had cleared all the hurdles and qualified for a coveted slot in the track wherein fledgling pilots graduate as fledgling *fighter* pilots.

Then, these fledgling fighter pilots were dropped into combat survival training at Fairchild AFB near Spokane. After a couple of days of deceptively cushy classroom work, they suddenly take you up over the Colville National Forest in a C-130, tell you to survive, and kick you out the door—and there's one more thing, you also have to evade capture by the teams of 22nd Training Squadron instructors who play the role of bad guys for the fledglings.

The Combat Survival, Evasion, Resistance, and Escape (SERE) exercise is just as difficult as it is straightforward. All you have to do is parachute into a national forest and walk out. The not-so-easy parts include the terrain and the fact that under the best of conditions, it's a four-to-five-day hike.

To be captured means four days of browbeating interrogation in a mock POW camp. Here, the mock bad guys from the 22nd were tasked with tormenting their captives with experiences that simulated the worst that might be inflicted upon them in a real prison camp. The point of SERE is to prepare downed pilots to be captured, but most of the people who go through it do their damnedest *not* to be captured.

A lot fewer than four out of five who start actually evade capture—almost nobody ever does.

Most get caught.

"We better get going," Troy said. "It's gonna be dark soon."

"Man, I just need to rest awhile longer," Hal Coughlin complained. "We been climbing this ridge all day."

"So have they," Troy said, nodding at their unseen foe, who were somewhere below them on the slope. "And they aren't stopping for anything until they catch us. They're better equipped than us, and they know this country like the backs of their hands. They know all the shortcuts, and they probably know where we are."

"How could they see anything in all this clutter?"

"I bet they do," Troy said grimly. "I'll bet you ten bucks they got their binocs locked on us right this minute. If we get across that ridge, we'll be out of sight. We'll also be going down while they're still going up. We can move faster than them."

"Maybe we should just let 'em catch us?" Coughlin suggested. "They'd have to feed us . . . I'm starved . . . wish we hadn't lost all our gear . . . and rations . . . in that stream yesterday. Even an MRE would taste good right now."

"Shut up, you're making me hungry." Troy laughed. He *was* hungry, and he *was* so cold that he was shivering and yearning for some calories. The only good thing about the light drizzle was that a drink was always as close as the nearest large leaf.

"Let's just let 'em catch up to us, then. We gave a good go. We've outrun 'em for two whole days. We did pretty good."

"You *want* to go through that interrogation they do when they catch you? Man, that's a bitch."

"*This* is a bitch," Coughlin whined. "It's a cold, wet bitch."

At least Coughlin had gotten up and they were moving again. Every step took them closer to the top and extended the distance between them and those who were trying to capture them. Troy and Hal knew that for those guys, it was a matter of pride to catch every single little bird who was dropped into this wilderness.

"What would your daddy say if he heard you wanted to give up?"

"Don't bring my father into this," Coughlin snarled.

"Sorry," Troy said, half meaning it. He knew that he had touched a nerve—a very raw nerve.

Hal's father, Illinois congressman Halbert Coughlin, Sr., was the chairman of the House Military Appropriations Subcommittee and a powerful force inside the Beltway. He had pulled a lot of strings for Hal through the years, but he could pull no strings out here.

In the early days, Hal relished the fact that strings were pulled on his behalf. He had gotten into a good

Washington prep school and had gotten out of it quite smoothly, despite some hijinks whose consequences his father's string-pulling made go away. Ditto with Northwestern. Hal probably wouldn't have gotten in without the congressman's off-the-record phone calls, and he certainly would not have graduated.

Since being in the Air Force, though, Hal had begun to see and understand the downside of Daddy's influence, and he had come to yearn for the opportunity to do things for himself—on his own.

He craved the opportunity to get out from beneath his father's shadow, to make his own choices, to guide his own life. Most fathers would encourage this, but the Illinois congressman had been more interested in molding his son as he thought best than in allowing Hal to develop as his own man.

The two men resumed the climb without speaking, concentrating on grabbing branches and half-pulling themselves up the slope. As the sopping wet brush got thicker, climbing the hill was almost like swimming upstream.

The injury to his arm that Troy had suffered when he made a bad landing in his parachute two days earlier made this whole process difficult and painful. He wasn't about to complain, though—certainly not to Hal Coughlin.

They made the crest of the ridge before dark, as Troy had hoped, and started down the other side. On this side of the ridge there was significantly less brush, although the grade was slightly steeper. At least they now had gravity on their side. They were headed down, while the bad guys were still climbing.

Nightfall came quickly, its black glove hastened by their descent into thicker forest in the lower reaches of the canyon. Not far below, they heard the rattling of a stream running off the hillside.

"Ouch! I can't see a thing," Hal complained. "Just almost poked out my eye on a branch."

There was a quavering in Hal's voice that he could not control. Troy had been recognizing the signs of hypothermia in his fellow pilot since early afternoon. Crashing through wet brush all day had soaked them to the bone, despite the water-resistant flight suits they were wearing. When darkness came, the plummeting temperatures didn't help.

"Keep moving," Troy said, repeating a phrase that he had been using and abusing all day long.

"Move where? I can't see where I'm going."

"Down," Troy said as he paused to catch his breath.

"Down where?"

"Stop your bitchin', Hal."

"I'm serious, man. How the hell do we know where the hell we're going?"

"We're going down," Troy repeated patronizingly as he nodded toward the nearby sound of running water.

"On this side of the ridge, all the streams lead down to the Kettle River, and the Kettle River leads out of here."

"You want to follow a stream?"

"Yeah, it's the road out of here. Not only that, the noise of running water will mask the sound of running pilots."

They clambered down a few dozen yards and took a look at the stream. It was very dark, but the trace of ambient light from a mist-shrouded moon highlighted the stream well enough for them to make it out as it cascaded down a narrow V-shaped crotch in the hillside.

"There ain't no riverbank on it," Hal exclaimed. "It's too steep. We can't follow it without falling *into* it."

"So that's the way it'll have to be," Troy said impatiently.

"We'll get more soaked than we already are!"

"You more afraid of a little water or a lot of interrogation?" Troy asked. "They're gonna do a Gitmo on your ass if you get caught."

"I say we stop here and build us a fire and dry out and rest awhile," Hal proposed.

"Fucking start a *fucking* fire?" Troy exploded. "That's a beacon for them to catch us! They'll see a fire from a mile away and we're only about a mile from the top of that ridge."

"Fuck *you*, man. We've been walking for two days. We barely slept last night. You're fuckin' nuts. If we go splashing down that creek, the odds are even we'll end up with hypothermia. I'm shivering already, man."

"We're out here to *evade*, man," Troy retorted. "We're not out here to fuckin' *submit*."

"There's no guarantee that if we do that we're gonna get away," Hal insisted.

"I *can* guarantee we *will* get caught if we stay here and start a fire," Troy countered.

It was like debating with one of the wet logs over which they'd been stumbling. It was clear that Hal had reached the end of the line.

Troy looked back up the slope into the wall of damp darkness. The only sound was the chirping and gurgling of the stream, but somewhere up that hill was a team of men with night-vision gear coming toward them. To be captured probably meant days of hell, but none of the people who went through SERE knew exactly what it was like until it happened to them.

Looking up and down the indistinct hillside, and at Hal, Troy knew that he had to make a decision, and make it *now*. If he was going to continue to try to evade, he had to go, and go *now*.

CHAPTER 4

Fairchild AFB

LIEUTENANT JENNA MUNROUGH LOOKED ACROSS THE
room at two dozen people whose lives had been irrevocably altered by their experiences over the past week. It
was a week that seemed like ten.

As she looked at the faces, and as her eyes fell on
empty chairs, she realized that the most graphic aspect
of this morning was not the expressions on those faces,
but the memory of faces not present.

The Combat Survival, Evasion, Resistance, and Escape (SERE) exercise had begun here in this classroom.
It was a classroom like any other; it was a class like any
other. The instructors had a lot to say, and the students
absorbed the class content to varying degrees. Nothing,
though, had prepared them for what was to come.

Many of the more macho guys were cocky, sure that they would get through the exercise with ease. The four women in the group had known that they were perceived as weak links, and they were determined to prove their detractors wrong.

Three of the four had. Jenna was one of this trio.

No woman who had sat in this room a week ago was more determined to triumph than Lieutenant Jenna Munrough. Born in the Ozarks, about fifty miles southeast—as the crow flies—from Fayetteville, Arkansas, she was no stranger to hill country. She had spent the first ten years of her life roaming those hills, and the second ten years of her life yearning to get as far from those hills as she could.

Life in a double-wide is fine when you're seven, but by the time you're seventeen, you start thinking that there has to be a better way.

Jenna had been raised in a world where women are bred not to have ambitions beyond the confines of the community where they were born. A third of the girls in her high school class were mothers by graduation day. Jenna rebelled. Beginning with community college, she had climbed a ladder that led to Air Force Officer Training School, to flight school at Laughlin AFB, and now here. Her yearning to get away from the Ozarks had led her to the rugged wilderness of the Kettle River Range.

It was a hell on earth that not everyone in their section of thirty-two had gotten through—but Jenna *had*.

So too had her partner in the exercise, a young lieutenant from upstate New York. His twisted ankle had meant that they were finally captured on the fourth day, but he acknowledged that without Jenna's ingenuity, they would have been captured the first day.

The mock POW camp had been its own special kind of hell, but being among those who were captured last, they had endured less of it. After the whole experience, there were several dropouts from the program who had simply given up on a career path as a combat pilot.

Only two in the entire section were never captured—Lieutenant Troy Loensch and Lieutenant Hal Coughlin. Loensch had successfully evaded capture and had walked out. He had walked into a gas station on Highway 395 and asked to use the phone. Hal was found on the third day of the exercise, suffering from hypothermia and near death. He wound up in the hospital, and Loensch had wound up with a reprimand for having abandoned his partner.

As she glanced around, Jenna saw Loensch sitting stoically in the back of the room. On one hand she admired him for successfully evading teams of well-equipped troops with night-vision gear, but on the other hand she despised a man who would go off and leave someone who was physically unable to carry on. This especially angered her, given that she had also been with an injured partner.

As the debriefing session concluded and everyone began getting up to break for lunch, his eye caught hers. He stood, deliberately not making eye contact.

"Don't say it," he said. "I've already heard it. I know I screwed up."

"It's good you know that," Jenna said, her eyes drilling into his guilty conscience. "Because you sure as hell *did* screw up . . . big-time. I know what you're thinking."

"What *am* I thinking?"

"You're thinking that crap about how the ends justify the means," Jenna replied in her Ozark drawl. "You're thinking how evading and getting out at all costs is what it's all about."

"And it's not?" Troy parried. "Seems like this deal was named Survival, Evasion, Resistance, and Escape . . . not 'do good for your neighbor.'"

"You're an asshole," Jenna said, shaking her head. "You know that?"

"I know," Troy agreed. "I've been told that, and I cop to it. I am. I know it. Coughlin knows it. But this world is full of assholes and we're in a business where we gotta deal with some of the worst assholes on earth."

"Nice guys finish last, huh?" Jenna said sarcastically.

She wondered whether she would have made it herself if she had abandoned her partner. The idea had occurred to her while she was out there, but she had never seriously entertained the thought.

"Maybe it's just a case of assholes finishing first." Troy shrugged.

Jenna looked into his hard eyes and wondered what it

was about him that would make him react one way, and about her to make her react another.

"What if Coughlin had died up there?" Jenna asked. "How'd that have made you feel?"

"Like shit. It would have made me feel like shit . . . like I was a bigger asshole than I already am."

"So, why'd you do it?"

"I told you," Troy said coldly. "I went up there to survive and evade, so that I wouldn't have to resist and try to escape."

As he watched the slender woman with the short blond hair walk away in disgust, Troy still felt the sting of her words and the tone of her voice with a trace of a hillbilly accent and more than a trace of seething anger.

He had been honest with her. He *did* know that he had screwed up. When he heard how Coughlin had been found, nearly unconscious, only about thirty feet from where they had parted company that night, Troy had felt the sharp sting of guilt ripping into him like a combat knife with an eight-inch blade. Hal would survive and make a full recovery—but it had been touch and go.

He had rationalized his guilt to himself as he had to Lieutenant Munrough.

The mission of the downed pilot really *is* to survive, evade, resist, and escape. If it really had been an operational mission, one pilot who escapes is better than two that are captured.

What probably bothered Troy the most was that in his gut, he really *was* starting to believe in the survival of the asshole at all costs.

Eight years of football had taught him the importance of being and functioning as part of a team.

The past days and months on the track toward being a fighter pilot had taught him that he was alone in the world, and responsible for himself first—and perhaps for himself *last*. His survival, whether in the cockpit or on a cold, miserable mountain, depended only on the asshole that he had become.

CHAPTER 5

Souda Bay, Crete

THEY SAY IT TAKES ONE TO KNOW ONE.

To a lot of people who had crossed him through the years, Illinois congressman Halbert Coughlin, Sr., was an asshole. For someone doing business in the kill-or-be-killed cauldron of Illinois politics, it is almost a prerequisite.

It takes one to know one.

Illinois congressman Halbert Coughlin, Sr., knew an asshole when he saw one, and Troy Loensch, the asshole who had left his son to die on a mountainside in the middle of nowhere, was definitely an asshole.

As if his guilt were not bad enough, Lieutenant Troy Loensch had found out the hard way that having left the son of the chairman of the House Military

Appropriations Subcommittee on a mountainside in the middle of nowhere was definitely something that would change your career path.

One week, Lieutenant Loensch had been fast-tracked for a seat inside the cockpit of an F-22 Raptor, the Air Force's premier air-superiority fighter. The next week, his career had taken a turn for the dark side. Calls had been made, favors called in. Thanks to the strings pulled by Hal's influential father, Lieutenant Loensch would *not*, after all, be getting his assignment to Air Combat Command.

However, the Air Force does not like to throw pilots away, especially ones who slide through SERE without getting caught. Lieutenant Loensch was ordered to report to a nondescript building at Lackland AFB on the edge of San Antonio. On the door was a black and blue shield on which was inscribed a sword crossed with a key under a black chessman. Behind the carefully guarded door marked with this insignia was Troy's new life as part of the secretive Air Force Intelligence, Surveillance, and Reconnaissance Agency (ISR).

The ISR is into a lot of things, some of which you see, some of which you don't. The agency is into a whole host of disparate activities, all of them classified, including signals intelligence, cryptography, cyber warfare, and harvesting intelligence on foreign air and space weapons and systems. Its personnel spend their days in windowless bunkers or flying missions in electronic warfare and reconnaissance aircraft around the world.

The ISR's 55th Wing used to fly Looking Glass, the Strategic Air Command's airborne nuclear command post. Since the first Gulf War, the 55th has flown intelligence, surveillance, and reconnaissance missions in support of the U.S. Central Command.

The first eighteen months of Lieutenant Troy Loensch's career with the 55th were spent in the right seat of an EC-32 electronic surveillance aircraft, a modified Boeing 757 airliner, flying around the world in a white paint job, while the spooks in the back did their snooping.

On his rare trips home, he had confided in Cassie Kilmer that he felt like an airline pilot. She suggested sarcastically that maybe he ought to get out of the Air Force and get a real job. If he felt like an airline pilot, maybe he ought to be one. Of course, he couldn't just quit. She knew that and she told him so. She just found herself caring less and less about what he did. From her perspective, Cassie had made the transition from "the girl left behind" to someone who was living her life regardless of a man who happened to drop in for a few days every nine months or so—and Troy could sense this, even though it remained unspoken.

Their relationship was definitely unraveling. He should have foreseen this when he had joined up—but foresight had not exactly been the strong point in Troy's life.

The last few weeks of *Captain* Troy Loensch's career were spent with the 95th Reconnaissance Squadron, a unit of the 55th Wing based at RAF Mildenhall in the United Kingdom, and flying missions out of Souda Bay on the Mediterranean island of Crete.

"Falcon Four . . . you're cleared for Runway Niner Left."

"Roger, Souda Approach." Troy smiled. "Falcon Four on Niner Left."

In the distance, Crete was a dust-colored patch in the deep blue Mediterranean Sea. He could see the white wake of a ferry headed into the bay, and two miles ahead on the crescent of the Akrotiri Peninsula, he could make out the two runways of the Souda Air Base.

Troy was happy to finally be off the flight deck of the EC-32 and into a fighter. Actually, he was now flying a *modified* fighter, but it was still a fighter. His new airplane was one of several similar Block 40 F-16C Fighting Falcons that had started their combat career flying combat air support in the Balkans but had later been retrofitted for electronic reconnaissance. Smart eavesdropping pods replaced smart bombs.

Although the bird was still armed with AIM-9 Sidewinder air-to-air missiles for self-defense, it was a snooper, not a fighter. Technically, it was now an EF-16C, but the Air Force didn't apply such designations for fear of tipping its hand as to the actual function of such birds.

The aircrews in the 95th had hoped for the new

Lockheed Martin EF-35Cs, but the Air Force budgets had been running a little on the tight side lately. Troy didn't mind. Whatever the mission, the F-16 was still a fighter, and at last, he was in the cockpit.

As he turned onto the taxiway after a perfect touchdown, Troy noticed two other U.S. Air Force F-16Cs parked near a pair of Hellenic Air Force F-16Cs, which were marked with the red and blue shield of the 115th Combat Wing, the main Greek unit based at Souda. The American Falcons had 95th Reconnaissance Squadron insignia—the bucking mule on a blue disk was a relic of the squadron's heritage as a bomber squadron in World War II—but their tail numbers were not ones that he had seen around Lakenheath since he had arrived.

"Welcome to scenic Souda, Captain." The man in the garrison cap with the bronze oak leaf on it smiled.

Troy had raised his canopy and was removing his helmet when Major Russ Smith of the 95th approached his aircraft. He was surprised to have the commander of the squadron's Falcon Force come out to meet him, but pleased that Smith seemed to be in such a good mood.

Troy forgot for a moment that in the military, good news is usually followed by bad news.

"Wish I could say you have time to enjoy the scenery, Loensch, but Falcon Force will deploy at 1300 hours . . . *today*. Don't worry about unpacking your gear. Briefing in twenty minutes in Ops. See you then."

With that, Smith had turned and was headed back to

the Detachment Operations shack adjacent to the nearest hangar.

The twenty minutes proved long enough for a pit stop and for Troy to find the vending machines to get a soda and a candy bar.

Stepping away from the soda machine, however, he came abruptly and unexpectedly face-to-face with his past.

It was Hal Coughlin, also now sporting captain's bars and wearing a flight suit.

It was Hal who broke the ice.

"Hello, Troy," he said, hesitantly extending his hand.

The two men had not seen each other since that night in the Colville National Forest.

"Hal," Troy said, shaking Coughlin's hand. "Long time, y'know . . ."

"Yeah . . . long . . . long time."

"What are you doing here?" Troy asked.

"I'm with the 95th. Just reassigned. I was at Luke with the 425th, y'know . . . just got reassigned . . . what about you?"

"I've been with ISR for a year or so, and with the 95th for a month or so," Troy acknowledged.

With the "what's-ups" out of the way, the two men just stared at each other awkwardly.

This time, Troy broke the ice.

"I shoulda called you . . . y'know . . . after . . ."

"For a long time, I thought about what I woulda said if you had . . . but I haven't thought about it for a long time."

"I woulda said . . . I shoulda said . . . that I fucked up, Hal."

"When I was thinking about it . . . lying on my fuckin' back in the hospital, I went back and forth between thinking you were an asshole and thinking that I was a wimp."

"What did you decide?" Troy asked.

"I still haven't."

The awkward moment of unresolved tension seemed to last an hour.

This time, the ice was broken by Captain Jenna Munrough.

"Loensch," she said loudly as she entered the hallway. "What are *you* doing here?"

"I was just asked that," he explained, nodding at the 95th Squadron patch on her shoulder. "I guess I'm doing the same thing as you are."

As she glared at him across folded arms, Troy could sense that the anger in her eyes had not diminished, even after nearly two years.

"Guess that means that we *all* have the same briefing . . . about now," Hal said, walking away.

Inside the briefing room, Major Smith had his laptop plugged into a slim projector. The first image cast on the wall was a map of Sudan. Troy noticed that among the several people in the room, the only three in flight suits were Hal, Jenna, and himself.

"As you know, the United States has had combat forces in Sudan since the beginning of the year in support of government forces fighting the Al-Qinamah rebels backed by Eritrea," Smith droned in a description that sounded as though it had been lifted straight from a briefing paper. This was, after all, a briefing. Troy shrugged.

"Joint Task Force Sudan has been operating out of Atbara, about three hundred clicks northeast of Khartoum," the major said, pointing to a spot on the map next to a squiggly blue line that Troy guessed was probably the Nile River. "The air component of the JTF is the 334th Air Expeditionary Wing . . . commander is General Raymond Harris. . . . Falcon Force . . . the three of you . . . will be attached to the 334th under his direct command."

"Doesn't he have any other recon?" Troy asked. It was unusual for a wing not to have tactical reconnaissance assets.

"Your job is to get the recon that the strategic planners need to plan *beyond* tomorrow," Smith replied. "Harris can use the recon he has now for strike assessment and so forth."

The image on the screen changed to a Google Earth aerial view of a city with a river snaking through it. In one corner, the pilots could easily make out the runways of an airport.

"The Atbara Airport here has a 5,905-foot runway," Smith continued. "Harris has got F-16s operating out of here, flying strike missions in Sudan, and C-130s hauling personnel from Khartoum to fields closer to where the action is along the Eritrea border. Technically, the UN mandate won't allow combat ops inside Eritrea, but that apparently doesn't apply to recon flights. Your job is to fly into Eritrean airspace to gather intel."

"Does that mean we can't shoot back if they shoot at *us*?" Jenna asked. Because she had grown up in rural Arkansas, shooting was second nature for her.

"Fire only when fired upon." Smith nodded. "That's the basic rule of engagement here. Fire only to defend yourself."

"We have to let them shoot first?" Jenna pressed.

"That's what's in the rules of engagement here," Smith confirmed.

"But—" Jenna started to say.

"You are flying *recon* missions, not combat missions. Our rules of engagement preclude offensive operations in Eritrean airspace."

"What if somebody gets shot down while playing this game?" Jenna asked.

"If you get shot down, we can prove from your reconnaissance gear that you were *not* on an offensive mission," Smith said in an ominous tone.

CHAPTER 6

Atbara Airport, Sudan

"FUCKIN' DUST IS EVERYWHERE," SAID A DISEMBODIED, half-asleep voice in the darkness.

Coughing sounds came from various corners of the darkness, and another voice angrily admonished the first voice to "Shut the fuck up and go back to sleep!"

Troy had awakened coughing the grit and phlegm out of his throat. He rolled over on the cot and took a breath. Again, the dust flooded into his mouth and nostrils, again causing him to gag. He opened his eyes to the stinging crud and wiped his forehead. Instead of sweat, it felt like mud.

The three F-16Cs of Falcon Force had arrived at dusk. The pilots had reported to General Harris's command post, but he was in the field, so they went to base operations to scrounge temporary quarters. Having flown all the way from Lakenheath to Souda, and from Souda to Atbara yesterday, Troy had been exhausted, so he took the cot in the tent to which he had been assigned, and just crashed.

Now it was nearly 0500, and he was awake. He couldn't possibly nod off again without hosing the dust off his face. He had two hours before Harris's operational daily briefing, so he decided to try to find a shower and get something to eat.

Finding a shower turned out to be a joke. The base was so new that such amenities didn't exist here yet. However, Troy was able to find water to wash the dust from his hands and face. The "officers' mess," with its lukewarm powdered eggs and cold hash from a can, was a bit like a Boy Scout camp gone terribly wrong, but Troy did manage to get fed.

Atbara Expeditionary Air Base was a sprawling, hastily assembled tent city across the runway from the main buildings of the Atbara Airport. Two C-17s were landing as Troy finished his plate of reconstituted eggs. It was always amazing to see such high-tech equipment in such a primitive context, but outsiders more technologically savvy than the locals had been waging war in Sudan since Lord Kitchener beat the Mahdist Army out here in 1898—or since the pharaohs battled the Nubians in these shifting gravel hills thousands of years before that.

When he had flown in yesterday, Troy had seen no

paved roads until he was well into final approach, and out beyond the perimeter wire, a few guys in turbans riding along on donkeys could have been a blast from centuries past.

The briefing, in a large room in the general's command post, was another incongruous display of the latest gadgetry in the primeval landscape. Live, subtly changing satellite photos were displayed on two large screens, and between them was a screen with an animated situation map of Sudan and Eritrea. It was similar to the map that Major Smith had shown them the day before in Souda, but much more detailed. The word *Classified* appeared at the bottom of the screen.

There were about fifty people in the room, and seating for just the first three dozen early arrivals. There were officers, including pilots and navigators, and enlisted personnel, mainly loadmasters from the transport aircraft. Troy stood in a place near the back of the room and noticed Hal Coughlin standing in the opposite corner. He thought he saw Jenna Munrough seated in the second row. A young captain stood on a raised platform before the group and explained the daily situation, told of the strike package that had gone out at 0400, reported the results, and pointed out enemy positions on the animated map. Finally, it was time for the star of the show to take the stage.

General Harris was a bear of a man, with close-cropped hair and a ruddy complexion.

"Bastards are on the move," he began, wasting no time getting to the subject. "They hit the UN troops here, there, and there yesterday. We hit 'em at 1800 yesterday and at 0400 this morning. Initial reports of the strike pack that came back from this morning's hit-and-run shows a concentration here, with supply lines running up here. Those of you who I briefed for the 0900 package will hit them *here*."

The general used his laser pointer like a light saber to stab the *here* to which he referred.

"The distance is short," he explained, looking at the pilots who had been assigned the 0900 sortie. "You won't need extra fuel, so double up on JDAMs and blow the shit out of those bastards."

He sucked a mouthful of tepid water from a plastic bottle and looked out into the crowd.

"I'm looking for mules," he said, scanning the shoulder patches of the assembled pilots for the insignia of the 95th Reconnaissance Squadron. "There's one. Did you come alone, Captain?"

"They're in the back, sir," Jenna Munrough confirmed.

"Good, I'm glad y'all didn't oversleep. See me after class, we need to talk."

With that, Harris turned to a mission overview for the C-130 crews, whose difficult mission for the day would be flying into Khartoum to pick up a UN regiment and haul them into a makeshift field that was only about three kilometers from the shooting. Troy had always been glad *not* to have wound up flying transports. Flying into harm's way was one thing—landing and taking off there was another thing.

"Let's get down to business," Harris said, eyeing the three pilots from the 95th who had moved down to the front of the room when the rest of the personnel had moved out to go to work.

"This is Eritrea," he said, changing the image on the screen. "This is the source of all our migraines. This is the snakepit the Al-Qinamah rebels crawl out of . . . and this is the snakepit that the Al-Qinamah bastards crawl back into. We can't hit 'em there . . . same old drill, y'know."

The three pilots from the 95th nodded. It had indeed been the same in numerous wars into which the United States had been pulled through the years. The bad guys had a safe haven—a safe snakepit in Harris's lexicon—where they could hide, untouched by American bombs or bullets, and where they could plan attacks against American troops or their allies.

"We got *some* wiggle room, though." Harris nodded. "The UN resolution *has* okayed recon flights over Eritrea . . . which is obviously where you come in. I have birds that conduct photorecon over Eritrea, but I need Sigint. That's why they sent you. Only ISR has the gear that can capture signals intel the way we need it captured."

"I wouldn't have thought these guys were that sophisticated, sir," Hal replied.

"That's what we all thought initially, but we thought wrong," Harris replied. "These bastards may look like a bunch of bush bunnies running around in makeshift uniforms, but they got people who are running some pretty complicated covert channels."

Harris proceeded to explain their mission for the day, and for the coming days. They were to enter Eritrean airspace at various points along its vaguely defined border with Sudan, from different and random directions each day.

The three Falcon Force pilots walked to their birds separately, a team in name only. They would work together because they were professionals, not because they were comrades. After their shared experience in the Colville, Hal and Troy could share no camaraderie, only awkwardness. Though she had reamed Troy for what he had done, Jenna kept her distance from both. She had her own agenda to fulfill. Like so many female pilots tasked with flying combat missions, she was single-minded in her determination to prove herself at least an equal to those of the traditional combat pilot gender.

Hal, by virtue of his having logged slightly more time in an F-16, was designated as flight leader, and he took off first. Once they were airborne over the desert east of Atbara, Troy and Jenna tucked their Falcons into an echelon formation off his right wing.

Troy sat back in his cockpit and relaxed. It was all very orderly, just like many of the training missions that he had flown in an F-16, but today would be different. Unlike the training flights, and unlike all of his missions in an EC-32, today he would be over territory where people really might be shooting at him.

He wasn't scared. His emotions varied between a sense of unreality and an adrenaline-fueled excitement. Ever since he had been bounced off the fighter track and shunted into ISR, he had imagined that he would never get a chance to fly a fighter into combat. Today, all that changed. He caught himself worrying that he might *not* get shot at.

A few minutes later, Hal called the initial point and all three F-16s banked left and dropped to one thousand feet. As briefed, they separated to a distance of about a kilometer to provide greater triangulation on the electronic whispers they scooped into the AN/APY-77 and AN/ASD-83 surveillance pods that hung on pylons beneath their wings. Troy didn't understand exactly how those things worked, but that wasn't his job. His job was to get them where they needed to be in order to do *their* jobs, then flick the switch.

As the concrete-colored desert flashed beneath him, Troy kept his eyes on the horizon and on the countdown clock that told him when the flight had passed into Eritrean airspace. The little LED stopped at triple zero, and he engaged the surveillance gear. That was it. There was nothing else to do but fly the mission as briefed, making a series of coordinated turns until the flight path took him back to Atbara.

The Eritrean desert looked identical to the Sudanese desert—an endless sea of rolling hills, an occasional deep gully or canyon, and rarely any sign of habitation. What villages there were flashed by in an instant. Anyone below would not hear the fast-moving, low-flying Falcons until they had passed.

Hal led them into a slight left turn at the appointed moment and dropped to five hundred feet. The large town of Barentu was straight ahead. The turbulence stirred up at the lower altitude rocked the aircraft as they passed over the rooftops.

Hal was first and Jenna second.

About half a kilometer off his right wing, Troy saw a flash out of the corner of his eye. Someone down there was firing tracers, probably from an AK-47 or some such infantry weapon. They missed by a wide margin. It's very hard to hit an airplane at five hundred feet and nearly five hundred miles per hour with an AK-47 and little or no warning.

Suddenly, it was over. The F-16s were back over the open desert, making the series of turns that would take them back to Atbara.

As they climbed back up to a higher altitude with less turbulence, Troy realized how tightly he had been gripping the stick to control the aircraft at low level. He relaxed a bit and thought back to that thirty-second pass over Barentu.

Was that all there was to it?

This is a piece of cake.

Then he remembered the tracer rounds.

It was the first time in his flying career that somebody had been shooting at him for real. He guessed that it would not be the last.

CHAPTER 7

Denakil Desert, Eritrea

EMERGENCY EVACUATION?

In the six weeks that Troy Loensch and the other ISR pilots had been attached to Task Force Sudan, enemy strength and enemy brazenness had increased, and now even the sprawling base at the Atbara Airport was in danger of being overrun by Al-Qinamah rebel forces.

Despite American air support, the Al-Qinamah had beaten Sudanese and UN troops in several key battles. There was even some doubt as to whether the UN could protect Khartoum itself from being sacked by the Al-Qinamah. At Atbara, the Task Force was formulating an emergency evacuation plan.

As Falcon Flight streaked across the border for the second mission of the day over Al-Qinamah–controlled

Eritrea, Troy realized how tenuous things had become. On their earlier couple of dozen missions, the war had seemed so abstract. For pilots of fast reconnaissance aircraft, small-arms fire was a negligible threat. Then the bad guys had imported ZSU-23 antiaircraft guns. Last week, there were reports of surface-to-air missiles. This morning, as Falcon Flight was exiting their briefing, they heard that an F-16 on a strike mission had been hit. There was no word yet on the pilot.

"Those bastards," General Raymond Harris growled out, using his favorite word for the Al-Qinamah, and a word that he also often used to describe the American and UN bureaucrats.

"Bastards sit in air-conditioned offices and tell us how to fight a war . . . then they tie one hand behind our backs . . . while Al-Qinamah is punching back with *two*. Those pinheads are so damned skittish that we're gonna 'escalate' this damned war. If they bothered to take a look at what's really going on out here, they'd see that this damned thing has *already* escalated, and that it's not us but the Al-Qinamah bastards who did the escalating!"

However, Harris had gotten creative in his interpretation of the rules of engagement. The Task Force Sudan aircraft were not permitted to fly strike missions against targets inside Eritrea, but anyone fired upon could return fire. Harris had decided that if one of his reconnaissance aircraft was fired upon by a missile site or a ZSU-23, the pilot could attack the site and destroy it.

A week ago, Harris had ordered all his reconnaissance aircraft to carry AGM-88 HARMs (High-speed Anti-Radar Missiles) and to attack any ground-based weapon that locked its radar on a friendly aircraft. Then he went a step further. In Falcon Flight, he ordered Jenna and Troy to specifically track enemy radar. Hal would fly at the center of the formation, running his Sigint pods as usual, while the other two flew off his wing to the right and left, concentrating their attention on killing the Al-Qinamah antiaircraft sites.

If Hal felt as though he were bait in the fishing expedition that Harris had concocted, there was a reason. He *was*.

If Troy felt as though he were a player in an increasingly competitive game that Jenna had concocted, there was a reason. He *was*.

"I'm gonna be the *first*, y'all."

Those words, which Munrough had spoken on the flight line three days ago, had startled Troy. He hadn't thought of being the first to kill an enemy antiaircraft site as part of a race, but if that was what she wanted to play, he was more than willing to oblige.

Thinking about it today, as he watched her Falcon in the distance off Hal's left wing, it startled him that he was startled. He should have predicted this. Competitiveness was in her nature. In the boredom of base life, he could see it in the way she played cards and the way she played basketball. In the air, aggressiveness *defined* Jenna Munrough.

Today's mission was taking them deeper into Eritrea than normal. The Denakil Depression was an uninviting wilderness where the Al-Qinamah were massing to infiltrate into Sudan by way of Ethiopia.

Eight clicks north of the town of Kulul, Hal dropped from fifteen hundred feet, and the others followed.

"Falcon One . . . flight level . . . two hundred feet," Hal reported.

"Falcon Three holding at four hundred," Troy confirmed.

"Falcon Two . . . let 'em start pinging *me* at four hundred," Jenna said. The girl who had carried a squirrel gun in the Ozarks when she was barely six was itching for a fight, and it showed. Being at higher altitude, Jenna and Troy were more likely to have enemy radar lock on to them than Hal.

"Let's do this," Hal said as Kulul came into view, the spire from its mosque clearly discernible.

Nobody saw them coming.

Nobody down there perceived the AN/APY-77 and AN/ASD-83 electronics pods sucking up data like milk through a straw.

Wherever in the vicinity of Kulul the Al-Qinamah nerds had their Wi-Fi connection, it was being routed into the surveillance pods at a bit rate that would have made their heads spin.

By the time the thunder of the three General Electric

F110 jet engines hit the town and rattled its windows, the Americans had come and gone.

"Falcon One . . . resuming flight level . . . turning ninety degrees . . . north."

"Roger, Falcon Three climbing out . . . right behind you."

Troy could see Jenna below and to his left as she started to turn to follow Hal.

"I've been made, y'all," Jenna shouted. "I'm going missiles hot."

She'd been pinged. Somewhere, someone had locked on to Falcon Two.

Troy had to hand it to her, she had reacted instantly.

Suddenly, he too heard a pinging in his headset, and he turned hard to line up on the source.

As Jenna and Troy banked hard to get into firing position, Hal was getting farther and farther from the other two. Carrying the heavy surveillance pods, he had a harder time turning at high speed than did the others, who were encumbered only with the lighter HARMs.

When the formation turned left on exiting the Kulul area, Troy, being on the right wing, came around at a higher altitude. Jenna, being on the left, was closer to the ground. So Troy had a cleaner shot as he came around and locked his HARM onto what he could now see was a surface-to-air missile battery on a hilltop.

"Fox One," Troy said. He decided that he'd be damned if he'd wait for Jenna to take her shot.

"Damn you," Jenna barked as she saw Troy's HARM streaking toward the SAM site at supersonic speed.

Troy missed seeing the impact but saw the column of smoke beginning to rise as he came around.

He had no time to gloat. The sound of another radar lock-on was screaming in his ears.

"This one's *mine*," Jenna demanded.

"Not if I get to him first," Troy replied.

He knew he shouldn't have. It was all about impulse, and Troy didn't have the best head for sorting out his impulses.

He cut Jenna off, firing his second and last HARM less than a quarter kilometer from the SAM site just as a surface-to-air missile left the tube.

As the SAM site erupted in smoke and flame, he could see the contrail of the SAM as it arced up and away.

"Bogies at eleven o'clock," came the call.

It was Hal.

Bogies?

Bogies were enemy aircraft. In nearly two months in country, nobody from Task Force Sudan had ever been challenged by enemy aircraft.

There has to be a first time for everything.

"I got two MiGs incoming," Hal said.

Troy jerked his head around, trying to spot the flight leader in the dome of blue sky as he turned.

He saw the lead F-16, the pods heavy under its wings, making a slow banking turn.

He also saw the enemy, a pair of dark check marks maneuvering in the sky, too far away to identify as to type. They had apparently made one pass to check out the American Falcon and were banking around for a second pass—their kill pass.

For the first time during their series of encounters since exiting Kulul, Troy felt the creepy sensation of dread.

If Hal was planning to try outmaneuvering the MiGs, he was a goner. He was between a rock and a hard place. The surveillance pods inhibited his ability to turn, but to drop technology so sophisticated inside Eritrea would compromise the whole Falcon Force operation.

There was no way that Troy could get there before they pounced on Hal.

As he lit his afterburner, Troy spotted another aircraft.

It was Jenna.

She had executed a Split S maneuver and was above the enemy and beginning to dive. The bad guys were so focused on getting into firing position behind Hal that they hadn't seen her.

Troy saw a flicker of orange flame erupt as an AIM-9 Sidewinder air-to-air missile left the rail at the tip of the F-16's wing. From above and behind, it was a no-miss shot, and it didn't.

It was over in a second.

Troy watched the contrail of the Sidewinder as it overtook an aircraft that he could now make out as a MiG-29 Fulcrum.

The fireball briefly continued the forward momentum that it had when it was an airplane, then fell like a rock.

The other MiG broke off his attack against Hal and ran.

Jenna, whose higher altitude could be translated into speed, gave chase.

There was another flicker of orange flame, but this time the MiG jinked at the last moment. The contrail shot past with inches to spare.

It seemed as though the panicked pilot had just caught a lucky break, but his turn brought him face-to-face with Troy.

Two fighters closing on each other both face a difficult shot. With an aggregate speed of more than a thousand miles per hour, a second is a long time.

Troy impulsively thumbed the trigger of his M61 Vulcan cannon. Had he had a moment to think, he'd have known that a heat-seeking Sidewinder would have a hard time acquiring the MiG in a head-on dash, but something in his instinct had told him to use his gun.

The MiG raced through the wall of tracers that Troy had put up, and kept coming—on a collision course toward him.

Troy broke left.

He was lucky that the MiG pilot broke right.

He was also lucky that the MiG pilot decided that now was a good time to turn.

Troy never had time to wonder whether the breaking turn was the MiG pilot's attempt to turn and fight or whether it was just an evasive escape maneuver.

It didn't really matter.

The turns bled off a great deal of speed for both aircraft, but it also brought the MiG directly into the circle in Troy's head-up display. The red, green, and blue insignia of the Eritrean Air Force looked like a Christmas tree ornament.

This time, training and instinct converged.

The Sidewinder left the rail on Troy's wingtip.

It is a cliché to say that the speed of the missile made the slow-turning MiG seem as though it were standing still.

There was still smoke and debris in the sky as Troy's momentum brought him hurtling through that place where once there was a MiG.

CHAPTER 8

Atbara Airport, Sudan

UNTIL FURTHER NOTICE.

The words stung.

Nothing inflates a fighter pilot's balloon more than his first kill in aerial combat. As Falcon Flight dashed home after their dogfight over the Denakil Depression, Hal Coughlin was breathing a sigh of relief, but for Troy Loensch and Jenna Munrough, the mood was the exhilaration of victory. Two MiGs down.

Nothing *deflates* a fighter pilot's balloon more than to hear the words *grounded until further notice*.

If Troy and Jenna had harbored any illusions about a cheers and champagne reception back at Atbara, they were mistaken. General Raymond Harris was livid. He had already caught a hellstorm from the chain of command above him, and he was passing it down.

Eritrea was swift to lodge a protest with the UN. Two of their half dozen MiG-29s were now debris fields. Two of their "brave aviators" had been "murdered" by pilots operating under the mandate of a UN resolution.

"Self-defense?" Harris queried angrily when Troy and Jenna explained what had happened, his normally ruddy cheeks redder than usual. "That's what you're saying?"

"Begging your pardon, sir," Troy replied. "But you *did* authorize us to return fire when attacked . . . as I recall, sir, you went so far as to *encourage* us to return fire."

"I believe that we were discussing Al-Qinamah ground fire when we had that conversation, Captain. The emphasis here is on *Al-Qinamah*. Our enemies are the Al-Qinamah rebels, *not* the Eritrean government. The fact that the Eritrean government is sloppy about controlling the rebels inside their porous borders is beside the point. The fact that the Eritrean government is probably complicit in the rebel activity and giving aid and comfort to the rebels is beside the point."

"Yes, sir," Troy said.

"Off the record, I don't care if you take out the whole damned Eritrean Air Force," Harris said. "But I'm reprimanding Loensch and Munrough because the higher-ups demand it . . . and for showing bad judgment in not paying attention to what was going on and letting the bastards get the drop on you. Coughlin, you're off the hook this time, but I hope you're learning a lesson here."

"Yes, sir."

"It *was* self-defense, sir," Jenna interrupted. "As we explained, those MiGs were going after Captain Coughlin at the time we opened fire, sir."

"At the time that *you* opened fire, Captain Munrough," Harris clarified. "It seems from what I've seen on the gun camera footage that Captain Loensch attacked a fleeing aircraft."

"He was coming right at—" Troy said.

"He was running," Harris replied. "The gun camera footage shows him coming at you, but he never fired. He could have fired and he didn't. You were shooting at a scared rabbit."

"Or one with malfunctioning fire control," Troy suggested. "I've heard their maintenance is lousy."

"That's beside the point," Harris said. "This whole damned incident came about because you weren't paying attention . . . none of you . . . but especially *you*, Loensch. You were showboating with Munrough, cutting her off and trying to blow up every damned SAM site in that desert and you missed the fact that enemy air was in the area."

Jenna took the opportunity to give Troy a dirty look.

"That's why I'm reprimanding Munrough and *grounding* you, Loensch. Your little game with the SAM sites endangered a fellow pilot . . . your shooting at a fleeing aircraft gets me in hot water with the big bosses, and all of the above show piss-poor judgment. Am I making things perfectly clear?"

"Yes, sir."

"Loensch, just so that you don't get too bored on your 'vacation,' I have a team that needs a hand installing some software upgrades in about four dozen targeting systems. I overheard them saying that it would be useful to have a pilot involved in their work. You could report to the major in charge at 0700 tomorrow. You wouldn't mind, would you, Loensch?"

"No, sir."

"Don't get too smug, Munrough," Harris added. "If I could afford to ground *both* of your sorry asses, I would. But I need at least two aircraft in Falcon Force to carry on with operations tomorrow and the next day . . . and the next day . . . *Dis*-missed."

Troy and the others went their separate ways. Once again, as in the Bruins locker room and in OTS, a big screwup had gotten Troy in serious trouble. He guessed that he was lucky that the general didn't put him on KP. Installing software beats peeling potatoes.

When he had finished an early dinner in the mess hall, Troy decided to seek out one of the satellite phones that were made available for the troops to call home. He hadn't talked with Cassie for a while, and to his parents for even longer.

"What time is it there?" Cassie asked after he said hello.

"Quarter after six. What time is it there?"

"Shit, it's after seven already," Cassie said, sounding distracted. "I gotta get ready for work."

"What's up?" Troy asked.

"Not much . . . just going to work and . . . hanging out . . . How about you?"

"Oh, not much . . . just going to work and hanging out," Troy said, deciding not to tell her that he had just "murdered" an Eritrean pilot and had been grounded. "Same old thing."

"Have you seen any camels over there?"

"Only from the air . . . we don't get off base much . . . there's a lot of rebel activity not too far away, so we're staying inside the wire."

"You're not in any kind of danger or anything?"

"Naw . . . not here. What's the weather like there?"

"Pretty warm . . . and crazy smoggy in the Valley . . . what's it like there?"

"Hot as hell with a ninety-nine percent chance of dust storms."

"Sounds like beach weather." Cassie laughed.

"Yeah . . . I sure am looking forward to getting back home and going to the beach with you."

"When's that going to be?"

"I dunno. Like I said in my e-mail . . . tours keep getting extended. Not long, I hope . . . I'm sure missing you."

"I'm missing you too, big guy," Cassie said in a matter-of-fact way. Troy was just happy to hear her using her pet nickname for him. "Listen, I gotta run . . . gotta get to work. Love ya, big guy."

"Love you too," Troy said as the click of Cassie hanging up echoed in his ears.

"I thought that absence made the heart grow fonder," he said out loud to himself as he dialed his parents' home.

"Heard the smog's been pretty bad," Troy said after exchanging greetings with his mother. She too had wanted to know what time it was.

"Yeah, very bad here in the Valley. I'm going up to that needlepoint shop in Santa Clarita later. Guess I'll make a day of it."

"No work today?"

"It's Saturday. . . . What day is it over there?"

"I guess it must be Saturday night," Troy said. "The days just run together. One's the same as the next."

"You sound despondent," she scolded. "Gotta get your blood sugar up. Did you get those cookies I sent?"

"Not yet. When did you send them?"

"Last week."

"They'll get here. They're pretty good about getting our mail to us . . . not necessarily in a timely way . . . but it seems to get here sooner or later. . . . So where's Dad, if it's a Saturday?"

"He went in to work . . . something about the warehouse . . . I don't know."

It was his mother's turn to have a despondent edge to her tone of voice. Troy decided to change the subject, a subject that worked its way around to the question of when he'd be coming home.

Again, he explained that tours were being extended.

"What exactly is going on over there?"

"You know I can't talk about what we're doing," he explained, mad at himself for his patronizing tone.

"I watch it on the news, and it just doesn't make sense. These guys look like just a bunch of ragtag punks, but they seem to be winning. Can't you stop them?"

"We're trying, Mom. We're trying."

"This morning there was a thing on the news . . . they said that the Americans shot down some planes that belonged to one of those countries over there . . . not to the punks . . . but to a country. Did you hear about that over there?"

"Yes, Mom, I did," Troy answered, suppressing the urge to tell her that he was one of the Americans.

"Is it true?"

"True, what?"

"That Americans are shooting down planes."

"Yes . . . it *is* true."

"What's gonna happen?"

"That's up to the politicians to decide."

"Promise me one thing, Troy."

"What's that, Mom?"

"Promise me you'll stay away from where they're shooting down airplanes."

"Ummm . . ."

"Promise me."

"Yeah, Mom . . . I promise I'll do my best."

CHAPTER 9

Atbara Airport, Sudan

"THANK YOU, SIR."

Eight days and five or six dozen software upgrades later, Troy Loensch had just gotten restored to flight status.

Eight days of grunt work—albeit high-tech grunt work—had gotten Troy's attention. A 1.8-millimeter Phillips screwdriver and a pair of needle-nose pliers were not exactly like the control stick of a jet fighter. The first couple of days of plugging, playing, and running diagnostics with a laptop had made Troy feel a bit humiliated. For the next few days, humiliation had gradually turned to humility. Troy found himself working side by side with people who did this for a living, day in and day out. They crouched in awkward places in the fuselages of airplanes in hangars that felt like ovens so that hot-shot pilots like Troy Loensch could have the means to be hotshot pilots. When he finally got the word that his indentured servitude had come to an end, Troy was ecstatic, but at the same time, he would never again take the software geeks for granted.

"We need you back in the air," General Raymond Harris explained from behind his messy desk. "We can't afford a pilot off flight status with the situation on the ground as screwed up as it is. Besides that, your team needs you."

"Team . . . needs me?"

"Yeah . . . they've been on my case to get you back in the air. Both of 'em. Coughlin and Munrough . . . especially Coughlin."

Troy was dumbfounded that Hal and Jenna had interceded with the general to get him back in the air. Both had reasons to be glad that he *wasn't* flying with them. He was also surprised at his own reaction when the general had referred to the three of them as a "team." They flew together, executed missions in a coordinated manner, and got things done, but he had never thought of them as a team, certainly not in the sense of the football teams on which Troy had played such a long time ago.

He caught up to his "teammates" in the officers' mess, sitting together at a table on the edge of the room. Troy grabbed a cup of coffee and walked over.

"Guess what," he said in as cheerful a tone as he could

muster, given that the mere sight of them reminded him of the long-strained relationship. "You are rid of me no longer. I'm back in the air."

"Mission briefing at 1400," Jenna said, standing up to leave. "Check you then."

"I heard you put in a good word for me with the general," Troy said to Hal as Jenna left the room. "I don't deserve it . . . but thanks."

"Whatever your faults, man . . . you're still a helluva pilot."

"Thanks. It's appreciated . . . ummm . . . coming from you . . . I mean I don't deserve it from you."

"Like I said . . . you're a helluva pilot."

"It was Munrough who saved your ass in that dogfight," Troy reminded him. "It wasn't me. I was just watching and trying to get there."

"I know . . . I owe her big-time . . . but I appreciate that you *were* coming back."

"All's well that ends well, I guess."

"It ended well," Hal said. "Unless you count the reprimands."

"That's no big deal . . . anybody who reads those reprimands is going to see that we got into a fight and lived to tell about it . . . who would you want on *your* team? Who would *they* want on *their* team?"

"Haven't heard you use the word *team* before," Hal said. "Guess I'm glad to have people like . . . y'know . . . you and her on mine."

"Don't get all gushy on me now," Troy said, getting up to go. "See you at 1400."

Troy felt good, sitting in at his first briefing in nearly two weeks—even if it was a good news/bad news briefing.

The good news was that it would be a shorter mission than those to which Troy had been accustomed before his grounding. The bad news was that it was over Sudan. The front in the war had crept much closer to Atbara.

Troy was happy beyond words to be back in the saddle again, but he was hoping that his first mission after the grounding would be routine. The last time he had this stick in his fist, he had been thumbing a trigger that killed a MiG—and created an international incident.

About four hundred clicks south of Atbara, Falcon Force descended from a cool, cloudless fifteen thousand feet to a hazy fifteen hundred. In this arid desert, ground fog was rare. The haze that pilots often encountered was the remnant of the incessant dust storms that made life in Sudan generally unpleasant for aficionados of fresh air.

The target for the day was not a place on a map, but a set of coordinates in a trackless desert north of Al Qadarif. The ISR Sigint interpreters somewhere back behind the front lines had decided that these coordinates marked the spot where the Al-Qinamah had located the command post that directed their attacks on UN Forces east of Khartoum.

A bunch of ragtag punks. That's what Troy's mother had called Al-Qinamah. Others—a lot of others—had called them worse—a lot worse—and they *were*. It seemed counterintuitive that punks riding around on donkeys could be so sophisticated in their technological expertise that it took AN/APY-77 and AN/ASD-83 electronic pods to keep tabs on them.

Falcon Force dropped to two hundred feet.

It was showtime.

For today's mission, both Hal and Troy were carrying pods, with Jenna flying off Troy's left wing with HARMs.

Below, in the ocean of dirt, there would be no landmarks, no mosque spires of a rebel-held city, only a camouflaged communications hub that American eyes would not see but American ISR pods would hear.

If the bad guys were smart—as often they were—there would be no position-revealing ground fire. They knew that in Eritrea, rules of engagement prevented the Americans from attacking them, but here in Sudan, the American jets they heard approaching were likely to have a hellstorm of cluster bombs beneath their wings.

Today, at least one bad guy wasn't smart.

"Tracers at one o'clock," Jenna reported.

"ZSU?" Troy asked.

"Smaller. Just a quick burst. Probably a nut with an AK."

The pilots usually ignored small-arms shooters with no chance of hitting a fast-moving jet—and it was pointless for them to try to hit back at a target so small and so easily concealed.

"We're on top of the target . . . now," Hal reported.

It was merely a formality. Hal and Troy had already lit their AN/APY-77 and AN/ASD-83 gear, and it was working autonomously.

"Didn't see anything," Troy said.

There was nothing to see. A few seconds after Hal had said the word *now*, they were already ten miles from the target.

"Hiding in a hole probably," Jenna said with disdain for the Al-Qinamahs back there.

"Climbing to flight level one-five-five," Hal said.

"Roger one-five-five," Jenna said calmly.

"One-five-five and home," Troy said. "Ugh. Come on you, what's the—"

"Falcon Three, what's up?" Hal asked.

"Some kind of fuel issue . . . Getting sluggish performance."

"Can you climb to one-five-five?"

"Maybe . . . ugh . . . no. I'd better level out at five-five," Troy said, opting not to climb any higher because his aircraft was not behaving properly.

"We're with you, Falcon Three," Jenna said, leveling out at Troy's altitude.

"Roger, five-five," Hal confirmed, doing the same.

Guess we must actually be a team, Troy thought to himself.

It startled Troy to discover that the others were dropping back to his altitude. Long ago, deep in a wilderness, Troy had deliberately abandoned Hal. Today, high over another wilderness, Hal had deliberately *not* abandoned Troy.

A few minutes later, Troy's warm fuzzy feeling was jolted—literally—as his F-16 began to shiver. He looked at the fuel gauge. It was dropping much faster than it should be. His left wing tank was nearly empty, increasing the weight on the right and making the plane hard to control.

"Falcon Three here, I'm losing fuel . . . pretty fast, too."

"You okay to Atbara?" Hal asked.

"Think so," Troy said. "Left wing tank is dry and I'm having trouble pumping from the aft tank. Right wing . . . very heavy."

The F-16 shivered again.

Troy was doing his best to adjust the crossflow of fuel, but his whole fuel system was misbehaving, and not enough was reaching the engine. The aircraft was slowly losing altitude.

Would he be able to maintain his altitude long enough to reach Atbara?

Below, the trackless desert raced beneath his wings.

What if he had to punch out?

A SAR chopper could reach him in an hour or so. If there were no bad guys around, it would be a mere inconvenience. If there were bad guys, then it could be—probably would be—all over.

"Seven minutes out," Hal said calmly after what seemed to Troy like an eternity of fighting to keep his plane from slumping to the ground. "Falcon Three, go on in first."

"Atbara approach," Troy called. "This is Falcon Three . . . I'm declaring an emergency . . . coming in bingo fuel."

"Roger Falcon Three, we have your flight on the scope, you're cleared to land at your discretion. We are vectoring other traffic out of the approach pattern . . . will you need assistance on the ground?"

"Not if I make it as far as the runway," Troy said, half joking. He knew that he could land the F-16 if he could get it *to* the runway, if he could get it *on* the runway. If he didn't make it to the runway, they could take their time picking up the pieces.

As he banked left to line the aircraft up with the strip of asphalt in the distance, Troy felt the F-16 shudder and fall.

Starved of fuel, the 3,700-pound Pratt & Whitney F100-PW-229 had just quit.

The lump in Troy's throat seized like the fuel line to the engine, and he yanked back on the stick in an effort not to lose any more altitude until he reached the runway.

He was coming in fast and low, low enough that he imagined he could see the expressions on the faces of the guys on the donkeys in the desert just beneath him.

The higher-than-normal airspeed kept his momentum up and contributed to his keeping the aircraft up, but coming in fast and low was not the best way to land an F-16.

The fast-forward momentum was not Troy's best friend, it was his only friend. It was the only thing that was keeping his nose above the top of the perimeter fence. It would also mean that if the F-16 hit the ground before the runway, the destruction would be so complete and so fast that Troy would feel no pain.

From above and behind, Jenna watched Troy's F-16 racing toward the runway, flying in formation with its own shadow. She watched the airplane and shadow merge into one as the F-16 dropped to an altitude of practically zero.

Jenna gritted her teeth, noting that Troy still had a quarter of a mile—an endless distance under these circumstances—to go before he was over the runway.

She expected at any moment to see the F-16 suddenly turn into a tumbling cartwheel of scrap metal.

Through her mind dashed the images of this aggravating asshole of a man and his self-centered behavior at every turn. Yet despite this, she yearned, even prayed, that he would not die.

She stared at him, ahead and below, for those few seconds that stretched to eternity.

Suddenly, the airplane was engulfed in a gray cloud.

In less time than it took for the image to travel from eye to brain, she realized that this was merely the burning rubber of a dead-stick aircraft's tires hitting a runway at high speed.

Aboard that dead-stick aircraft, Troy had waited painfully long before dropping his landing gear, so long that he was not sure the gear was fully extended when he hit the runway.

He clenched his teeth, waiting for the ground loop that never came.

The hotdogger quickly replaced the man who had almost died, and Troy used his last spurt of momentum to turn neatly off the runway and onto the taxiway as though nothing had happened.

CHAPTER 10

Atbara Airport, Sudan

"THANKS, MAN," TROY SAID SHEEPISHLY.

"Thanks for what?" Hal Coughlin asked.

The two men were walking from their quarters to the briefing room. Barely eighteen hours after Troy had landed with two lucky nine-millimeter holes in his fuel system, the Falcon Force was going out again.

"I thought about that day, that night, y'know, out in the Colville," Troy said. "I thought about how I left you . . . and then . . . I was in trouble out there yesterday by Al Qadarif . . . and you *didn't* leave me."

"You made it back on your own," Hal said. "You didn't need anything I did . . . nothing that Munrough did. We couldn't do anything but watch."

"Still, it's the thought that counts," Troy said appreciatively.

"I don't want you dead," Hal said. "As hard as that may be for you to believe, I don't want to see you dead. When I was lying on my back in the hospital, I probably would have shot you if you came through that door . . . but . . ."

"Thanks for that . . . I guess . . ."

"I don't want you being dead on my conscience," Hal said.

"I don't want it there either," Troy agreed, ducking into the head, as much to get away from an awkward moment as to get rid of the remnants of the three cups of coffee in his bladder.

As he emerged, he noticed Hal at the end of the hallway. Jenna was there too. Neither saw him or looked in his direction. This was not the least bit unusual; everyone was headed to the same briefing. However, they were standing awfully close to one another, closer than two pilots usually stood next to one another—much closer.

Pilots who were part of the same flight were supposed to work closely, but there was something more to this. Troy was about to accuse himself of overthinking the situation when he saw their hands touch—not accidentally, nor for just a split second. Then, for a split second, he saw Munrough's hand touch the back of Coughlin's flight suit. Aha, there *was* more to it than met the eye.

* * *

ANY BRIEFING THAT BEGINS WITH A SENTENCE containing the phrase *not going to be easy* is one of those that gets your attention.

The first slide on the screen looked like someone had splattered pink paint on a pale blue wall.

"This is the Dahlak Archipelago," Harris intoned. "Bunch of islands east of Eritrea in the Red Sea. Intel had it that the Al-Qinamah heavy weapons are being transshipped through here. They get shipped out of Iran or North Korea or wherever, come into the Red Sea, and get landed here. Then they shuffle 'em onto small boats and bring 'em ashore on the mainland."

"Lot of islands there," Hal said. "I lost track counting at two dozen."

"They tell us that there's a hundred twenty-four of 'em," Harris said. "Trouble is, we don't know where the hell they're bringing the stuff in."

"And so you send a recon flight out there to find out," Troy suggested.

"Clever boy, Loensch." Jenna laughed sarcastically.

"Obviously it's better that nobody with radar sees you coming," Harris said, ignoring her taunting banter. "You'll fly low, so you'll need to carry extra fuel. Fly east, cross over the coast and turn south across the Red Sea at two hundred feet or less. You'll be sucking whitecaps as you go."

"Why not head due east? It's a lot shorter," Hal suggested, pointing at the screen. Harris had a map of the entire region up now. The route that Harris had described took a roundabout track to the target.

"Because," Harris said in an exasperated tone. "The shortest distance between two places takes you right over the Eritrean population centers . . . practically over their capital . . . I do not think you clowns want to be tangling with the Eritrean Air Force again. . . . Am I right?"

"Right," Hal agreed. "I guess we don't want any more international incidents."

"Guess *not*," Jenna agreed, glancing at Troy with a wry grin.

It was the kind of glance that instinctively elicits a wink when you see it, but remembering what he'd seen in the hallway before the briefing, Troy simply stared back, his expression unchanged, then glanced back at the screen.

The flight out of Sudanese airspace was uneventful, but the wavetop run over the Red Sea was challenging. The guidebooks all tell you that the daytime weather over this placid lake between two deserts is clear and sunny ninety-nine percent of the time, but pilots know that the same unsettled air at low altitude that kicks up killer sandstorms over land can also kick up killer turbulence over the water. At two hundred feet, it was a white-knuckle ride as they dodged both downdrafts and the masts of supertankers bound for the Suez Canal.

At last the khaki-colored lumps of the Dahlak islands loomed ahead.

"Dropping tanks," Hal said.

"Tanks," Troy confirmed, feeling the F-16 bob upward as his auxiliary fuel tanks tumbled into the Red Sea. Without them, the aircraft would be lighter and somewhat easier to manage, but each plane was still encumbered with more than the usual payload of recon gear.

"Falcon Three, breaking right," Troy said. Each member of the team had a particular flight path and a particular set of islands to survey.

"Falcon Two, left," Jenna confirmed.

"Falcon One, cameras on," added Hal.

"Cameras on," Troy and Jenna said, almost in unison.

The recon payload that each F-16 carried included not just camera pods, but their AN/APY-77 and AN/ASD-83 pods, as well as AN/AKR-13 telemetry receivers and other equipment. Because each member of Falcon Force was surveying a separate path, there were no HARMs today. They each carried recon gear.

Troy glimpsed a few small boats—they came and went in a split second—and wondered if any of them were carrying weapons or contraband.

As usual, everything on the ground flashed by too quickly for any of the pilots to make out anything useful.

It was up to the interpreters who plowed through the data the pilots were collecting.

"Dammit," the other pilots heard Jenna say.

"Falcon Two, whazzup?" Hal asked, more than a trace of concern in his voice.

"Damned AKR-13 went FUBAR on me just as I came over Dhuladhiya," Jenna said.

The island of Dhuladhiya was one of the key islands on her recon track, and a screwed-up telemetry receiver meant incomplete coverage.

"Falcon Three breaking left," Troy said. "I'm only about ten clicks off. I can be there in half a minute."

"What about your track?" Jenna asked.

"I can bounce over and bounce back," Troy said.

"Thanks," Jenna said.

"General Harris thanks you," Hal added.

Troy banked hard, heading north toward Dhuladhiya.

This will make them feel special, he thought to himself, *to get buzzed by two American jets from two directions in one day.*

The large island lay like all the others, flat and dust-colored, a few boats clustered around an inlet on one side.

By the time Troy had zigged back to the recon track assigned to him, Falcon One and Falcon Two were far ahead, no longer visible to him, exiting Dahlak airspace and turning for home.

"Falcon Three, we're gonna orbit at the egress point and wait for you to catch up," Troy heard Hal say.

"Roger that, Falcon One," Troy replied. "Thanks. I appreciate the company."

After all the months of internal antagonism, it was beginning to seem as though the three pilots of Falcon Force had finally reached the point where they could function as a team.

CHAPTER 11

Joint Task Force Sudan Compound, Khartoum

"WHY THE HELL *CAN'T* WE?" GENERAL RAYMOND Harris demanded. "Why the hell *not*?"

"Because it's Eritrea, that's why," the man in the suit said angrily.

Harris had been sparring with the man from the State Department—an under-undersecretary of some sort—practically since the conference began.

"I don't know why I bothered to come down here from Atbara, if I'm just going to be told what my guys *can't* do."

There were a dozen people in the room, including the JTF commander and his staff, as well as the CIA reconnaissance interpreters who had sifted through all the data that Falcon Force had collected over the Dahlak Archipelago.

Essentially, Falcon Force had found what it had been sent to find—a good overview of the what and how of arms trafficking through the islands. The purpose of the meeting was for JTF Sudan to figure out what to do about it. Harris was present because attacking the traffickers with JTF assets would fall to his 334th Air Expeditionary Wing. The man from the State Department was there—pretty much as Harris had pegged it—to tell the JTF what it *could not* do.

"General, let me put it as clearly as I can," he said in a patronizing tone. "This, these islands, are part of Eritrea. The UN mandate says we are not to bomb Eritrea, which is technically neutral in this conflict. May I remind you that we had to do big-time, *very* big-time, damage control a few weeks back when your joyriding jet jockeys shot down a third of the Eritrean Air Force."

"Technically neutral, my ass," Harris replied. "Begging your pardon for my choice of words, I take exception to the undersecretary's characterization of a country where Al-Qinamah has command posts, a country through which Al-Qinamah is hauling weapons and ammo that are being used to target American troops."

"That's why I used the word *technically*," the man said, loosening his tie.

"And one more thing," Harris said, having sensed that the man was momentarily on the defensive. "My aircrews were not on a joyride, they were not out there looking to attack somebody. They were shot at first. . . ."

"Enough," interrupted the JTF Sudan commander, the three-star who was Harris's boss. "Both of you have made it abundantly clear where you stand on this thing. Now, let's figure out what we *can* do, and decide what we *will* do to stop this crap from getting from those islands onto the mainland."

"If I might interject," one of the CIA analysts interjected.

"Please do," the JTF commander said, happy to have a fresh voice shoehorn its way into the dialogue.

"The rules of engagement prohibit attacking Eritrean surface targets unless a JTF asset is fired upon," the analyst said. Everyone nodded. This was a well-known given fact.

"We're also prohibited from attacking the Iranian ships that deliver the hardware."

"We certainly wouldn't want to offend the poor Iranians," Harris said sarcastically.

"But there is nothing to stop us from attacking extranational ships in these waters," the CIA man continued. "Thanks to the data we have now, thanks to the 334th, we know that the barges go in and out from Dhuladhiya Island. There's miles of water between there and the mainland."

"That's territorial water, Eritrean territorial—" the State Department man interjected.

"Under the UN resolution on piracy," the analyst retorted. "I think we are not prohibited from attacking extranational vessels engaged in—"

"Then I think we have our work cut out for us," the JTF commander said, happy to have a plausible resolution to the problem. Turning to Harris, he asked, "When can you . . . ?"

"The 334th will have 16s armed and ready to go by this afternoon," Harris asserted happily. "But it's probably best to go at night; they're not used to us flying at night, and that's when they're more likely to be at sea with their garbage scows . . . I'll have an attack plan by the end of the day."

"I'll have to run this past State," the under-undersecretary said cautiously. Things were suddenly moving fast, and he did not like being out of control.

"Do you want me to look up the pertinent resolution number?" asked the CIA man.

CHAPTER 12

Atbara Airport, Sudan

TROY LOENSCH HAD A RARE AND UNEXPECTED DAY off.

It was the first time since he was grounded that he had time to himself. It was the first such time in weeks without it being overshadowed by a reprimand. The 334th Operations Center was abuzz with the upcoming action in the Dhuladhiya Channel. Harris had all the F-16 crews who flew strike missions pulled into a big briefing, and this left Falcon Force sidelined for the next forty-eight hours. They were, as people say in recon circles, snoopers, not shooters.

He thought about calling home, but it was the middle of the night in California. He thought about reacting to his status as *not* a shooter by going to the primitive

Atbara O-Club and shooting pool, but decided to go shoot some hoops instead. He realized only as he started scrimmaging with a couple of other guys that he had unconsciously made the decision to play a team sport rather than a solo sport.

What had come over him? Had the self-centered asshole become a team player?

For Troy, the realization that Falcon Force had melded into a team had come on the same day that he had first gotten an inkling that his teammates, Jenna Munrough and Hal Coughlin, were *more* than teammates. Why hadn't he seen it earlier? He guessed that either they had done a very good job concealing their "special relationship" or it had only just started.

Once again, he was the outsider in the small group of three—not that he really wanted to be a third party in a three-way relationship of that kind.

As far as his relationship with Coughlin and Munrough as pilots went, Dhuladhiya had been the turning point, although the turn had begun over the desert north of Al Qadarif. When he'd gotten his fuel tank punctured, they had stayed with him. There was little they could do for him, but they had stayed with him.

Then, Dhuladhiya. It was a place name that none of them had ever heard until that morning when the mission was briefed. Troy didn't have to double back to provide the coverage that Jenna could not—but he had, and he did so immediately. It wasn't that he had done her a huge personal favor, but he had displayed the action of a team player.

It was new for him. In football, wide receivers don't really have to be team players. They catch what the quarterback throws, but other than that, they don't have to be team players. Their job is to run, catch and run. They don't have to do for others. They have other people blocking for them. Their job is *not* to worry about covering for a teammate whose AN/AKR-13 craps out.

Today, out on the court—which was just a dusty patch of asphalt with a pair of mismatched hoops—he found himself passing as much as he was shooting.

Why not?

He was as good as he was, and he was not the best player on the asphalt. He was better than most, though not as good as the new guy with the short, blond Mohawk. The guy was good, he knew it, and Troy had no interest in proving he wasn't.

"This a boy's game, or can a girl play?"

Troy turned; it was Jenna Munrough. He almost didn't recognize her in shorts and shades rather than a green flight suit.

Someone passed the ball; Troy caught it, dribbled once, and snapped it off to Jenna.

She caught it and shot it in with almost a single motion.

One of the other players grunted his approval as it went in.

The guy with the short, blond Mohawk got the rebound and slammed the ball through the hoop.

This time, Jenna was under the hoop.

She scooped up the rebound as one of the guys grabbed and missed.

She passed it to Troy.

He found himself wanting, more than ever in this game, to make this shot. What was it about boys and girls that makes a guy want—no, *need*—to make the shot while the girl is watching?

The ball bounced off the rim and Mohawk reached for the rebound.

Suddenly, Jenna was between him and the ball.

As he leaped up and came down empty, she shot up and slam-dunked the ball.

Troy seized the rebound and scored, and suddenly the two Falcon Force teammates were teammates on the dusty patch of desert.

Jenna missed her next three shots in a row, but Troy scored two. This was not to say that anyone was really keeping score as Troy and Jenna scrimmaged against three other players. Ultimately, the trio of others probably outscored the two Falcons, but everyone played well. Jenna startled the guys with her skill at first, but soon they were treating her not as a girl in a boys' game, but as just another player to be guarded.

When it was finally over, and as everyone shook

hands and said "Good game," it was Troy's turn for a surprise.

"Buy y'all a beer?" Jenna asked as she wiped the sweat from her face with the T-shirt she had been wearing over her tank top.

"Umm . . . thanks . . . but I got some stuff I gotta take care of. . . . Rain check?"

He had no "stuff." He did have an aversion to this sort of camaraderie with a teammate—a female teammate— especially one with whom his relations had, until very recently, not been good.

There had long since ceased to be a gender gap on the court, but the ritual of "having a beer" meant something completely different when two people were from oppo- site sides of that gap. Beyond that was Troy's sense of that "something" that apparently existed between Jenna and Hal.

"Rain check." Jenna smiled broadly as though her suggestion had been far less complicated than what Troy had read into it. "See you at the briefing in the morning."

With that, she was gone.

As he picked up his gear, Troy noticed his watch. It was still too early to phone California, but by the time he finished his shower, he figured that his mother would probably be up.

Nobody was home when he called home, so Troy

decided to phone his father at work. "Office Tech, this is Carl."

"Hi, Dad, what's up?"

"Troy . . . is that you? Good to hear you. Where are you?"

"Sunny Sudan. Actually, the sun's down, but it's still Sudan," Troy said. His father seemed to be in a good mood. After the usual exchange over what time it was, Troy asked his father about how business was.

"Little slow," Carl said. "Y'know, ups and downs, but everybody still needs paper . . . and ink for those damned computer printers. You have to spend more on the damned ink than you do for the printers. . . . What are you doing? Are you flying much?"

"Most days. Had a day off 'cause they've got a big thing going that doesn't involve us . . . can't talk about it."

"Yeah . . . I understand," Carl said. "When you comin' home?"

"Can't say. You know these open-ended enlistments. Used to be that there were tours of duty, y'know. Now, nobody knows. It will be a while."

"Take care of yourself."

"I will."

Troy signed off with the usual niceties and tried his mother. Still nobody home. She didn't like carrying her cell phone.

He started dialing Cassie's cell phone, stopped after the 310, hesitated, and dialed again.

"Hey," Cassie said, sounding distracted.

"Hey, babe, it's Troy."

"Wow, hey . . . what's up?" Cassie said after a pause.

"Just thought I'd give you a call."

"Cool . . . that's great," she said, sounding distracted. "What time is it over there?"

As he answered, he could hear her telling someone that she was talking to Troy.

"Where you at?" he asked. "Who you with there?"

"Yolanda and Trina, everybody's in the office today. . . . Yolanda wants to know what you're doing over there."

"Flying jets." That was the simplest way to describe it.

"Yolanda says 'cool,' wants to know when you're gonna give her a ride in one."

"Tell her if she shows up here, I'll try to squeeze her in."

"You gonna squeeze me in, big guy?" Cassie asked.

"You know it, girl."

"When you comin' home?"

"I don't know . . . this thing keeps dragging on."

"What's going on that it's taking so long?"

"Endless supply of bad guys, I guess . . . can't say more than that. . . . I sure am looking forward to . . . y'know . . . getting back there and squeezing you in and . . ."

"Me too, big guy," Cassie interrupted hurriedly. "Listen, I gotta run. Talk to you soon . . . love you lots."

Troy was about to reply in kind, but Cassie had already hung up.

CHAPTER 13

Atbara Airport, Sudan

"DIDN'T THINK WE WERE ON FOR THE DHULADHIYA mission," Jenna drawled as she caught up to her Falcon Force teammates heading for a rare late-evening briefing. "Thought it was a strike mission. I thought I was a snooper, not a shooter."

"I heard that Harris wants us to snoop on the shooters," Hal said. "I guess we'll fly in right after they shoot, and snoop on what's left."

"At least we had a day and a half and a good night's sleep," Troy Loensch added. He was walking behind them slightly, keeping an eye open for the kind of groping that he expected was going on between them, but saw none. Groping? Maybe he was reading too much into it. She had, after all, merely patted him—even if it was on his ass.

They arrived in the briefing room, finding it unusually full. The forty-eight hours of downtime had become thirty-six hours, and now it was over—before the second of the two good nights of sleep for which they had hoped.

The strike mission was due to launch at 0300 so that they would be over the target in the predawn darkness. Indeed, Harris had decided to have Falcon Force fly a poststrike assessment package.

The 334th Air Expeditionary Wing planning staff, standing in the front of the room, looked exhausted. They had pulled an all-nighter and had been working all the next day. After they unveiled their master plan, they could all sleep—while the aircrews went to work.

There was an air of excitement in the room, the anxious excitement born of the anticipation of a larger-than-usual mission. After the conference at Joint Task Force headquarters, General Harris was anxious to prove that his airpower could do the job, and he was making it a maximum effort.

There were two fighter/ground attack squadrons assigned to the 334th. Between them, they could muster thirty-four F-16s. In normal operations, some of these were routinely reconfigured from carrying ordnance to flying reconnaissance missions such as poststrike assessment. Tonight, he wanted all of them carrying weapons.

This left the three Falcon Force ISR birds as the only F-16s available for snooping, and they got the job.

On the screen were images that Troy had brought back of Dhuladhiya. Overlaying these were circles and arrows that indicated where the barges carrying weapons would be. In a satellite image less than six hours old, a freighter labeled as Iranian by the intel analysts could be seen unloading crates onto a barge near an inlet on the island. This was the smoking gun—or rather the guns that would be smoking as soon as the bad guys could get them within range of UN or U.S. personnel.

"FALCON ONE, CLEAR FOR RUNWAY TWO-NINER."

Troy breathed a sigh of relief. Hal was now taxiing toward Atbara's runway. Next, it would be Jenna's turn, and finally his. After an hour of sitting in their cockpits watching the strike package take off—tongue after tongue of flaming turbofan engines—it would be good to get moving.

They flew the same flight plan as they had on their earlier reconnaissance of the Dahlak Archipelago. This time, though, the distance ahead of them was filled with the winking red lights of the strike aircraft.

An hour later, as they descended to the flight level for the attack, Troy could hear the voices in his headset of pilots far ahead as they began to drop ordnance.

There were some excited boasts as hits were reported

on barges. The GBU-32 JDAM smart bomb was deadly accurate, and it was also just plain deadly.

Suddenly the tone of the chatter changed.

"Aspen Four . . . taking ground fire."

"Maple One . . . I see tracers at two o'clock . . . one o'clock."

"Aspen One . . . I got tracers at eleven . . . everywhere!"

"Think I see a SAM . . . Ponderosa Two . . . SAM incoming . . ."

"Mayday . . . repeat . . . mayday . . ."

"This is Ponderosa One . . . we are egressing over Eritrea and walking into a wall of SAMs."

"We got SAMs coming off that damned island *too!*"

"Aspen Four looks like he got hit . . ."

"Aspen Four, this is Aspen One, can you read me . . . come on, talk to me . . . Aspen flight . . . climb to . . ."

"Mayday . . . this is Maple Four . . . I'm hit!"

The lump rose in Troy's throat. In the distance, he could see the carnage, a sky full of explosions and white-hot streaks of SAMs climbing through the darkness.

The American F-16s had raced into the target area in close formation and were too close to take evasive action without risking in-flight collisions. They had to just grit their teeth and plow though it.

"Why?" Jenna said out loud. "How?"

"Somebody got tipped we were coming," Troy snarled angrily.

"Roger that, Falcon Three," Hal said, trying to remain calm. "Climb to ten thousand and maintain heading."

The surface-to-air missiles were fused for the altitude at which the bombers had been flying. Hal figured that Falcon Force could still complete its mission at a higher, safer altitude.

As they came across Dhuladhiya, the ground and sea beneath them were on fire with burning ships and the tracers and streaks from SAMs targeting airplanes.

In the distance, Troy could see the unmistakable plume of a burning aircraft falling to earth.

"Wish we were carrying HARMs on *this* flight," Hal said. The planners had taken the calculated risk of loading the attackers for strikes on boats and barges. Nobody had anticipated surface-to-air missiles, certainly not so many. Indeed, there had been no sign of them in the recon data brought back by Falcon Force.

The flight plan for their return called for the American aircraft to cross onto the African mainland by way of the narrow, lightly populated strip of Eritrea that led into the Denakil Depression where Troy and Jenna had earlier tangled with the Eritrean MiGs. Unfortunately, as soon as they made landfall, the aircraft came under attack from a second defensive line of surface-to-air missiles. The strike commander had ordered the aircraft to scatter, but not before at least three, and possibly more, had been hit.

Both the airspace and the airwaves were in a state of mass confusion.

"Falcon Two . . . incoming," Jenna shouted. "I've been pinged. See it coming . . . taking evasive—"

The next three seconds were the longest of her life.

She jinked and rolled as she watched the white-hot doughnut of a SAM coming at her head-on.

"Aaarrgh!"

She felt the Gs as they stacked up and pressed on her brain, but still the thing came, pursuing her like a shadow.

Her whole field of vision was filled by the thing.

Was this really the way her life would end?

Then came the impact as the heat seeker brought the SAM into contact with the tail of her F-16.

There was a thundering crash of metal onto metal and a jolt that was like being hit by a freight train.

But no explosion.

The aircraft shivered and shook, but it did not come apart in a cloud of burning debris.

"Falcon Two, are you there?" Hal said nervously. "Talk to me . . . are you there?"

"Falcon Two here . . . I've been hit . . . it was a dud . . . didn't explode. I've been hit . . . hard to control."

Troy let out a breath. At least she was alive.

"Falcon Two, can you eject?" Troy asked.

"Trying to get control," Jenna said. "Don't want to punch out . . . not here . . . get closer to home."

The streaks of purple dawn were starting to form along the horizon, and Troy could make out the silhouettes of the other two aircraft in his flight. Hal was about a quarter mile away at his altitude, but Jenna was a couple thousand feet below.

"This is Falcon Three," he said. "I'm going to descend to get a better look at the damage to Falcon Two."

"Roger that," Hal said in a tone of voice suggesting he wished he'd thought of that first.

"Falcon Two, that SAM must have hit you damned hard, your rudder is bent and there's a piece missing."

"No wonder it's so hard to fly this thing," Jenna replied.

"Do you think you can make it back to Atbara?"

"I'm losing altitude and can't turn," Jenna replied. "Other than that . . . no problem."

"We're with you, Falcon Two," Troy said.

"Mighty neighborly of y'all," Jenna replied.

"Falcon One, I have bogies," Hal said nervously.

"I see 'em on the scope," Troy said. "Probably stragglers from the strike pack."

"Negative Falcon Three, they're headed south, straight at us."

"Falcon One . . . I've been pinged," Hal said. Indeed, the incoming fighters had locked on to him first because he was flying at the highest altitude. "I'll ping . . . him back . . ."

Hal stood the F-16 on its tail, climbing to get above the incoming bogies, and then he looped as they approached. The added altitude gave him the advantage as they maneuvered to pursue him.

"Fox Two . . ."

While the other planes clawed for altitude, his loop brought Hal into firing position. He had a good shot, and he took it.

The first Eritrean pilot was so busy trying to get at Hal that he didn't realize until too late that he was about to get got.

The AIM-9 Sidewinder connected, and one of Eritrea's last remaining MiG-29s was gone.

The second MiG-29 broke and ran.

Hal, who had been in a diving attack, began his pullout.

Had the second MiG pilot been more professional, he would have rolled in behind Hal as the F-16 plummeted and picked him off.

As it was, he was so freaked out at watching his pal get popped that he decided to get out of the area.

However, as he ran east, he spotted two Americans below. The first rays of the morning sun striking the rudder on one of the F-16s illuminated what appeared to be serious damage.

How do you say *sitting duck* in Tigrinya?

Realizing that he had the altitude advantage that the American had in the previous encounter, he rolled out and dove.

"Falcon Three, bogie on your six," Hal shouted as he banked hard to intervene in the fast-closing battle about two miles away.

"Roger that," Troy said, instinctively turning to screen Jenna's damaged aircraft as the enemy's missile lock-on pinged in his headset.

Troy looked back. There was a bright yellow flash as the Vympel R-60 "Aphid" air-to-air missile erupted from the MiG's wing.

Making sure that it was tracking him, not Jenna, Troy banked as hard as he could, hoping to outturn the missile.

It came so close that the lemon-yellow flame from its solid-fuel engine illuminated his cockpit—just before the explosion illuminated his entire field of vision.

The concussion knocked Troy's helmet against the inside of the canopy, cracking it. The F-16, which was in a roll when the proximity fuse detonated, began to spin.

There was good news and bad news.

The good news was that the Aphid hadn't hit Troy. The bad news was that the explosion was close enough to cause severe damage to his aircraft.

"Falcon Three . . . g-g-g-going . . . d-d-d-down," he reported as he fought to control the shaking, shuddering, corkscrewing aircraft.

"Punch out, Falcon Three," Hal shouted, as Troy tried to control the spin long enough to do this.

Seeing the spinning desert rushing up at him, he decided that it was now or never.

In a blinding flash, he left the F-16, and for what seemed like an eternity he hurtled through the air, spinning like a Frisbee. Somewhere within that eternity, he might have blacked out, because the next thing he remembered was when the canopy of his parachute jerked him back to his senses.

In the distance, he saw an F-16 tumbling lifelessly toward the ground. He watched it hit and disintegrate, the pieces bouncing across the desert at impact speed, swathed in dust and smoke.

Then, out of the corner of his eye, he spotted something else. It was another F-16, twisting, gyrating, and falling.

Who? Hal?

Suddenly a third F-16 flashed past, and in the cockpit he caught a glimpse of the checkerboard pattern of Hal's helmet.

"Jenna!"

Troy realized as the second F-16 impacted the desert that one of these falling airplanes was Jenna's.

Hal came by again, so close that the shock wave caused Troy's parachute to bounce about twenty feet.

Below, the ground was rushing upward.

The last thought Troy had before the impact knocked him unconscious was that he had better prepare for a hard landing.

CHAPTER 14

Denakil Depression

TROY LOENSCH WAS UNSURE WHETHER HE WAS DEAD or alive, but he settled on something that was somewhere in between. His first sensation was one of being enveloped in a cocoon of excruciating pain. Everything hurt—his shoulder, his knees, his head. He gritted his teeth and felt the grind of a mouth full of sand.

He opened his eyes and saw only the gravelly ground.

He tried to move and discovered that his limbs were wildly contorted, as though he had been wadded up and tossed in a sandbox—which was more or less what had happened.

Troy had started to hope that nothing was broken, then settled on hoping that nothing was broken *off.*

He tried to summon enough saliva to spit the crud from his mouth, choked, and started to cough.

When his mouth was reasonably clear, he attempted to untangle himself and roll into a sitting position.

As he did, he saw a person standing over him.

"You look like shit, Loensch."

It was Jenna Munrough.

"Are you all right?" Troy gasped.

"Better than y'all by the looks of things," she replied.

She didn't look it. Her flight suit was filthy beyond any recognition of its true color—and so was her hair. Her face was so dirty that the only thing recognizable about her was her voice.

Amazingly, Troy discovered that he could stand—and take steps. It hurt like hell, but he could do it.

"Guess nothing's broken," he said. "Least nothing important. Glad to see you got out okay, Munrough . . . I saw your bird auger in . . . didn't see your chute."

"I was above you . . . I saw yours . . . figured you were toast from the way you were spinning."

"Me too," Troy agreed.

"Where do you suppose we are?" Jenna asked, looking around.

"We're in that desert . . . Denakil . . . y'know, where we shot down the MiGs. Do you have your GPS receiver?"

"It broke when I landed. Y'all have yours?"

Troy checked his gear and found that his GPS receiver

was working, though the information it gave them was of little practical use. They learned that they were fourteen degrees, forty-five minutes north of the equator and thirty-nine degrees, thirty-two minutes east of Greenwich, but that was merely of academic curiosity.

Troy's radio, like all of Jenna's gear, had been crushed on impact, but the transponder with which a rescue team could home in on his position still worked.

They could see on the GPS that they were fifty miles inland from the coast, and that the mountain they could see to the north was called Amba Soira. The GPS told them that there was a road on the other side of the ridge that lay to the west, but they could have discovered that by climbing to the top of the ridge.

"Haven't heard a chopper," Jenna said, looking skyward. "I'm sure that Hal would have reported our position . . . or they'd be homing in on the transponder."

"There were a lot of people shot down last night. I figure they're pretty busy . . . you suppose we ought to just hang in here and wait?"

"I really don't think that's a good idea," Jenna said. "Remember where we are and how we got here . . . we got shot down by Eritreans . . . this is Eritrea . . . I sure as hell don't want to be a female POW in Eritrea."

"Point taken," Troy said.

"I'll help you bury your parachute," Jenna offered.

After burying Troy's chute and trying to disguise it as best they could, the two pilots climbed to the top of the ridge to look at the road. It was deserted for as far as they could see, so getting across it without being seen would have been possible. However, it was what *lay* across it that was the decision maker for them.

"Look at that," Troy said, pointing to the immense desert, stretching into Ethiopia, that separated them from the Sudanese border by hundreds of miles.

"Sure hate to run out of water over there," Jenna said, instinctively glancing at the small flask from her survival kit that she had strapped to her belt.

"Let's head the other way," Troy suggested. "There are U.S. Navy ships in the Red Sea; if they are tracking my transponder, they may be able to get a chopper out from there to pick us up."

"Let's go and get gone before somebody comes to investigate where those two parachutes came down this morning," Jenna agreed.

They hiked for about two hours, suffering from the midday heat and pausing from time to time in the shade of the rock outcroppings that dotted the landscape.

"Gotta conserve water," Jenna said, scolding Troy as he reached for his flask.

"Maybe we oughta wait until dark?" Troy asked rhetorically. "They said in survival school that you shouldn't try to hike in the hottest part of the day."

"You oughta know, you were the one who aced the survival course."

Troy ignored her baiting, feigning distraction as he

reached into a crevice in the cliff beneath which they had stopped.

"Whatcha looking for?" Jenna asked.

"I dunno, just thinking there might be some condensation in the dark, deep corners here."

"Well . . ."

"Baked dry centuries ago."

"Hear that?"

"Hear what?"

"Thought I heard a chopper," Jenna said with guarded excitement.

"At last." Troy sighed, as the *whup-whup-whup* grew louder. "First thing I'm gonna do is get me a shower and a beer, or a beer and a shower."

"Where's he going?" Jenna asked as the *whup-whup-whup* grew more distant.

"Sounds like he's searching the place where we landed, maybe one of the crash sites?"

"Let's go get us seen," Jenna said, scrambling up a low incline that they had just descended a few minutes earlier.

Troy followed, nearly colliding with her when she stopped abruptly.

"What's the—"

"Oh shit," Jenna exclaimed. "Look at—"

"Oh double shit," Troy whispered.

The helicopter was orbiting the spot where they had come down, but it was *not* an American Black Hawk. It was a green and tan Mil Mi-8 with the Christmas-tree-ornament-colored insignia of the Eritrean Air Force.

Without a further word, the two Americans raced back to the cliff and shoved themselves as deep into the shadow as they could.

Jenna's hand went to her Beretta M9, as though merely touching the standard-issue automatic pistol would provide her some consolation. Each of them had two thirty-round magazines, but against an armed helicopter, or even an unarmed helicopter filled with armed troops, the Berettas were scant consolation.

"Maybe we can outshoot 'em." Troy smiled.

"Save the last round for yourself," Jenna replied grimly.

Troy looked at her expression. There was no way that she would allow herself to wind up as a female POW in Eritrea.

CHAPTER 15

Denakil Depression

"MAYBE WE CAN STEAL A BOAT." TROY LAUGHED.

"And sail off into the sunset," Jenna said with a growl of mock sarcasm, her voice raspy from too little water and too much dust.

"Technically, from this coast it would be the sun *rising*."

The two downed American pilots had been walking for three days in the tortuous heat of the Eritrean desert. Had it been summer, not spring, they could very well have died of heatstroke by now. Had they not pulled some only slightly brackish water from an abandoned well that they had found, they could well have died from dehydration.

No American rescue helicopter had come, despite

Troy's transponder broadcasting their position. They had given up trying to figure out why.

Fortunately, they had seen no further Eritrean choppers. They didn't *care* why. They were just glad.

Troy and Jenna had decided that it would be suicide to try hiking straight back to their base in Sudan. There was too much inhospitable distance, and too many Al-Qinamah bad guys. Therefore, they had decided to try to reach the Red Sea coastline. They hadn't yet decided what they'd do when they got there—except find a place to get a long, cold drink of water.

"I'm surprised that Hal hasn't tried to find us," Troy said, making conversation. Aside from walking eastward and worrying about water, that was all they had to do. "Like, y'know . . . you and him . . ."

"Me and Hal what?"

"Oh come on . . . I saw your hand on his ass . . ."

"So?"

"So I figured there was something going on . . . figure that on account of that . . . he'd come flying over this damned place trying to spot us."

"Maybe he did . . . Maybe he did back where we were . . . we're a long way from there now."

"Maybe."

"What?" Jenna asked in that "I-know-what-you're-thinking" tone that people have when they think they know what you're thinking.

"Whaddya mean, 'what'?"

"Are you jealous?"

"Well, I guess, y'know," Troy said, groping for words. "I've been listening to you snore every night and it's hard not to think about . . . when you're sleeping with somebody and all that's happening is that you're trying to *sleep* . . ."

"You saying I *snore*?" Jenna laughed.

"Yeah, but . . ."

"Okay . . . since we may never get out of this thing alive . . ."

"Don't say that," Troy interrupted.

"Okay . . . since we may never get out of this thing alive," Jenna repeated, "I should admit that I've . . . y'know . . . I've had those kinda thoughts about y'all."

"Really?"

"You're a hunk, Loensch," Jenna said in a matter-of-fact way. "Sometimes you're obnoxious, but you're a hunk and I have had . . . kind of a thing for y'all."

"What kinda thing?"

"Yesterday . . . all day when we were walking through that ravine, y'know," Jenna replied. "I had this fantasy about taking a shower with y'all."

"I've been thinking about showers a lot too," Troy admitted.

"I was thinking about what came *after* the shower," Jenna said with a hoarse chuckle.

At that moment, the two of them reached the crest of a ridge and looked down into a landscape totally unlike anything they had seen for days. They could see the Red Sea in the distance, probably no more than five miles distant. In the foreground were patches of vegetation, even a date palm orchard and clusters of buildings. They could even see the coastal highway.

"Green sure looks weird when you ain't seen leaves for a week or two," Jenna exaggerated.

"Green sure looks like there's water to me," Troy said.

"We better be careful," Jenna cautioned. "We get caught down there, we'll get ourselves turned in."

As painful as it was, they waited until dusk to approach the date palms. As they sat in the shade of the boulder, talk did not return to the after-shower fantasy, but to earlier fantasies of drinking water.

Unfortunately, when they reached the first irrigation ditch, the water failed to match the water of even the least-demanding fantasy.

"Nasty shit," Jenna exclaimed as they studied the greenish liquid in the half light of the evening.

"Probably really *is* a sewer," Troy said disgustedly.

"There's got to be a well somewhere. Let's move out while we got *some* light."

As they snaked their way through orchard, field, and vacant patch of ground, they were careful not to get too close to any buildings, and they took cover whenever a vehicle passed nearby.

At last they found it.

It was a simple hand pump on a rickety wooden platform. The water was not the best they'd ever tasted—but to them, it *was* the best water in the world.

Jenna cupped her hands to drink as Troy pumped the handle, then thrust her head beneath the flow, moaning gently as the tepid fluid poured through her hair and trickled down the back of her flight suit.

Next, it was Troy's turn, and Jenna pumped water onto him. He had never in his life been so happy to wash his face.

"All I need now is some aromatherapy gel and some cucumber slices for my eyes." Jenna giggled, her voice already sounding less gravelly.

"All I want is that shower you were talking about this afternoon," Troy said, looking at Jenna in the half light. She had peeled back her flight suit to the sports bra beneath. Seeing Munrough's breasts, nice ones at that, was like seeing foliage for the first time after an eternity in the desert. He knew that such phenomena existed, but actually seeing it made it so much more real, and so very appealing.

"Look, there's a dude under all that dirt," Jenna said as she leaned closer, reached out and put her hand on his cheek.

"*Ya nadil!*"

The two startled Americans turned at the sound of the voice. It was a short man in his early twenties who was missing several teeth. They had been so preoccupied with the sensual joy of the water, and so used to being alone in the desert with no one else around, that they had dropped their guard.

"*Ma-smuk?*"

Another man emerged out of the shadows. Both were short of stature, making the AK-47 that each carried seem enormous. By the way they had the muzzles pointed downward, it was apparent that neither had noticed that the two Americans were carrying sidearms.

"Sorry, we didn't mean to steal your water," Jenna said in an apologetic tone as her fingers crawled slowly toward her holster, which she had set aside when she pulled back her flight suit. She had no idea what they were saying, but hoped her tone would set the men somewhat at ease.

"*La 'afham,*" one of the men said with a shrug, as though he had no better idea of what she had said than she had of his earlier assertions.

"*Mundhu 'an kuntu murahiqan 'ahbabtu 'as-sayyidata s-suwidiyyat,*" the first man said to the other, nodding toward Jenna and obviously remarking about her blond hair. It was something these men didn't see every day. Perhaps never.

Having the attention focused on her allowed Troy the opportunity to get his hand around the grip of his Beretta.

"*Al-'an wajadtu imra'a li-z-zawaj.*" The man chortled.

"*Ana 'aydan 'uhibb 'as-sayyidata l-misriyyat, khassatan*

hawajibahunna s-sawda," the other said, shrugging as if to say that he didn't care for blondes.

Troy wrapped his finger around the trigger and gently slid his Beretta from its holster.

CHAPTER 16

Culver City, California

"THIS IS REALLY AWKWARD, TROY," CASSIE KILMER said nervously.

"Let me give you some space." The man in the coral-colored polo shirt smiled as he put on his sunglasses and stepped out the front door onto busy Sepulveda Boulevard.

Across the office, Yolanda Rodriguez watched him leave, then glared back at her keyboard, pretending that she hadn't been watching.

"Well, shit, Cassie, this is a little awkward for me too!" Troy said, looking at Cassie in disbelief.

"You were gone for two years," Cassie said angrily. "And back only twice in that whole time."

"That was my job . . . we talked about it—"

"What was *I* supposed to do?" Cassie interrupted angrily. "You had your job and it was your life. What was I supposed to do? Just put my life on hold while you were off somewhere living *your* life? You can't just go off and expect me to stay here all frozen in time like a state of suspended animation or something. I'm a person too. I'm entitled to live a normal life."

"How was I supposed to know you had this guy?"

"Enrique is not just *a guy*."

"*Excuse me*, how was I supposed to know you had this 'not just a guy'? Why didn't you at least tell me, so I don't come walking in here and make an ass out of myself."

"I didn't . . . y'know . . . I didn't know you were coming back," Cassie said, glancing at the large ring on her left hand. "Enrique and I didn't become officially engaged until . . . you know . . ."

"So you thought I was dead and you jumped into bed with *In-Reekie*?"

The inadvertent, giggly yelp emanating from Yolanda's desk indicated both that she had in fact been eavesdropping, and that she was well aware that Cassie had been in Enrique's bed long before she received the report that Captain Troy Loensch was missing in action and presumed dead.

"I'll run these down to the FedEx drop box," Yolanda said, standing up and grabbing a stack of important-looking orange and purple envelopes.

"I cried when I heard the news," Cassie said sadly,

tears forming in her eyes. "I cried all damned night when I heard that you weren't coming back. I cried for you and I cried for me. That was when I realized that it didn't matter . . . you were gone from my life a long time before that . . . and I realized that I should have moved on long before. I'm glad that you're all right . . . but I'm still moving on. There's nothing left for you here, Troy. There's nothing left in my heart for you."

"Hey, but Cas—" Troy started to say.

"There's nothing more to talk about, Troy," Cassie said emphatically. Her body language as she stepped toward him read not as a move to be close, but as pushing him toward the door.

Troy realized that it was neither possible nor desirable to beg her to reconsider. She wouldn't, and he didn't want it.

He left the real estate office wishing he could kick a dent into an expensive panel on Enrique's Porsche, but the punk had already driven off.

As he walked down Sepulveda, back to where his mother's car was parked, Troy thought about everything that had happened to him over the past months. They were the kinds of experiences that people describe as life-changing, but Troy couldn't tell. Everything in his life, every point of reference, had changed, so he couldn't really tell whether he had changed, or if it was just a case of everything changing around him.

His nearly three weeks of wandering in Eritrea with

Jenna Munrough had been like a bad dream, punctuated by experiences like that night at the well when they shot the two men, and the two desperate days of being chased by the local militia. When they had reached that Doctors Without Borders compound at the end of their wanderings, they had finally learned why the American helicopters never came.

After the calamity over Dhuladhiya Island, in which eleven American aircraft were shot down attacking the sovereign nation of Eritrea, the United Nations had pulled the plug on the operation and the United States was given forty-eight hours to withdraw its forces.

The fears that the Joint Task Force base at Atbara would be overrun were finally realized, but by that time only a few dozen Americans remained. They never made it home.

Troy Loensch had made it home.

The Doctors Without Borders people had gotten him and Jenna across the border into Djibouti, where the American embassy had arranged for a flight back to the United States.

As Troy climbed into his mother's Chevy Equinox, he thought about how strange it was to no longer be strapping himself into an aircraft. During his two years overseas, he had rarely driven a car, spending much more time in the air than on a highway. In Sudan, he hadn't driven at all. After four days back home he was only just reacclimating himself to Los Angeles traffic.

He didn't know whether he would ever be back in a cockpit.

So much had happened while he was on the run in Eritrea that he felt like Rip Van Winkle. When he and Jenna landed at Dulles Airport, they were met by Air Force personnel who whisked them to a military hospital to be checked out, rehydrated, and treated for dysentery. They expected to be promptly shipped back to the Intelligence, Surveillance, and Reconnaissance Agency and the 55th Wing, but instead they were given a thirty-day leave and told that their next assignments were not yet known.

As they began to catch up on the news from their lost weeks, they discovered that in the wake of the Dhuladhiya disaster, Congress had passed legislation terminating overseas peacekeeping operations by the American military.

As Troy and Jenna were being checked out of the hospital after two days, they were each handed a packet offering them a bonus for accepting an early discharge. The termination legislation carried a steep decrease in the Pentagon budget, and the Air Force had decided to stay ahead of the curve and to reduce manpower wherever possible.

"How'd it go with Cassie?" Barbara Loensch called from the kitchen when she heard her son slam the front door of the family's Northridge bungalow.

"Oh, all right . . . we decided to call it quits," Troy

answered. He thought about telling his mother the whole story, but decided it was pointless.

"Quits? That's too bad . . . I thought she was, y'know, a nice girl."

"Oh yeah, she's a nice girl," Troy said, pretending that he meant it. "But y'know, it's just not gonna work out. We're completely different people than we were back in college."

"Yeah, I suppose . . . sometimes I think that your father and I are completely different people than we were back then."

"You and Dad?"

"So, have you decided whether you're going to take that offer from the Air Force?" Barbara said, changing the subject.

"I dunno." Troy shrugged, grabbing a can of Hyper-X energy drink from the fridge. "They gave me a month to decide. The money's good if I take the discharge."

"Why would they pay to get rid of a good pilot like you?"

"They just have a whole lot less to do in the world now."

"What will happen in those places like over in Africa where you were?"

"They'll just fall apart," Troy said sadly. "Like what happened in Sudan. The Al-Qinamah just swarmed into that base where I had been. Killed a bunch of people. That was after we lost so many pilots that night when I got shot down."

"That was terrible," Barbara said. "Terrible that it had to happen like that."

"It was like getting stabbed in the back," Troy said angrily, slamming the remainder of his energy drink. "They gave the Joint Task Force the authorization to bomb those arms boats, but the State Department, some dude that was at the meeting, decided to try to do some diplomatic intervention and bad guys got wind of it. They had two days to set a trap . . . and we got trapped."

"I can sure understand you not wanting to go back," Troy's mother said sympathetically.

"On top of that, they want to *pay me* not to go back," Troy said. "That's a pretty sweet deal . . . I just don't know what I'm gonna do next."

CHAPTER 17

Glendale, California

"FIRST DAY ON THE JOB, HUH?" YOLANDA RODRIGUEZ said as she put on her mascara. "Like, I bet you're pretty excited, huh?"

"Yeah, it'll be pretty weird having to be somewhere after not having to be anywhere for a few months," Troy said, reaching for his jeans. "But I've been screwing around for long enough; it's time to get back to work and earn some cash."

"Hey, screwing around?" Yolanda giggled. "Is that what you call us?"

"Hey Yo, y'know what I mean," Troy pleaded. They both knew what he meant, and they both knew that their relationship really amounted to little more than screwing around. They had hooked up after Cassie dumped Troy. Yolanda engineered a "chance" meeting and turned on the charm, and their first night together was sufficiently memorable for there to be a second, a third, and so on. But they both knew it was just a lot of fun and little more.

"Hope you got a day off pretty soon, though," Yolanda said. "Sure missed you not drinkin' Corona and shots with us last night."

"You know I couldn't do that, especially on my first day," Troy said.

She understood. The job that Troy had taken was with Golden West Courier, piloting one of their Beech-craft Bonanzas between Burbank Airport and points throughout California and Nevada. Company rules prohibited alcohol consumption by pilots for twenty-four hours before wheels-up.

"So you gonna get your own place then, huh?" Yolanda said, slithering into a tight, teal-colored skirt.

"Yeah. First paycheck," Troy confirmed. "Gotta get out of that house."

"Must be weird watching your own parents split up, huh?"

"It's unreal."

"So your dad, he's got something going on the side?"

"No, it's not like that . . . least I don't think so . . . don't *want* to think so anyway. I think they're just tired of each other."

An hour after watching Yolanda drive away in her coffee-colored Sebring, Troy was in the cockpit of a Golden West Bonanza going through his final check for takeoff. At last, cleared for Runway 26, he cranked up the Continental E-185 and let its 205 horses lift him into the sky over the San Fernando Valley.

Climbing out over the San Gabriel Mountains, headed north toward his stops in Bakersfield and Fresno, Troy felt the elation of once more being in the air. The Bonanza was about as far from an F-16 as you could get and still be in an airplane, but that didn't matter. He was flying.

Just as Troy's life was starting to come together, his parents' lives were coming apart. When Office Tech downsized, the longtime employees with the biggest salaries were the first to go. Carl's being out of work put further strain on an already strained marriage. Barbara went up to visit her recently widowed sister in San Luis Obispo for a couple of weeks. That was a month ago.

Troy had started spending most nights at Yolanda's, but he was looking forward to getting off on his own permanently.

Watching the trees of the Angeles National Forest slip past beneath his wings, Troy was reminded of how desolate Sudan and Eritrea had been. He was glad to be out of that place, but he found himself missing Hal Coughlin and Jenna Munrough. After all that the three of them had been through in the early part of their knowing one another, a bond had finally formed. Now it had been broken.

He had gotten a couple of e-mails from Jenna, but they hadn't really kept in close contact. Like him, she and Hal had taken their discharge bonuses and had gotten out of the Air Force.

They had both taken jobs with one of those defense contractors that are clustered all around the Washington, D.C., Beltway. Troy had forgotten which one. There were so many, and he had never heard of this one. It sounded, from Jenna's e-mail, as if she and Hal were "together," but she hadn't actually said as much.

He occasionally thought about her in a "what if" sort of way, but the memories of the dirt-encrusted Jenna with her short, ratty blond hair in comparison with the reality of Yolanda's beautifully proportioned body and her long, well-kept ravishing raven hair kept Troy happily in the here and now.

The unspoken understanding between Troy and Yo was that they were each in it for the sex—but the sex *was* good.

The downside of their relationship, if you could call it a "relationship," was that Yolanda reminded him all too often of Cassie. The two women worked in the same office, and occasionally Yo would mention something in passing.

From what Troy had gathered, Cassie and Enrique

had hit a rough patch, and for a moment Troy entertained thoughts of phoning her—but only for a moment. The next he heard, they were back together, and he was glad that he had not called.

The ship of his once inevitable relationship with Cassie had long since sailed, and he was glad to have said bon voyage.

CHAPTER 18

Sacramento Executive Airport, California

TROY POPPED OPEN HIS LAPTOP. THE SUN WAS GOING down, and he had about forty-five minutes to kill before the Golden West Courier van arrived with baskets of letters and parcels from the sprawl of state office buildings in the city. He had been on the Valley route for a week, making stops up through the San Joaquin, culminating in an end-of-the-day run from the state capital to Los Angeles.

After nearly six months, he had come to really enjoy his job, which offered plenty of solitary flying time in airspace with generally good flying weather. To break the monotony, he and the other four Golden West pilots rotated routes. Last week he had been on runs up to Santa Rosa, Eureka, and Redding, and next week, who knows? The variety was nice.

He flicked idly though his e-mails.

There was one from his mother, responding to his response to her *Why haven't I heard from you in two weeks?* e-mail.

There was an urgent e-mail from a man in Nigeria who desperately needed Troy's help in transferring eight million dollars to a bank account in Andorra.

There was another one that asked *Any chance we can hook up?* in the subject line. He didn't recognize the name. Who in the world was jmm@fhcoherndon.com? Troy was about to delete that one, thinking it was just a come-on to a soft-porn site, but he decided at the last moment to take a look.

The *jmm* was Jenna Munrough.

She and Hal Coughlin were going to be in Las Vegas, attending some sort of convention, and she was inviting him to come up and join them for a day or two.

Jenna Munrough. As the months had gone by, Troy had thought less and less of her, and even less of Hal, and of their days with Task Force Sudan.

Could he hook up with them? The Golden West run to Las Vegas was an overnighter because of packages that the casinos needed flown to Los Angeles at the start of the business day. Troy hadn't been on this route for a few weeks. The guy who was due for it next week owed Troy a favor, so the answer was yes.

Would he hook up with them? If for nothing else, he was curious to hear about what they were doing. They could get together for dinner, hang out for a few hours, and that would be that.

Should he hook up with them? During their weeks in the desert, he had started to develop what chicks call "feelings" for Jenna, and she had expressed as much toward him. Evidently, she and Hal were still an item, so what should he do?

What the hell? Troy decided that he'd do it.

Five days later, he was climbing into an orange-roofed taxi from the Desert Cab Company at the McCarran Airport General Aviation hangar. He had stashed his gear at the cheap motel where he usually stayed, had combed his hair, and was headed for the Mirage, where Jenna and Hal were staying.

"Great to hear your voice, Loensch," she said affably as Troy reached her on his cell phone from the cab.

"Umm, good to hear yours. You sound the same," Troy said. Memories came flooding back at the sound of her voice.

"I don't know whether to take that as a compliment or an insult." She laughed. "Where are you?"

"Stuck in traffic on the Strip near the Tropicana. Where are you?"

"At the Mirage . . . I'll meet you in the lobby by the big fish tank."

In the late afternoon, traffic on the Las Vegas Strip moves at a snail's pace, but at last, Troy was walking through the wall of glass doors at the Mirage Hotel.

The lobby was a swirling sea of humanity. There were hard-core gaming types, convention-goers intent on shedding business suits to become swingers for the night, and swingers who came out only at night. There were bachelor partiers and bachelorette partiers. There were beautiful people, and the inevitable beautiful people wannabes.

But Troy saw no Jenna Munrough.

He found the fish tank and scanned the crowd. He walked to the opposite end of the fish tank and was wondering if there might be *another* fish tank.

"Hey, Loensch! Y'all just walked right past me."

It was Jenna's voice. Troy turned. He saw no one he recognized.

"What's the matter?" Jenna said in mock anger. "Y'all walked right past me like I wasn't there. Is that any way for ya to treat your old buddy, Falcon Two?"

Troy was speechless. He heard the voice, but it was not coming from a pilot with short-cropped hair and a dusty olive-green flight suit.

Her voice was coming from lips the color of rose petals. Her hair, once scraggly and spiked, now flowed to her shoulders in sensuous waves. Her flight suit was superseded by a shimmering black cocktail dress, her dog tags by a jeweled pendant.

"Jenna," Troy said, feeling himself starting to go red in the face. "Umm . . . you look great . . ."

"How 'bout a hug for Falcon Two for old times' sake?"

A whiff of her fragrance and the feel of her hair against his cheek, and Troy could not imagine this gorgeous woman as the pilot he remembered as Falcon Two.

"Hey, Loensch, good to see you."

Troy turned at the sound of Hal's voice. He was more or less as Troy remembered him, though he had traded his flight suit for an open-collared sport shirt and a blazer that looked expensive. The last time that Troy had seen his face was that day when he was dangling from a parachute harness over the Denakil Depression, and Hal had flashed past in his F-16.

"Let's go eat," Jenna said, taking Troy by the arm. "We got reservations at Carnevino over at the Palazzo . . . you still like steak, don'tcha, Loensch?"

She seemed taller, Troy thought as they walked toward Las Vegas Boulevard. It must be the four-inch heels.

She seemed unusually friendly, and so too was Hal. It must be that whatever had happened in their final weeks together in Sudan had erased the old animosities that had once hung over them.

"Guess you guys must be rolling with the high rollers," Troy said, looking at the menu after Hal asserted that their expense account would be picking up the tab. The dry bone-in rib eye was priced at about double Troy's typical weekly expenditure at Safeway.

Hal and Jenna laughed and said that they'd landed in a good situation, job-wise.

"We're working for a company called Firehawk?" Jenna said, framing the statement as a question as if to ask whether Troy had heard of them. "Consulting company in Herndon, Virginia?"

"I've heard the name," Troy said. It sounded only vaguely familiar. "What is it that you do?"

"It's a private military contractor, a PMC," Jenna said. "It's like an NGO, a nongovernmental organization, like Doctors Without Borders, but military."

"What does it . . . do you . . . actually do?" Troy asked.

"It's like a private security firm . . . only a lot bigger," Hal said. "It's almost like a . . . Well it *is* like a private army."

"Is that legal?" Troy asked.

"You can't swear allegiance to a foreign army," Hal said. "Doesn't mean you can't work for a private company."

"Now that Congress has curtailed overseas deployments, warfighting is gonna be outsourced." Jenna shrugged. "The Germans and the French have been doing this for years. The Bundestag won't let German forces operate overseas in a combat role because of that nastiness back in World War Two . . . so they contract with private firms."

"I thought the Germans were in Afghanistan," Troy said.

"But only in Regional Command North," Jenna replied, sipping her Merlot. "They were about as far from where the Taliban is shooting as possible."

The food had come, and Troy found the rib eye to be the best he could remember. It was probably not worth the price, but it was good, and he wasn't paying.

"What's the convention that brings you to Vegas?" Troy asked as he glanced longingly at the citrus mascarpone cheesecake with fried pumpkin on the dessert menu.

"Global Security ExpoCon," Hal explained. "It's a meet and greet for PMCs and suppliers . . . hardware . . . software . . . all that stuff. You oughta come by tomorrow."

"Sounds interesting," Troy said. It was a strange concept, but it sounded intriguing. "Wish I could, but I got a flight at 0730 . . . I fly for a courier company . . . the Vegas run is taking things back and forth to L.A. for the casino bosses."

"So you're still flying?" Hal said jealously, realizing that they'd been talking all evening about their company and hadn't asked what Troy was doing.

"Don't have the kind of expense account that you guys have, but I'm in the cockpit twenty hours every week . . . Sometimes more."

"Cool," Jenna said. "I sure miss it. That's the one thing about the Air Force that I do miss."

"What exactly do you guys do for Firehawk?" Troy asked.

"Operational planning," Hal said. "Figuring out what we need, and how to get the most out of it. It's a lot like the military, but the chain of command's a helluva lot shorter and decision times are a helluva lot quicker."

"I'm an administrative liaison," Jenna said. "I spend a lot of time schmoozing with customers—Pentagon, State Department . . ."

"State Department?" Troy said. "Weren't those the guys that got us shot down?"

"The person responsible for that took early retirement," Hal said conspiratorially. "Nobody really knows what happened to him."

CHAPTER 19

The Palazzo, Las Vegas

CONVERSATION TURNED TO LESS WEIGHTY TOPICS, and at last the threesome was strolling back toward the Mirage in the warmth of the Vegas evening.

"I know of a table that's got my name on it," Hal said at last. "Care to join me?"

"No, the tables are never that good to *me*," Troy said. "And it's getting close to taps for this old dude."

"Me neither." Jenna laughed. "No table ever been good to this old country girl."

They parted with Hal inviting Troy to look them up if he ever came to Washington, and vowing that he and Jenna would visit Troy when they came to Southern California.

As Hal dashed off to find that special lucky table, Jenna shook Troy's hand and bade him good night.

Troy was just savoring the way her skirt swirled as she turned, when she turned back.

"Hey," she said, tossing her hair and slinging her purse onto her shoulder. "It's still pretty early; could I buy y'all a drink? I owe you a rain check from once back in Sudan."

"You got a long memory, Munrough. . . . Would this be on the Firehawk expense account?" Troy asked.

"You betcha, Loensch."

Through the lobby of the Palazzo and down an endless hallway was the entrance to a small—by Las Vegas standards—bar, with low light and dark wood. It was empty except for a couple in a booth, and three guys, obviously conventioneers and probably ExpoCon conventioneers, watching and probably betting on a televised basketball game.

Jenna and Troy slid into a booth as an attentive waitress arrived promptly to take care of them. Jenna ordered a bourbon neat, Troy another glass of Sprite. She knew not to question the drinking habits of a pilot on the eve of an early flight.

"You know, y'all really ought to think about coming to work at Firehawk," Jenna suggested. "We're *always* looking for a few good men."

"Thought occurred to me," Troy admitted. "But I like doing what I'm doing . . . and after that deal at Dhuladhiya, I'm pretty soured on the military."

"This ain't the military," she said. "We don't play with red tape."

"Mmmmm," Troy replied in a tone that said he really didn't want to talk about it.

"Besides, looking back at the way it ended over there, I thought our little adventure was kinda fun." Jenna smiled.

In the flickering light of the single candle, Troy found her really gorgeous. He almost said it, and if he'd had a drink, he probably would have. Instead, he just watched the dancing reflection of the candlelight in her eyes and in the strings of jewels that dangled from her ears.

"Remember that night at the well?" Jenna said.

"How can I forget? We blew those poor guys away."

"One dude was getting pretty frisky with his AK, and I sure didn't like the way he was looking at *me*." Jenna shrugged.

It was hard to imagine this beautiful woman in the candlelight as the same person who'd put two nine-millimeter rounds into a person's forehead.

"I was thinking more about what we were talking about before all that," Jenna explained.

"About taking a shower?" Troy smiled.

"And about how I had a kind of a thing for y'all. By the way, you sure do look pretty good when you're all cleaned up."

"You too, Munrough."

She reached across the table and gently touched his cheek, just as she had that night at the well.

"We never had a chance to finish that conversation," she drawled. "Seems like we got some unfinished business."

In one fluid motion, she slid around the table, snuggling next to him and stroking his back.

He looked into her eyes, at the dancing light and at the irresistible woman beside him.

When her lips brushed his, he succumbed. One passionate kiss was followed by another, yet more passionate. She pressed her body against his, and he felt her hand suddenly beneath his shirt.

He placed his hand on her bare thigh, and she moved as though encouraging him to move it higher. It was a good thing that the bar was dark and nearly deserted. It was a good thing that the television set at the bar was loud enough to drown out the murmur of groans coming from the booth.

"Let's go up to your room . . . now." She gasped as she fumbled to unbuckle his belt.

"I'm staying at a motel down by the airport," he whispered, his hand massaging the bare flesh well north of her thigh.

"My room, then," she said breathlessly.

"Isn't that also . . . y'know . . . Hal's room?"

"He'll be at the tables all night."

"What if he's not?"

"I need y'all to—" she said, panting desperately.

So did Troy, but the image of Hal's face came to him, carrying the expression he'd had the first time they crossed paths after that night on the mountain in the Colville.

"We better not do this," Troy said, leaning back.

"What the hell?" Jenna said, her voice trembling with the desperation of interrupted passion. "I'm burnin' up here, y'all. I need you to come on in and finish me off."

"What are we doing?" Troy asked. "I mean besides the obvious. Why are we . . . I mean you and Hal . . . Why are you here with me?"

"Because I've wanted this for a long time, and it feels like you're wantin' it too."

"What are we doin' to Hal?" Troy asked.

"He's not here, Loensch," Jenna said, leaning back and straightening her disrupted underwear. "I'm tryin' to do *you*."

"Man, I left him on a goddamn mountain. You reamed me from one end of the hangar to the other for being the self-centered asshole who left him to die. Now, here I am with the woman he thinks he has something with . . . I just can't . . . as much as I want to . . . just can't . . ."

"This is sure a surprise from an arrogant, self-centered bastard like you," she said, sighing and smoothing her dress. "You got me all on fire, and then you want to pull back without completin' the deal."

"You know what I mean," Troy said.

"Yeah, dammit, I know what you mean," Jenna said, staring into space. "Let me catch my breath. I shouldn't have . . . we shouldn't have. I'm gonna go back to my room . . . alone . . . gonna take a cold shower . . . alone . . . and be glad this never went any further."

She reached into her purse and took out her brush, then looked sadly into Troy's eyes.

"You're right," she said, looking seductively into his eyes. "Tomorrow I'll be so glad we didn't, but right now, I want you *so* bad."

CHAPTER 20

Santa Barbara Municipal Airport, California

"**GOLDEN WEST EIGHT-SIX-FOUR, CLIMB AND MAINTAIN** heading and flight level one-five-zee-ro," crackled the voice in Troy's headset as he climbed out over a California coastline tinted gold by the rays of the late-afternoon sun. Beneath him, the ocean was a deep cobalt blue.

"Roger, this is Golden West Eight-Six-Four, climbing and maintaining," he replied. "Good day."

One thing about his job was that it gave him plenty of time to be alone with his thoughts and with the voices in his head.

More and more, the voices themselves were becoming his circle of friends. Cassie had left him—an old wound, healed but with permanent scarring. He and Yolanda saw less and less of each other, getting together every few weeks—then every few months—only to be reminded that they had little in common.

The voice of the woman in his headset reminded him of the voice of the woman in his head. Since Las Vegas, Jenna's voice bounced frequently into Troy's mind. He heard the Ozark drawl telling him he was an asshole for leaving Hal Coughlin on a mountaintop to die, and he heard it tell him that she craved the warmth of his body.

It seemed that his relationship with Jenna over the past months and years had been a series of unfinished conversations, a relationship that had not yet really formed into a relationship. From the night at the well in Eritrea to the night at the bar in Las Vegas, it was a series of conversations that ended in midsentence without reaching a conclusion. Maybe that was why his mind played and replayed them over and over, each time continuing them to an alternate, imaginary finale.

With Cassie, it was an intended life together of many decades that ended unexpectedly and suddenly on the second lap, like a multicar pileup on a NASCAR track. With Yolanda, it was mutually satisfying, mutually understood shallowness. With Jenna, it was an ambiguous something that was never truly defined, but that might have been defined any number of ways.

After Las Vegas, they had exchanged e-mails. On the surface, they ignored both the fact that something had happened in Las Vegas, *and* that *nothing* had happened—although innuendos flowed freely between the lines.

What had happened—or not happened—in Vegas had not stayed in Vegas, but over time, the e-mail traffic grew less frequent. Troy hadn't heard from Jenna in weeks.

That night, when Troy opened his laptop and saw the @fhcoherndon.com suffix on an e-mail, he thought for a moment it was Jenna. As he took a second look, though, he noticed that the *From* line read rhh@fhcoherndon .com, not jmm@fhcoherndon.com.

Who? What?

Troy clicked on it.

Dear Captain Loensch,

Your e-mail address was passed along to me by Captain Munrough. I understand that she and Captain Coughlin gave you a bit of background on what our company is doing. Getting straight to the point, I'm inviting you to consider employment opportunities here. Please advise if you would be interested in visiting us in Herndon. I would be pleased to give you a personal briefing. I look forward to hearing from you.

General Raymond Harris (USAF, Ret.)
Director of Air Ops, Firehawk, LLC

As a word to describe Troy's reaction to an e-mail from Harris, two years after Dhuladhiya, *surprise* would have been a serious understatement. How should he respond to such an invitation from his old commander?

He recalled Jenna suggesting such a thing, but he had given it no more than a passing thought since Vegas.

Troy started several replies to Harris and deleted them all. He decided to sleep on it, and he woke up deciding, "Why not?"

CHAPTER 21

Headquarters, Firehawk, LLC, Herndon, Virginia

IT HADN'T TAKEN TROY LOENSCH LONG TO FIND THE place. Herndon is practically in the shadow of Dulles Airport.

Firehawk's unmarked and nondescript headquarters building was a seven-story steel and glass structure, set amid a landscape of steel and glass structures that make up the office park sprawl along Highway 267 between Leesburg and the nation's capital. On the wall of the lobby was a stylized aluminum rendition of the company logo, a bird's head surrounded by flames.

"Troy Loensch to see—" he started to explain to the receptionist.

"He's expecting you, Captain Loensch," she interrupted in a crisp, efficient tone. "Fill out the sign-in sheet, don't forget your social, and show me some ID, if you please."

These formalities done, she handed the retired Air Force captain a badge, directed him to an elevator away from the other elevators, and told him to push seven.

The seventh-floor lobby was clean and corporate modern, trimmed in light wood with large photographs of soldiers in the field wearing very clean uniforms that carried the Firehawk logo as a shoulder patch.

Just as he started to look around for a seventh-floor receptionist, a door swung open.

"Well, hello, Falcon Three, it's good to see that y'all finally made it to Herndon."

It was Jenna Munrough. It was the same Jenna Munrough he had seen in Las Vegas: the one with lips the color of rose petals and with the long blond hair. It was the same Jenna Munrough who had made him *almost* defy his better judgment—and wish later that he had. She was wearing a straight, businesslike skirt with her photo ID clipped to the waistband.

"Good to see you too, Munrough." He smiled, extending his hand.

"Glad you could make it," she said, ignoring his hand to give him a polite hug and a quick I-haven't-forgotten-our-last-meeting-even-if-you-pretend-you-have pinch.

She escorted Troy to Harris's office, and after an exchange of pleasantries, she smiled and left, closing the door behind her.

The room befitted the image of a military man gone corporate. There was a flagpole and the obligatory $\frac{1}{32}$-scale mahogany models of aircraft that Harris had flown, as well as framed photos of him with various notable people.

"Please sit down, Captain," Harris said, using Troy's last military rank and gesturing toward a comfortable-looking chair. Harris seemed in good form. He was a big man, but Troy noticed that he seemed to have lost a little weight, as though he had been working out. "I appreciate you coming to see us."

"Let's say I was intrigued, General." Troy smiled, politely using his host's last military rank.

"So you're still flying. That's a good thing. Great that you're able to get the hours. I wish I could spend more time in the cockpit myself."

"Looks like you've done okay as it is, sir," Troy said, nodding at a picture of Harris with the vice president.

"We've had some challenges, but we've built a solid business," Harris agreed. "Tell me about what you're doing."

Troy explained what he was doing for Golden West, and about how he liked being able to fly at least four days a week.

"Ever wish you could be back in jets?" Harris asked.

"Of course," Troy answered. "But I like my job better than dealing with commercial airline schedules."

"What are they paying you?"

When Troy told him, Harris leaned back and thought for a moment.

"What if I double that and throw in a bonus for overseas operations?" Harris asked.

"Mmm," Troy said thoughtfully. "Tell me more."

"Okay, here's the deal," Harris said. "Without going into operational details, let me say that the world that was always full of bastards is *still* full of bastards. Uncle Sam's government, which used to be in the business of taking on and taking down the bastards of the world, has grown squeamish about such things and finds it easier to outsource the dealing with bastards. That's where the PMCs come in. For Uncle Sam, it's like calling in a cleaning service to clean up a problem . . . or an exterminator. They don't ask . . . don't have to, or *want to* ask . . . *how* it's done. We just tell 'em *when* it's done."

"That's a novel idea."

"Actually, it's not new at all. Up until the eighteenth and nineteenth centuries, a lot of the armies fighting in Europe were professional armies that had no political connection at all to the country they were fighting for. For small countries, it was a lot cheaper and more efficient than having a standing national army. That's how the Hessians ended up fighting in our own Revolutionary War."

"How does this work?" Troy asked. "You don't read much or see much on the Net about PMCs."

"The guidelines are pretty simple," Harris said. "As

authorized by the United Nations and ratified by more than a hundred countries, PMCs can act as international and independent entities, although we have to be contracted by a sovereign state to get involved in a conflict. They then have the status as official combatants, but we're required under the UN resolution to use our own equipment to fulfill our missions."

"That includes jets?" Troy asked.

"Because we're required to use our own stuff, we're authorized to purchase heavy equipment on the international arms market. With a few exceptions, such as nukes and a few other things, PMCs are exempted from restrictions on conventional weapons sales."

"That was sort of how Coughlin and Munrough explained it to me," Troy said. "They said there was a lot less red tape."

"The concept is as old as before the eighteenth century, when the Hessians were hired out to fight for the Brits, but at the same time, PMCs are the way of the future for peacekeeping forces," Harris said. "Fewer political entanglements and quick response times . . . which theoretically makes us the perfect first responders to crises and humanitarian missions."

"And you're running airpower as well as ground forces?" Troy asked.

"Firehawk is mainly air," Harris confirmed. "Other PMCs do ground, blue water, covert stuff, whatever. Others do cyber warfare . . . everybody sorta specializes."

"What sorts of jets?" Troy asked, glancing out the window.

"You won't see them around here." Harris smiled, noticing Troy's glance. "They're all based at remote sites, or forward deployed to where we need them. We run a mix of fixed-wing aircraft. Can't say exactly which, but I will say you'd be able to step right in."

"Where did you get F-16s?" Troy asked, noting Harris's comment about "stepping right in."

"Can't confirm that Firehawk operates 16s," Harris said. "But there's a lot of good used equipment on the market around the world if you know where to look. We can get our hands on whatever is for sale on the international market. Mainly it's older, previously owned stuff, but you'd be surprised. Remember that guy a few years ago who was selling a Soviet-era nuclear submarine?"

"Did you guys buy that one?" Troy asked.

"No." Harris smiled. "But we've done some deals with the same broker who was handling it."

Troy nodded. He knew there was indeed a lot of high-tech hardware on the used-equipment market.

"What if I said I was interested?" Troy asked after Harris had spent about fifteen minutes giving him an overview of how Firehawk worked, and for whom.

"I'd ask when you could start."

"And if I said I needed to give three weeks' notice?"

"I'd get you to fill out some paperwork, y'know, a

nondisclosure and all the usual stuff, and tell you where to report in three weeks."

"Where would I be reporting?"

"Pack for the tropics." Harris smiled. "And don't worry much about dust storms."

CHAPTER 22

Mundo Maya Airport, Santa Elena, Guatemala

AS THE GULFSTREAM 5 BANKED HARD TO LINE UP with Runway 28, Troy Loensch could see the red roofs of the town of Flores tightly clustered on an island in the middle of Lago Petén Itza, the second-largest lake in Guatemala. Flores is the capital of the state of Petén, one of twenty-two states, but one that accounts for about a third of Guatemala's land area.

After a two-week refresher course in a T-38 trainer at one of Firehawk's remote sites in eastern Colorado, Troy had been handed his first assignment, which consisted merely of orders to report to a nondescript hangar at the Denver Airport. It wasn't until he boarded the Firehawk Gulfstream that he was handed his briefing packet, or that he knew he was headed to Guatemala.

It seemed that the Zapatista Army of National Liberation, which had been trying for years to overthrow Mexican government rule in the Mexican state of Chiapas, had decided to also try to overthrow Guatemalan rule in neighboring Petén. The U.S. government didn't want Guatemala to be destabilized but could not have intervened directly. When the Zapatistas started using jet attack aircraft against the poorly equipped Fuerza Aérea Guatemalteca—the Guatemalan Air Force—Guatemala called for help.

When Troy had boarded the Gulfstream last night, the pilot asked as a courtesy whether he'd like to take a turn at the controls. However, he soon nodded off and did not wake up until they were an hour out of Mundo Maya, which served as the airport for Flores.

As he was waking up with a paper cup of strong coffee, Troy looked out across the endless green of the Petén jungle. What a difference from Sudan, with its endless dirt and gravel landscape. With an area about the same size as West Virginia, Petén had fewer people than Charlotte, North Carolina, but twelve hundred or so years ago, millions of Mayans lived here and it was one of the most densely populated places in the world. *What a difference a dozen centuries can make,* Troy thought as he read the background page in the briefing book.

As the G-5 taxied to an unmarked hangar across the runway from the main terminal, Troy saw two unmarked vans driving to meet them.

"*Buenos dias*, Captain Loensch," said a man in a Firehawk Windbreaker who greeted Troy as he emerged from the cabin. "I'm José Turcios, but most people call me Joe."

"*Buenos dias*, Joe," Troy said, shaking the man's hand. He recognized Joe's name from the briefing book as the Firehawk station chief in Petén. "Most people call me Troy. By the way, your English is flawless."

"That's probably because I was born and raised in Pasadena." Joe laughed. "Learned Spanish from my grandparents."

"Great," Troy said. "I'm from Northridge."

"Small world," Joe said. "Twenty miles from me. Let's get you situated. We have a safe house in town, but I need you and Andy to bunk here at Mundo . . . come on into the hangar and meet Preston. He's gonna be your wingman."

Troy blinked a couple of times as he entered the dimly lit hangar and did a double take. There were two Lockheed Martin F-16C aircraft parked side by side, each with AIM-9 Sidewinder air-to-air missiles attached to its wingtip rails. Neither carried any markings except consecutive civil registration numbers. They were registered in Guatemala as civilian aircraft.

"You must be Loensch," a red-haired man in jeans and a T-shirt said to Troy as he approached from behind and extended his hand. "Preston, Andy Preston . . . used to be with the 35th Fighter Squadron, deployed overseas to Kunsan, Korea."

"Right," Troy said, shaking Preston's hand. "Troy Loensch. I was with the 334th Air Expeditionary Wing in Sudan."

"Heard you got a MiG," Preston said.

"Yeah," Troy confirmed. He was going to clarify that by saying that he'd also been shot down by one, but he decided to leave it at that.

"I'll let you boys get acquainted," Joe said. "Preston, show Loensch to his quarters. Briefing at 1300 hours."

"How long you been in country here?" Troy asked.

"Twenty-three hours," Preston said, looking at his watch.

"Look like almost new birds," Troy said, walking over for a closer look at the nearest F-16. "Where'd they come from?"

"I was told that they were bought from Chile out of the ones they got from Lockheed back in 2006."

"Don't look like they have much time on them," Troy said. "That's good. Have you picked one?"

"Neither one has a serial ending in thirteen, so I say we flip for first choice."

"Tails," Troy said as Preston pulled a quarter out of his pocket.

CHAPTER 23

Mundo Maya Airport, Santa Elena, Guatemala

"YOU'RE BOTH FAMILIAR WITH THE SU-25 FROGFOOT, right?" Joe Turcios said, glancing up from his clipboard. They were sitting around a desk in the shack adjacent to the hangar that served as the Firehawk command post.

Troy Loensch and Andy Preston both nodded. The Frogfoot was a twin-engine ground attack jet designed in the 1980s by the Soviet design bureau, Sukhoi, and widely exported to Soviet client states. Hundreds were still in use throughout the Third World, most having been passed from one air force to another to another a time or two.

"Well, our intel says that at least two, and possibly as many as four or five, have wound up with the Zaps," Turcios explained, using the popular slang for Zapatista rebels. Despite the presence of state-of-the-art weaponry, the briefing was extremely low-tech and informal by comparison to the slide shows and live satellite feeds that the pilots had experienced while serving in the U.S. Air Force.

"They appear to be based here in the jungle up in Chiapas," Turcios said, unfolding a fairly detailed Michelin road map. "The Russkies designed the plane to operate from crude landing fields, and that's exactly how they're being used. In the past two weeks, Guatemalan government convoys have been hit here, here, and here in three separate raids. Our job is to intercept the Frogfoots or Frogfeet, or whatever the damned plural is, and shoot 'em down."

"How will we know where and when?" Preston asked. "Are we supposed to fly combat air patrols?"

"No, you don't have to fly a CAP," Joe assured him. "That would be a waste of Firehawk's gas. No, we got a guy working ATC radar in the main tower across the runway here at Mundo. He gets a little on the side from Firehawk to help take care of us. His air traffic control coverage includes the border region. You guys will be on alert. When we get the word, you launch and track the Zaps on your own radar."

"What if they see us coming and run across the border back to Mexico?" Troy asked.

"Go get 'em." Joe smiled. "The Mexicans aren't gonna complain if you kill a Zap airplane. You get one free ride in this deal. The Zaps have no idea that we're here with F-16s. The first time you go out on an intercept and they see you coming on radar, they'll think you're commercial traffic, and they won't run. They know that the Guatemalan Air Force consists of pretty much nothing but helicopters and trainers. They will *not* be expecting F-16s."

"That's just the first time," Preston said. "After that, they'll know about us."

"I expect that they will have lost half their air force in the first engagement, so there shouldn't be much more than two or three for you guys and the job will be done."

"Speaking of *air force*, I guess I can't really imagine that the Zapatistas are sophisticated enough for this kind of equipment," Troy said.

"I don't imagine that the guys flying these Frogfeet are actually Zapatista rebels," Turcios said.

"Who are they then?" Preston asked.

"Firehawk isn't the only PMC in the world," Turcios said. "And not all the PMCs in the world are working for Uncle Sam and his friends."

OVER THE NEXT TWO DAYS, TROY AND PRESTON LOGGED more than eighteen hours in the cockpits of the two F-16s. Unfortunately, during all of the hours, the cockpits were parked ten feet off the ground in the hangar. They ran up the engines a few times, but other than that, time was spent in the most boring form of just sitting around.

It was at about 0945 on the third day that Joe Turcios came into the hangar shouting, "Crank 'em up and roll 'em out!"

At last.

The man in the Mundo Maya tower quickly put a ramp hold on an Aviateca flight that was about to take off for Cancún and cleared the Firehawk F-16s for a runway.

Other than the thunder of two fighter jets taking off, the passengers hardly noticed. Their delay getting off the ground was about four minutes.

Troy and Preston climbed out fast and leveled off at about eight thousand feet, high enough to avoid ground turbulence but low enough to intercept an aircraft on a ground attack mission. Troy took the lead with the call sign Firehawk One, but the two F-16s flew in tight formation so as to appear as one on the radar in the Frogfoot cockpits.

On the F-16 scopes, the two Frogfeet were distinctly separate, circling a point about sixty kilometers inside Guatemala and ignoring the oncoming Americans.

Within ten minutes of wheels-up, Troy had a visual on the two Su-25s. He even glimpsed a contrail leaving the wing of one of the aircraft. It was possibly a Kh-25 air-to-surface missile, although the Frogfoot was often equipped with simpler, unguided ground attack rockets.

Two plumes of smoke were rising from the jungle canopy beneath. The attackers had found some targets. However, these attackers were about to become targets themselves.

As the F-16s approached, neither Su-25 seemed to notice.

When he was sure that he was close enough, Troy locked on to one of the Sukhois and fired a Sidewinder. With only seconds to live, the pilot continued his attack. Troy saw ordnance drop from the pylons beneath his wings just as the aircraft erupted in a ball of fire.

The pilot of the second Frogfoot pulled back on the stick and started to climb when he noticed that his wing-man had been hit.

"Fox Two," Preston said in a low calm voice.

Troy broke right as he saw the Sidewinder streak toward the climbing Sukhoi. The pilot's urge to climb away from danger proved fatal. It reduced his already slow airspeed and made him an easy target.

Preston banked left and formed up on Troy, who was already headed back toward Mundo Maya. He gave Troy a thumbs-up, and Troy waved back. They deliberately kept their communications to a minimum to avoid the prying ears of eavesdroppers. Even with state-of-the-art encryption, there was always someone who cracked into secure channels.

Both pilots made tracks for Mundo. The less time they spent over the target area, the better. They had caught their quarry completely by surprise, and perhaps neither of the Frogfoot pilots would have had a chance to report that he was being attacked by another aircraft.

"DAMNED GOOD SHOOTING, BOYS," RAYMOND HARRIS shouted as Troy opened his cockpit.

The two pilots were surprised to see the Firehawk, LLC, Director of Air Ops standing next to Joe Turcios in the hangar when they returned. He had arrived on an inspection tour just after the two F-16s had departed. "If I had known you were out on a mission, I woulda had the G-5 pilot follow you out so I could watch."

Troy and Preston glanced at each other. It was a good thing he had not. To have an unexpected airplane show up in airspace where ordnance was flying around would have been dangerous.

"Scratch two, sir," Troy said succinctly. "We were engaged for only a couple of minutes, but both of the bogies were destroyed."

"Good work," Harris effused. "If our luck continues like this, we'll have this thing wrapped up in about five minutes . . . ten at the most."

CHAPTER 24

Mundo Maya Airport, Santa Elena, Guatemala

THE TEN MINUTES HAD A SLOW WAY OF MANIFESTING themselves. Troy and his wingman stood by, suited up and ready to respond to word that the Zapatista Air Force had shown themselves again. A week and a half later, they were still lounging in their hangar, ready to scramble into their cockpits and take off. They had set up a ready area twenty feet from their F-16s with folding aluminum longue chairs and a television set.

Harris had remained at Mundo for a couple of days, hoping to be on hand for a quick second round in Firehawk's air war against the Zapatistas, but he was disappointed and had flown out on his G-5 for parts unknown.

The two pilots speculated on whether they would

fly another mission. Preston figured that the remaining enemy aircraft would lay low indefinitely.

"We may never see those clowns," Preston postulated as he sipped a Coke and leafed casually through a magazine. "They saw what happened to their buddies and they've been hiding under their beds ever since. They don't wanna die . . . but who can blame them? You tangle with the best . . . you die like the rest."

Troy was more pessimistic.

"I'm worried that they've spent the last ten days shopping for Aphids or Atolls," he said, using the common nicknames for widely available Russian air-to-air missiles.

"Maybe, but we've got the edge on the Frogfoot in terms of performance," Preston said, turning the page of his magazine.

Troy was about to reply when Joe Turcios entered the hangar.

"We got incoming," he said. "The general's back. His G-5 is on final."

The two pilots folded their chairs, tossed their empty soda cans in the trash, and were standing next to their aircraft when the G-5 rolled in.

"Still no action?" Harris said as he exited the forward door.

"Still no action," Preston confirmed.

"Guess we scared 'em off." Troy laughed.

"I only wish," Harris said, shaking his head. "We got

word from a guy who knows a guy that they're shopping for air-to-air missiles."

"Told ya," Troy said, looking at Preston.

At that moment, Joe's cell phone rang.

"Turcios, what's up? . . . There are?" Joe asked. "Okay, give us a window of five."

"Speak of the devil," he said, closing his phone.

The two pilots were already on their ladders.

The Zapatistas had crossed the border about a hundred kilometers east of the previous incursion and were attacking a Guatemalan army post. This time Preston was flying as Firehawk One, while Troy flew behind and to his left. On their radar they saw two aircraft orbiting a common point, occasionally breaking into the center of the circle to attack. There was other traffic on the radarscope, but it was well away from the action.

On their previous mission, the Americans had seen plumes of black smoke just as they made visual contact with the aircraft. This time, though, they watched them break off their attack and climb out quickly. These pilots had been paying attention to their own radar and were not taken off guard. Knowing that they were outclassed by the F-16s, they were taking their Su-25s and heading for the border.

"They're running," Troy said impatiently. He had been sitting on his ass for ten days doing nothing, and the thought of these targets getting away was more than he could bear.

Taking the lead, Preston banked left and accelerated. Troy followed, eager to overtake the fleeing Frogfeet. Though the Su-25 is essentially a slow-moving bomb truck, its twin Tumansky R-195 turbojets gave it considerable power in a pinch, and these two pilots felt pinched.

"I think we're close enough," Troy suggested after two long minutes of pursuit. As Firehawk Two, he had to follow Preston's lead in launching an attack, and he was recommending that *now* was the time to take that first shot.

"Firehawk Two, I wanna get closer . . . don't wanna miss."

Troy impatiently moved his thumb above the trigger. If Preston wouldn't, he would.

"Fox Two," Preston announced, just as Troy was about to fire.

The two Su-25s broke hard, left and right.

The contrail from Preston's Sidewinder followed the aircraft that broke right.

For a second the two hard-turning objects looked like they would merge, but the Frogfoot turned harder and the Sidewinder slid by.

Troy broke left to follow the other Frogfoot and jammed his throttle forward.

"Fox Two," Troy said, finally taking the opportunity to thumb the trigger.

The Su-25 had been turning hard, the idea being to

outmaneuver any missile launched by his pursuer—the same tactic that had worked for his wingman. However, the turn also eventually bled off momentum, slowing the aircraft ever so slightly.

The slight reduction in velocity meant that Troy's Sidewinder did not lose its lock on the target.

"I've been made," Troy heard Preston say just as he watched the Frogfoot explode. "Taking fire."

Where was he? How did he let the other Su-25 get behind him?

Troy put his F-16 into a four-G turn and scanned the sky for Preston.

"Firehawk One, I'm on it," Troy promised. He wasn't, not yet, but he would be and he wanted Preston to know that he was coming.

A patch of sky a couple of miles distant was filled with the streaks and dashes of tracer rounds.

Just as Troy was wondering how the other pilot had managed to let a Frogfoot outmaneuver him, he saw the Su-25 that Preston had missed with his first shot. The one that was now diving on him was a *third* enemy fighter, and one that both of them had missed. It had been flying a CAP high above the other two, expressly for this purpose, to attack anyone who attacked them.

He was going after the F-16, with his GSh-30 cannon blazing. Designed for the Frogfoot's ground attack role, the two-barreled automatic cannon was a formidable gun. Preston was rolling and dodging, trying to stay out of the stream of thirty-millimeter shells that it was pouring out at a rate of fifty rounds per second.

With its altitude advantage, the Frogfoot had Preston like a cat with its paw on a mouse.

Even though the F-16 had a far better thrust-to-weight ratio than a Frogfoot, Troy knew that he did not have time to try to get above the Su-25, so he maneuvered in below and behind.

It was a dangerous place from which to fire a Sidewinder.

If the heat-seeking missile missed the Sukhoi, it would be headed straight toward the heat of Preston's F-16.

Fortunately, the Firehawk pilots caught a break.

The weather over Petén that day was mostly clear, but the rolling, twisting chase had rolled and twisted toward a line of cumulus that was starting to form. Preston ducked into a cloud, and the Frogfoot pilot pulled back slightly. He had been firing on the F-16 visually, not using his radar, and this was a reflex reaction as he looked around for his prey.

Rapidly overtaking the Su-25, which was now in level flight, Troy fired his second Sidewinder. The distance was short, and the missile was much faster than the Zapatista aircraft.

Troy was dodging pieces of Frogfoot six seconds later.

He stood the F-16 on its tail and grabbed at the altitude he figured to be necessary if other bandits appeared.

Rolling out at nearly ten thousand feet, he checked his radarscope.

The original Frogfoot, which Preston had missed with his first shot, had escaped across the border into Mexico. Troy thought of giving chase, but realized he had shot both his Sidewinders.

Far below, Preston was climbing out of the cloud tops.

There were no other aircraft anywhere to be seen, either visually or on radar. The score was Firehawk two, Zapatistas zero, but the game was not over.

CHAPTER 25

Over the Petén Jungle, Guatemala

"FIREHAWK ONE," TROY SAID, WATCHING ANDY PRES-
ton's F-16 running westward through the cloud tops
below. "Shall we call it a day?"

"Roger that, Firehawk Two," Preston replied. "I'm
making a slow ninety-degree turn here."

By the way he described his turn, Troy knew that
something was wrong. In the spirit of keeping their communications to a minimum, he would not have explained
the details of any problem that he might be having. The
airwaves have prying ears.

As Troy took his own bird down to Preston's level, he
could see that a few of the thirty-millimeter rounds fired
by the Sukhoi had connected. None of the hits had been
sufficient to knock down the plane, but a punctured left

aileron had "potential disaster" written all over it. The sight of the damaged F-16 reminded Troy of that morning over Eritrea when he was watching Jenna's F-16 just before it went down.

"I'm with you," Troy said, pulling in next to the other aircraft and snapping off a friendly salute. He had appreciated a similar offer when his own aircraft had been riddled with gunfire.

Despite some close calls when the marginally controllable aircraft was hit by turbulence, they made it home. When Preston asked the tower for permission to land, there was no other traffic in the area, so he decided to keep a low profile and not declare an emergency. If he crashed, his would be the only day ruined.

"You got one of my airplanes into a fender bender, I see," Raymond Harris said as he greeted the two Firehawk pilots at the hangar. The shorter chain of command within Firehawk meant that he was much closer to the budget discussions than he had been in the U.S. Air Force.

"Two planes got home," Preston said as Harris walked beneath the wing to investigate the damage.

"And two pilots," Troy added.

"We'll have to fly in a repair crew and some parts from the States before we can fly this one again," Harris said, shaking his head in disgust.

"The damage cost the Zaps a lot more . . . cost them two Su-25s," Preston said defensively.

"The Su-25 is an attack plane, not a fighter," Harris

said. "You *ought* to able to outfly and outshoot an Su-25 in a dogfight when you're flying an F-16."

"We *did*," Troy interjected. "We left two of their 'air force' smoldering in the Petén rain forest, and we left both F-16s parked in this hangar."

"For that I'm grateful," Harris said in a conciliatory tone as he emerged from beneath the wing. "Tell me all about it."

"We engaged two, as we had on the previous mission," Preston began. "The first one evaded my Sidewinder, but Loensch nailed his."

Preston wanted to say something about Troy's over-eagerness in urging him to take a shot too soon, but so much had happened since—including his coming to Preston's defense moments ago—that he chose to let his feelings about the earlier incident slide.

"There was a third one flying CAP that jumped us using guns," Troy interjected. "That's where the damage came in."

"Loensch got him," Preston said, giving credit to his wingman. "But by that time, the lone survivor was well into Mexico."

"I didn't pursue him because I was out of missiles and I didn't want to have to chase him back to his home turf in order to get close enough to engage him with my gun," Troy explained. "Besides, the other plane in my element that day had been battle-damaged."

"These guys were pretty damned good," Preston

said. "A lot better than you'd expect of some guys who are used to living in jungles."

"Like I said earlier . . . I don't think you'll find too many native Zaps among the people who are flying those Sukhois." Harris smiled.

"Who in the hell *are* they?" Preston asked. "Who is this other PMC?"

"We found out that's a European outfit," Harris said in a matter-of-fact way. "They're called Svartvand BV."

"I knew that the aircraft were bought on the open market," Troy said. "But it still amazes me that the Zapatistas can afford to hire professionals to fly 'em."

"There's a lot of money in marijuana." Harris shrugged. "Follow the money . . . just like it was with the Taliban and opium in Afghanistan."

"The Zaps make enough selling weed?" Preston asked.

"They've always made money protecting the growers," Harris explained. "The growers sell to the cartels and the cartels have the money to buy the weapons and hire the hired guns. It's complicated, but if you follow the money, it all makes sense."

"Why are they attacking the Guatemalans, then?" Troy asked.

"Because it's in the interest of the guys with the money to keep the Guatemalan army out of the Chiapas pot fields and get control of the Petén pot fields. Pot knows no borders. It grows as well in Petén as it

does in Chiapas. They also like to control governments
of smaller countries . . . and Central American governments are so ripe for influence. Y'know, forty, fifty years
ago, it was the Communists who wanted to control all
these places. Before that it was the banana companies.
It's been like this for years."

"These guys that the Zaps hired," Troy asked, "where
did *they* hire the pilots that we've been flying against?"

"On the international market." Harris smiled. "There
are guys just like you two all over the world who used to
fly jets in some air force or other who want to get back
into action. There's probably quite a few Russians . . . a
Brit or two . . . there may even be some Americans. The
guy who put the holes into that F-16 may have *flown*
F-16s once upon a time."

CHAPTER 26

Mundo Maya Airport, Santa Elena, Guatemala

"INTEL SHOWS THAT THE ZAPS ARE DOWN TO JUST one Frogfoot," Joe Turcios said, placing an aerial photo on his desk for Troy and Andy to examine. "As you can see, there's only one parked here in this picture."

Troy picked it up and studied it. The single Su-25 was parked in a clearing in a jungle. There were a few buildings and a long runway camouflaged to look like a straight stretch of crudely paved country road. In fact, the more he looked at it, the more it looked as though the thing being used as a runway really was a straight stretch of crudely paved country road.

"How do you know this is current?" Troy asked. "I thought these Google Earth images were usually weeks or months old."

"The Google Earth ones are." Turcios grinned. "I downloaded these from a SPOT satellite less than an hour ago."

"How . . . ?"

"Don't ask."

"Okay, then how do we know that they don't have more Su-25s parked in the woods? The jungle is really thick around there. You could park a jetliner in there and it wouldn't show up in a SPOT image."

"Good question," Joe acknowledged, opening a drawer in his desk. "It's a calculated conclusion, based on these."

He fanned out a selection of photos of the same place, with dates written in the corners.

"These pictures were taken over the past few weeks. You see in the earliest picture that they hadn't cleared the brush from the runway areas. Then there's cleared brush and then two Sukhois arrive. Eventually there are four. Some pictures show three, but those correspond with dates we know that they had one out flying."

"What about the fifth?" Troy asked.

"The contacts that General Harris has in France told him that Svartvand approached a broker there about getting a single Frogfoot. We thought at the time that they were replacing one that had been lost in an accident, but we now know that there were five flying at once."

They compared a picture of the clandestine airfield with five Sukhois to the image that was hours old.

"What you see is what you get," Turcios said. "It doesn't seem that they ever made any effort to hide any of their jets. Just like you, they thought the Google Earth picture was months old. Now they're down to just one."

"So are we," Troy reminded him, nodding toward the hangar. "Until those parts get here from Texas, our squadron strength stands at one."

"Doesn't stop us from running a solo mission," Joe said. "General Harris wants to finish this operation sooner rather than later. This deployment is costing X millions of dollars a day, even without the price of fuel. And Firehawk is on a fixed-bid contract."

"Who flies?" Troy asked.

"You do. The general wants you to head up there and destroy the single Sukhoi on the ground."

"With what ordnance?"

"We don't have any air-to-ground missiles, but we did bring in a stock of JDAMs," Turcios explained. "You also have your cannon. One strafing pass and a couple of bombs ought to do it."

"What about air defenses?" Troy asked. "Can I expect any Triple-A . . . or SAMs?"

"I've studied these pictures myself, and there's no sign of SAMs. Wouldn't be surprised if they have thought about it, and I'm sure that they'll be thinking about it a whole lot tonight."

"What's to stop them from using this base again?" Preston asked. "They could bring in more jets and this thing could go through the same cycle. Harris would have to send us back down here for a million dollars, or whatever, a day."

"That's a good question." Turcios nodded. "The answer is that DefenseCo is going in there to sabotage it after you shoot it up."

"Who's DefenseCo?" Troy asked.

"They're the PMC that's handling ground ops up on the border between Petén and Chiapas."

"Why can't they go in there now and blow up the Frogfoot on the ground?" Preston asked.

"It's not in their contract," Turcios said, as if this were understood.

"How many PMCs are there in this part of the world?" Troy asked. "Seems like every time I turn around, there's another PMC popping up."

"There are three on this side," Turcios said thoughtfully. "And there's at least two on the other side . . . that we *know* about. That doesn't count the contractors who are handling logistics."

AN HOUR LATER, TROY WAS AIRBORNE OVER THE PETÉN jungle in the lone Firehawk F-16. There was some low cumulus off to the west as a rainstorm moved into the

area, but otherwise the sky was clear. He carried two
five-hundred-pound GBU-38 Joint Direct Attack Muni-
tion smart bombs on his underwing pylons, either of
which would total the lone Svartvand Frogfoot.

Troy's mission was to depart Mundo Maya on a commercial aircraft heading and altitude so as not to appear
conspicuous on radar, fly to the closest point on this
flight path to the target, drop to a thousand feet, and
conduct his bomb run. This latter action, Turcios and
Harris had calculated, would take the F-16 about six
minutes. It was unlikely, though still possible, that the
Su-25 could be scrambled fast enough to be airborne
before the bombs hit.

At the appointed time, Troy rolled the F-16 into a
dive, leveled out at his strike altitude, and accelerated
toward the coordinates of the patch of Chiapas where
Svartvand parked its airplane.

The anticipation made the six minutes seem longer
than they were, but finally, Troy could see the straight
line in the jungle that marked the runway. He adjusted
his heading slightly to line up on the runway and engaged
his targeting device.

The straight strip in the jungle pointed straight to
the cluster of buildings at the end of the runway like
an arrow drawn on a map with a ruler and a wide-tip
marker.

He grew closer and closer. At any moment now, he

expected to see the familiar profile of the stubby-winged Frogfoot parked in this area.

"C'mon . . . c'mon," he whispered with impatience. "Where . . . ?"

Suddenly there was a pinging sound.

This couldn't be!

He had been made.

The Su-25 wasn't there. It was airborne—and it was targeting *him*.

Seconds later, Troy was over the target—or what was to have *been* the target.

He released the two JDAMs as planned. They would hopefully do some damage to the base, and they were of no use to him now. In fact, their weight and drag would seriously degrade the maneuverability of the F-16, whose role had abruptly changed from bomber to fighter—a fighter fighting for its life.

He hadn't seen the Frogfoot on his radarscope because it had been playing Troy's own game: flying low, hugging the ground to conceal itself in the ground clutter.

Somehow, its pilot had taken off undetected before Troy arrived.

How?

That did not matter now.

The pinging had stopped. The same ground clutter that had hidden the Frogfoot had interrupted its missile lock.

For Troy, this was two pieces of good news rolled into one pleasing, but momentary, package.

Having had his foe lose his lock-on was good in itself, but this illustrated the better news that his foe was armed with semiactive radar homing missiles, rather than infrared heat-seekers—like Troy's Sidewinders. The Vympel R-60 Aphid air-to-air missiles often carried by Su-25s could be configured either way, and this Su-25 was flying with infrared Aphids.

The radar-guided missiles are good at long range, but inferior to heat-seeking missiles at dogfight range because they use tracking radar to acquire their target and illuminator radar for lock-on. Thus the radar lock has to be locked on from the time the target is acquired until the time the missile connects with it. At close range, this is more difficult. It was probably why yesterday's Frogfoot had resorted to using his cannon against Andy Preston.

Troy processed this information in about a second and concentrated on turning himself from hunted to hunter ASAP.

He scanned the sky, trying to get a visual on the Su-25.

On his scope, the aircraft popped in and out intermittently.

He was still flying low.

Troy accelerated upward. The best tactic now was to induce the enemy aircraft to come and get him. As

Harris had pointed out to Preston—not that he needed to be told—the Su-25 is a bomb truck, and hence slower and less maneuverable than an F-16. Luring him into a dogfight on Troy's terms was the key to success.

The Su-25 pilot had no choice but to take the bait. There was nothing else that he could do. He had no place to run.

Knowing he was low and slow, the Sukhoi pilot now needed to grab altitude. If Troy pounced while he remained low, the F-16 would have all the advantages. If the Su-25 pilot could increase his altitude, he would erase one of Troy's advantages *and* he could convert altitude to speed using the power of gravity.

His first move was to run away, climbing as he went. This would either give him a chance to increase his altitude while he was momentarily out of Troy's reach, or lure Troy to dive to attack him, thus costing Troy altitude.

For a split second, it occurred to Troy that the Sukhoi was escaping, but he saw him climbing and understood that he was planning to fight.

As much as Troy's adrenaline-fueled eagerness longed for a dogfight, he defaulted to that old adage that says, "He who fights fairly, dies."

The Su-25 had gotten about five miles away as he ran and climbed, but it was still within the range of the Sidewinder.

"Missiles hot," Troy whispered to himself as he locked

on the still-climbing Sukhoi. His foe was at his slowest as he climbed. It was not really fair, but it was oh so easy.

He thumbed the trigger, expecting the rocking motion that one felt as a missile left its rail.

It didn't happen.

Was the missile a dud, or was something wrong with his fire control system?

His dilemma cost Troy valuable seconds.

The Su-25 was now at Troy's altitude and climbing.

Troy was already headed in his direction, and he pulled back on his stick. As he climbed to match the Sukhoi's flight level, he watched the aircraft turn toward him.

The two miles of distance melted quickly as the two aircraft closed on one another.

Troy heard the pinging of a missile lock-on just as he pickled off his other Sidewinder.

The F-16 jerked slightly as the AIM-9 left its rail.

Knowing an R-60 Aphid was coming at him, Troy ignored his Sidewinder and broke hard to the right to evade the other guy's missile.

The Sidewinder was fire-and-forget, so he fired and forgot. Getting out of the way of the Aphid headed toward him was suddenly the *only* thing on his mind.

At this range, Troy had the offensive advantage with the heat-seeking missile, but avoiding an incoming infrared missile took a lot of skill—and an equal measure of luck. Having been shot down over Eritrea, he was not anxious for a redo. He had been very lucky that day not to have been killed in the explosion.

The trick, far easier said than done, is to outmaneuver the incoming missile without straying so far that it can match your evasion maneuver.

Troy turned and watched the faster Aphid turn with him and gain on him.

He jerked back on the stick and felt the G-force crumple his body.

It's funny, the kinds of things you notice at times like this. For Troy, it was that the Gs clinched his jaws so tight that his teeth throbbed. Better that than being blown into a zillion pieces.

Troy sensed for just milliseconds the ambient glow of the solid-fuel engine flame from the Aphid growing brighter and brighter.

Troy next sensed for just milliseconds the ambient glow of the solid-fuel engine flame from the Aphid growing dimmer and dimmer.

Out of the corner of his eye, he watched the Aphid as it arced away from him and raced at supersonic speed toward the Chiapas jungle.

It had missed him by about fifty yards. For a moment, he felt like a wuss for having let the damned thing worry him.

Okay. Now that *that* was over, where was the damned Su-25 and what happened to his Sidewinder?

Theoretically, the Sidewinder shouldn't have missed. But it had. Its glow, like that of the Aphid, was gone, as the two hundred pounds of ordnance had fallen into the triple canopy below.

The Sukhoi was still there, and a lot closer than he might have been after the past long seconds of wild maneuvering by the two aircraft.

Instinctively, Troy grabbed to fire again, but instantly realized that he had shot his only viable AIM-9. All he had left was the dud. He would have to go to guns.

To use his M61 Vulcan multibarreled twenty-millimeter Gatling gun, Troy would have to close the distance on the Su-25.

There wasn't much distance to close, but the Sukhoi pilot saw him coming and broke left just as Troy lined up on him.

Just as he touched his stick, Troy realized that he would be unable to stay inside the Su-25's turn radius. Troy couldn't afford to overshoot the guy's turn. He had to do what fighter pilots call a "yo-yo."

In the textbooks, they tell you to maintain back stick pressure and slightly decrease bank relative to the other guy. This allows you to arc up your nose. In other words, the effect of gravity on turn and velocity, combined with a turn in the vertical rather than horizontal, enables you to reduce angle-off, maintain your distance, and not overshoot.

That's what the textbooks say.

In reality, you don't have time to think about all the physics. You just pull back the stick to bleed off enough speed to be able to turn and still wind up on the other guy's tail.

He came out of the maneuver just where he needed to be and pressed the red button. Tracers swirled around the Sukhoi for less than a second. The bogie had turned again.

Once again, Troy turned, and once again he squeezed off a burst of twenty-millimeter cannon rounds.

Suddenly, the Su-25 was gone and everything around Troy had turned light gray. The F-16 bucked violently.

The cumulus!

Troy had plowed into the rainstorm that he had seen moving across the jungle earlier in the day.

"Gotta get out," he whispered to himself as he pulled up.

There was a sudden flash.

Was it lightning or another Aphid?

Seconds later, he was in smooth air and staring at blue sky.

He banked around to look for the Sukhoi.

It was nowhere to be seen—except on his radar.

His foe was somewhere below, somewhere in the clouds, out of visual contact.

Now was the time for the missiles he did not have.

Troy took a deep breath.

The Su-25 driver was taking a pounding down there inside that storm, and sooner or later, he'd make his break. Troy would be waiting, guns ready.

CHAPTER 27

High over the Chiapas-Petén Border

"FIREHAWK ONE," A VOICE IN THE HEADPHONES crackled urgently. Troy was startled. Communications were supposed to be minimal, and he didn't expect any calls on this frequency while he was operating solo over Chiapas. "Do you read?"

"Firehawk One, roger," Troy answered hesitatingly, trying to figure out why the Firehawk base would be calling in such an earnest tone.

"Terminate, Firehawk One. Cancel."

It was Raymond Harris's voice.

"Return home immediately . . . no further action . . . *over.*"

The way that Harris stressed the word *over* underscored an intense finality to his orders.

"But—" Troy started to say. He had been involved in—was still involved in—an intense dogfight during which either he or the Sukhoi pilot might have died. Several times over, either of them might have killed the other, and Troy was seconds away from delivering the coup de grâce and successfully completing his mission.

Terminate?

Why should he stop now? He had almost given his life to get to this point in the battle.

"Terminate. *Now*," Harris said.

Troy wondered. Should he just ignore Harris for thirty seconds?

He ignored Harris for ten seconds, maintaining his position above the cloud in which the Su-25 was flying.

He ignored Harris for twenty seconds, waiting and gritting his teeth, ready to dive, open fire, and get this over with.

"Terminate. *Now*," Harris repeated.

He ignored Harris for thirty seconds, and still no Sukhoi.

"Roger, Firehawk One . . . message received and understood."

As Troy banked to turn back toward Mundo Maya, he hoped that the Su-25 would suddenly break out of the clouds and come for him.

But it did not happen.

* * *

AS HE TAXIED INTO THE FIREHAWK HANGAR, TROY
could see Joe Turcios and Raymond Harris waiting.
Turcios had a sort of bewildered expression, but Harris
wore an ear-to-ear grin.

Troy shut down the Pratt & Whitney F100 engine and
popped open the canopy. As he climbed out, he looked
down at the black powder stains around the M61's muzzle and thought of what might have been.

Why was Harris grinning so broadly?

The mission had *not* been accomplished. The Svartvand, or Zapatista, or whatever it was, Sukhoi was still
there. It was still flying around on the Chiapas-Petén
border when Troy left it.

Maybe Harris *thought* Troy had downed the aircraft?
Maybe he'd better just play along and break the news to
him gently?

"Great news," Harris shouted.

Troy merely nodded. If the boss was happy, who was
he to complain?

"We're done." The retired general smiled as he patted Troy on the shoulder. "We're out of here. Dinner in
town tonight . . . It's on Firehawk . . . We'll celebrate."

With that, and without asking Troy for a mission
debrief, he turned and strode out of the room with Joe
Turcios.

"What was that all about?" Troy asked Andy Preston.

"I'm not sure," Preston replied. "He was pacing the floor for about an hour after you launched this morning, then he got a phone call. He had the driver take him somewhere. He came back all excited, ran into the radio room, and contacted you to stand down."

"Why?" Troy asked. "I was in the middle of fighting that guy in the Frogfoot."

"We're not here to ask questions, man," Preston said. "We're here to follow orders, and my last orders from him were to pack my gear and get ready to move out tomorrow. He said that the same applies to you."

RORY'S STEAK HOUSE, AS ITS AMERICAN-ACCENTED name implies, is one of those places that caters to gringos and to the members of the Guatemalan elite who find themselves in the provincial city of Flores. If nothing else, the prices on the menu—printed in English and Spanish, with English first—keep the riffraff at bay.

As with all such places in less-than-stable corners of less-than-stable banana republics, Rory's has high security, with razor wire atop the pinkish, hacienda-style wall that surrounds the palm-studded compound.

Subtly armed security welcomes guests, and the only people carrying weapons inside are bodyguards who have been prescreened by Rory's and issued photo IDs.

Beyond the perimeter, Rory's is just a typical Spanish-colonial style restaurant, with ceiling fans and heavy, dark wood furniture.

Harris had booked a private room in the back. Margaritas had already been poured when Troy and Andy Preston arrived, whisked from the Firehawk hangar in one of the bulletproof cars leased by the company. In all their weeks in Guatemala, the short drive from Mundo Maya was the only time that either of them had seen anything that could be construed as the "real" Guatemala. Certainly Rory's could have been anywhere in Florida or Southern California.

A dozen people were standing around in the room. In addition to the two pilots, Harris, and Turcios, there were four other Firehawk employees, including two mechanics, the radio operator, and another man to whom Troy had never been introduced. The four others were men whom Troy had never seen.

"Nice party," Troy said, approaching Joe Turcios. "I hear that we're headed out tomorrow."

"Yes, the steaks are really good here in this place." Turcios nodded. "Really a cut above what we're used to out at Mundo."

"So are you pulling up stakes tomorrow, too?" Troy asked.

"I expect so," he said, glancing at Harris, who was across the room talking to one of the men whom Troy had not previously seen. "My orders haven't quite been finalized."

"This deployment sure ended kinda suddenly, didn't

it?" Troy asked, hoping to elicit some sort of clarification from Turcios.

"It sure did." Joe nodded as he stepped away to refill his margarita glass.

The head waiter entered the room, announcing that it was time for everyone in the room to take their seats and open their menus.

Troy picked the bone-in rib eye, which was listed a few price points below the one he'd eaten on Firehawk's tab in Las Vegas, and turned to the man seated next to him to make idle conversation. His name was Aron Arnold, and he was from near Orlando, Florida. He was a slender man with dark, short-cropped hair who looked to be about Troy's age. They had gotten past exchanging pleasantries and had ascertained that they both had served in the U.S. Air Force as pilots when Raymond Harris stood up from his place at the head of the table, tapping the back of his steak knife against his water glass.

"I'd like to thank all of you for coming tonight." He smiled. "But I think the prospect of a free steak dinner was ample inducement."

Everyone chuckled at the lame humor. The Firehawk people were there under orders, and yes, the prospect of a free steak dinner *was* ample inducement.

"Some of you know already, but for the benefit of all concerned, I'd like to take this opportunity to announce the merger of Svartvand BV and Firehawk, LLC. From this point forward, Svartvand will be known as the

Svartvand Division of Firehawk, LLC. Let's all raise our glasses in celebration."

Troy was stunned. Less than seven hours earlier, Firehawk and Svartvand had not merely been competitors, they had been *at war*. Troy had been on the front lines, risking his life.

"With this turn of events, I'm pleased to announce a full cessation of air combat between Zapatista forces and the Guatemalan government. If diplomats could cut deals as easily as we do in the private sector, there would be a lot less war in the world."

There was a murmur of chuckles around the room at Harris's second attempt at lame humor, although on second take, the Firehawk people realized that he meant it.

"I'd like to introduce Enrique Girarcamada of Svartvand, who has a few words."

Another Enrique? Troy growled to himself. He had bad memories of the other Enrique in Culver City, and he had bad recent memories of Svartvand, the company that had tried to *kill* him.

"Thank you so much, Raymond; it is such a pleasure to be here with you and your people tonight," this Enrique said in polished but accented English.

Pleasure? Troy couldn't get out of his mind all of what this guy represented.

"The merger of our two PMCs is an important step forward for us, but especially for our customers. The diversification of capabilities brought about by this . . ."

Troy tuned out and took another sip of his margarita. Enrique sounded like he was reading from a press release. He probably was.

Soon the blah-blah-blah was over and there was a polite but halfhearted round of applause.

"This is a good steak," Aron Arnold said as he and Troy dug into their dinner. "I haven't eaten like this in months. Sure hits the spot."

"Don't you know it," Troy said, savoring a slice of the nice, lean beef. "How long you been with Firehawk? I haven't seen you around."

"Oh, I've been with Firehawk for about seven hours," Arnold said. "And you?"

"About four months," Troy said. "So if you've been with Firehawk for seven hours, that means that . . ."

"Yeah, I'm a Svartvand guy. I've been working up in Chiapas."

Troy stopped chewing and just stared at the guy. Svartvand? Pilot? Chiapas?

"We met earlier today." Arnold smiled. "Now that we're both on the same side, I look forward to flying *with* you someday."

CHAPTER 28

Headquarters, Firehawk, LLC, Herndon, Virginia

"TROY LOENSCH TO SEE JENNA MUNROUGH."

She surprised herself by how quickly she was on her feet when she heard his voice in the outer office. In the eight months since the Svartvand takeover and the termination of operations in Guatemala, Loensch had been on two high-profile assignments for which he had become somewhat of a legend within Firehawk.

"Hail the conquering hero." Jenna smiled, stepping out of her private office.

There he stood, the tall, muscular hunk who had become the worst enemy of Cambodian MiGs over the Gulf of Thailand during those past few months.

"I heard you were in the building," she said, giving

him a hug. "How come y'all didn't send me an e-mail lettin' me know you were coming in from the field?"

"Wasn't sure of my schedule," he said. "Didn't really know until yesterday when I'd be coming in."

"Well, your reputation precedes you," Jenna said. "I want to hear all about it. Let's go get a cup of coffee."

In those eight months, she had sat at her desk and at boring meetings over at the Pentagon, reading the communiqués of his exploits and jealous that she was at the controls of nothing more powerful than a Porsche 997 Carrera. Of course, a car that can do zero to sixty in less than five seconds is not *just* a car.

"Mr. Loensch," Jenna's secretary said timidly as her boss and the famous fighter pilot started to walk away. "Could I get you to . . . ummm . . . y'know . . . sign this . . . autograph this?"

She handed him a copy of the corporate magazine with a picture of Troy standing next to an F-16 on the cover.

"Sure, I guess so," he said, obviously still unaccustomed to his celebrity status.

"Hail the conquering hero," Jenna repeated, half-mocking him.

There were more smiles and glances of recognition as Jenna and Troy made their way through the hallways on their way to the Firehawk executive coffee room.

"You really made a name for yourself out there over

the Gulf of Thailand," she said as they sat down to savor their paper cups of French roast. "Just as you did in Guatemala, and in Zambia, too."

"Cambodian pilots aren't the best." Troy shrugged. "Zambia was pretty easy. The fight was pretty much a ground operation, and the guys from DefenseCo rolled that up pretty fast. Guatemala was just plain weird."

"How do you mean?" Jenna asked.

"I guess I was pretty naive in those days. One morning, I was fighting a Zapatista Su-25. I knew that Svartvand had supplied it to them, but in my mind, the pilot was a bad guy . . . any guy trying to kill you with Aphids is a bad guy, right?"

"Sure, y'all would naturally think of someone trying to kill you as a 'bad guy.' "

"Well, here I am that same night. I sit down to a nice dinner in a pretty fancy steak house, and I start talking to the guy next to me . . . and it's the guy. The guy who tried to kill me in the morning is the same guy who is asking me to pass the salt and pepper."

"That's the world of the PMC." Jenna smiled. "It's all just business. No hard feelings. By the sounds of what you did to the Cambodian Air Force over in the Gulf of Thailand, you seem to have gotten over your naïveté."

"Yeah, guess so. But since Guatemala, I haven't sat down to dinner with anybody that had spent his day shooting at me."

"Speaking of dinner," Jenna asked. "What are you doing for dinner tonight?"

"Harris has me down for some kind of meet and greet, but that's early, so I could probably do it around eight o'clock if that works for you?"

"That works for me." Jenna smiled. "Where are you staying . . . I can pick you up at your hotel."

TO JENNA, THE CONQUERING HERO LOOKED VAGUELY vulnerable as he stood in front of the Marriott Courtyard in Arlington waiting for his chariot and its charioteer. She imagined him as a puppy dog in need of a good petting—or as a small deer as viewed through the eyes of a tigress.

Jenna had mixed feelings. Was she heading for trouble with the thoughts she was thinking of Troy? There were many reasons to keep this idea filed under "what if," as it had been since Las Vegas. Most of these other reasons contained the word *Hal*. On one hand, she found Troy hands-on sexy in that bad-boy sort of way that is often so appealing, but on the other, she knew that bad boys can be a lot of fun.

Jenna had mixed feelings about Hal, too, though. The fire was definitely gone from their relationship. Both of them had moved on emotionally. She knew there were many reasons why she shouldn't be moving on in the direction of Troy Loensch. She knew that boring people like Hal were good in the long term, while bad boys were always a potential for trouble.

"Business must be good here at the home office," Troy said, looking over the Carrera. "Very nice-looking ride . . . and a fine-looking chauffeur too."

Jenna was pleased that he thought her to be "fine-looking," but felt a little peevish that this comment was an afterthought tagged on to his gushing about the Porsche.

"Where are we going for dinner?" Troy asked.

"Didn't feel like D.C. traffic tonight," Jenna said. "Thought we'd head out sixty-six. Feel like country food tonight, y'all. I made a reservation at a little place out on Fox Mill Road—chicken-fried steak and hush puppies and all. Sound okay?"

"Sounds good to me."

When they got past the Beltway on I-66, she glanced in her mirror and depressed the accelerator with the pointed toe of her Jimmy Choo and opened up the Carrera. If he liked the car, she'd show him the car. She noticed a smile. She also noticed a bit more than a glance at her leg.

"Nothing like a jet," she said casually. "But if y'all gotta be on the ground, it's the way to go."

"I asked around about Hal when I was in Herndon this afternoon," Troy said. "They said he's not at Firehawk?"

"Oh, yeah, I shoulda mentioned," she said apologetically. "Thought you probably heard. Yeah . . . Hal took a job with Escurecer, y'know, the PMC. He's been with them about three months . . . based out of their Alexandria office."

"Didn't know that," Troy said. "Guess it's my fault for not staying in closer touch."

"Y'all *aren't* very good about answering your e-mails," Jenna said in a mock scolding tone.

"Yeah, I'm a bad boy."

Jenna thought about saying something about how the teacher would have to punish the "bad boy," but she bit her lip.

"So, why'd he leave?"

"Escurecer offered him a job that has some flying involved," Jenna explained. "He really wanted to get back into the air. . . . That and umm, y'know . . . Firehawk has this thing about not wanting employees married to other employees."

This time, Jenna bit her lip *after* she let slip something that she wanted not to have slipped.

"Married?" Troy asked "Who? Wait . . . you guys got *married*?"

"No, not yet." Jenna shrugged. She hadn't planned to be discussing wedding plans with the conquering hero tonight, but she knew she was foolish to delude herself into believing it would not come up. "We've been together a long time . . . talking about it . . . so it was finally time to commit."

"Congratulations." Troy smiled.

She was pleased to have detected a trace of disappointment in his tone.

"Didn't notice a ring," Troy said, glancing at her hand.

"Oh, it's at the jeweler . . . umm . . . getting sized," Jenna lied.

The ring was in her purse.

"Is Hal gonna be joining us tonight?" Troy asked after they had been seated at the restaurant.

"No, he's out in New Mexico for a training thing . . . not sure exactly what . . . He can't talk about it, y'know."

The dinner conversation grew more and more relaxed, measured in increments by the number of drinks they had. It had started out as typical co-worker chitchat. They talked at length about Firehawk. Troy spoke of mutual acquaintances with whom he had worked in the field, and Jenna regaled him with amusing and occasionally ridiculous stories of home office politics.

"Glad that you and Hal are finally making it . . . um . . . official," Troy said at a break in the conversation.

"Girl's gotta think about her future," Jenna said. "Biological clock, y'know."

"So you're thinking of having kids?"

"Probably . . . sure . . . I guess."

"Can't picture Falcon Two all settled down in the suburbs with a minivan and soccer practice." Troy laughed.

"Where *do* you picture me?"

"Well . . ." Troy felt himself going red.

"Yeah," Jenna said. "You and me both."

"I'm sorry I didn't . . . y'know . . . back in Las Vegas that time."

"I'm sorry too," Jenna said. "But you were right . . . Hal and me . . ."

"Doesn't mean that I haven't wished that . . . things . . . well, would have gone different . . . and if you and Hal hadn't been . . ."

"He's a rock," Jenna said. "He's the kind of guy that a girl thinks about as a father of her children. He's solid . . . he's a good guy."

"What about me?"

"I'm sorry, but when I think about you, I see this crazy dude taking shots at SAM sites . . . the dude who smoked all these MiGs over there . . . a dude who's gonna be impossible to tie down. Did you ever think about settling down, y'know, *really* settling down?"

"Well . . ." Troy's expression told all that needed telling. The notion of settling down was an anathema.

"And what about monogamy?" Jenna said. The wine was talking. "How many girls do you have waiting for you in all your ports of call?"

"What is this? Twenty questions?" Troy said indignantly.

"I'm sorry," Jenna said soothingly. She reached across

the table and gently took his hand. She felt him willingly let it be taken.

"I'm sorry," she repeated. "It was none of my business . . . it's the same things that make you not husband material that make you so very . . . *very* appealing to me."

CHAPTER 29

Firehawk Compound, Kota Bharu, Malaysia

"WE'LL HAVE TO GIVE THE SANDIES SOMETHING TO chew on," Raymond Harris said as he walked Troy back to the operations building from the Gulfstream that had just flown him in from Bangkok. "We'll have to show them that this is damned serious."

The "Sandies" were the firm of Sandringham Partners, Ltd., one of the other PMCs operating in Malaysia. The name made it sound like a firm of London chartered accountants, but in fact, the company was a Cayman Islands–based gang of what Harris referred to as "damned mercenaries who change sides more often than most people change their shirts."

"What do the Sandies have to do with *us*?" Troy asked. "I thought they were mixed up in some sort of special ops thing way down near Kuantan. We're not even really engaged in country here."

The compound in Kota Bharu Province, officially sanctioned by the Malaysian government, was Firehawk's base of operations for the Gulf of Thailand missions against the Cambodian Air Force, but Firehawk was not actually running operations within Malaysia.

"We're not functioning in a vacuum here, Loensch," Harris said. "Guarding the perimeter at these bases is key. It's not something that you'd notice, but you'd sure as hell notice if it *wasn't* being taken care of. Whenever we go into one of these Third World shitholes like this, Firehawk has to pay the right people to take care of us . . . usually local people who know the lay of the land."

"I understood that, but I admit that I didn't think about it too much," Troy admitted.

"Well, it's something that I *have to* think about when I set up an operational base anywhere," Harris explained. "In this case, we've been paying this organization run by a guy named Buddy—that's not his real first name, but he calls himself that—Keropok, Buddy Keropok. We've been paying Buddy to take care of us, and his people have been doing a damned good job. There weren't any perimeter incidents when you were serving your first tour out here, right?"

"Right, I mean there were no problems that I knew of," Troy said.

"Anyway, Buddy and his people are also doing some

other sorts of operations down around Kuantan. That's where they've been having some trouble with the Sandies. The Sandies have killed about a dozen of Buddy's people, and he's getting real pissed off."

"As well he should," Troy agreed.

"Buddy's people killed some Sandies too," Harris conceded. "But only in retaliation. It's an eye for an eye in this culture, same as any. So Buddy came to me and asked me, since I'm running PMC ops here and the Sandies are another PMC, couldn't I just talk to them and figure out a way to end this."

"Were you able?" Troy asked.

"I went down to Singapore for a sit-down with Sandringham's station chief. He's got a real nice flat in a modern building down there. I told him that Buddy's people were doing a good job of taking care of us, and asked what his problem was."

"And . . ."

"Turf war. Buddy's got a little contraband transfer thing going on south of Kuantan."

"You mean smuggling?" Troy asked, interpreting the phrase *contraband transfer*.

"I wouldn't *exactly* call it that, but whatever it is, it got in the way of something that the Sandies were doing."

"Smuggling?"

"Probably."

"Not enough for both?"

"Trouble is that the Sandies have been fighting the

rebels for so long down in that area that they essentially control the whole east coast of Malaysia. This includes contraband transfers. The rebels used to run all that, but now the Sandies do."

"And they don't want to share?"

"The Sandies are dealing from a position of strength. They have the government wrapped around their proverbial fingers since they beat the rebels. They don't feel that they need to share with anyone. I told him to cut Buddy some slack, and he said he'd think about it. He got cagey and told me we'd talk in the morning."

"That sounds indecisive."

"Well, he needed to talk to his bosses," Harris said. "And his bosses talked to our bosses, and that night, I got a call from Herndon. The Firehawk board of directors had gotten a call from the head Sandy down in the Caymans. They came up with a novel solution."

"What's that?" Troy asked, intrigued.

"The head Sandy said make us an offer, and Firehawk offered to *buy* Sandringham," Harris said. "The Firehawk board figured that if Firehawk *owned* Sandringham, then they would just tell the Sandies down at Kuantan to back the hell off."

"That sounds like it ought to work," Troy said, thinking that all's well that ends well.

"Except for one little detail . . . it *didn't* work. The Sandies turned down the Firehawk offer. They didn't even counter. Firehawk upped the bid and the

Sandies just hung up the phone on 'em. I went back to see the bastard in Singapore the next morning, and he basically told me to go fuck myself . . . and take Buddy Keropok with me. That's why we gotta get involved and show the bastards that Firehawk means business."

"How can we do that?"

"We have seven F-16s here at Kota," Harris said, thinking out loud. "We'll load up with JDAMs. The Sandies have a staging base down on the coast near Kuantan. We'll just teach 'em a lesson the old-fashioned way."

"Can we do that?" Troy asked. "I mean, does our mandate, our contract, allow us—"

"Sure as hell," Harris said. "Remember when we were out in Sudan and the Al-Qinamah were hiding in Eritrea and we needed to go after 'em, but we had those damned 'rules of engagement'?"

"Yeah . . ."

"We were allowed to fire if fired upon?"

"Yeah . . ."

"Well, every PMC contract that's been written has a provision that permits every PMC to defend itself . . . and the lawyers have told us that this means we can go after the *sources* of threats just like we did with the damned SAM missiles over there in Eritrea."

"Just to clarify, then," Troy said. "Our job would be to curtail the Sandringham threat against Buddy Keropok, who is our protector here in Malaysia?"

"Screw it," Harris said. "This is a fuckin' *war*. We're gonna do more than that. We're gonna blow the Sandies the hell out of Malaysia."

"Do they have any airpower, any fighters that might oppose a bomb run?" Troy asked, interjecting an element of practicality.

"Nothing more than a few choppers and a Gulfstream or two."

"Should we do a recon flight over their base just to make sure?"

"Absolutely, but we'd better do it quick," Harris said, eager to get his operation off the ground. "I want to feed real-time data back here so that we can launch the strike package as soon as possible . . . like I mean within an hour or two."

"I'll volunteer to fly the recon flight," Troy said.

"Plan on a long day, then," Harris said. "I want a maximum effort on that target, so as soon as you touch down after the recon flight, I want you to load up and fly as part of the strike package."

"Absolutely." Troy smiled. His job was to kill bad guys, and if the bosses at Firehawk said the Sandies were the bad guys, then it was them he would kill. However, he thought it so ironic that had the acquisition negotiations, handled between people safe in their comfortable offices, gone differently, the killers and victims would suddenly have been friends. After his last mission in Guatemala, though, these ironies were no longer surprises.

"Isn't this great?" Harris asked as the two men parted company outside the operations shack.

"What's great?"

"Being able to declare a war when it needs to be declared, and then just go do it."

"As opposed to . . ."

"Having to wait for a big room full of politicians to argue and bicker about it and quibble over rules of engagement. That's why all wars ought to be run by the PMCs. We're a hell of a lot more efficient than governments . . . don't you think?"

"Absolutely," Troy said, not quite able to get his head around what Harris perceived as the logical future of armed conflict.

CHAPTER 30

Flight Level 220, over the South China Sea

TROY WAS TAKING THE LONG WAY AROUND. FROM THE Firehawk Compound at Kota Bharu, Malaysia, he had flown due east, rather than south to Kuantan. Over the South China Sea, he leveled out at twenty-two thousand feet and snuggled into the flight path, the highway in the sky that was traveled by commercial flights between Manila and Kuala Lumpur or Singapore. The odds that Sandringham was tracking Firehawk flights on radar was remote, but Raymond Harris was taking no chances.

Troy might have climbed up to a commercial altitude above thirty thousand feet, but he didn't want to be seen visually by the airliners on their highway, and he wanted to be closer to his operational altitude when it came time to turn on his camera pod. He would cross the Sandringham base at around ten thousand because a low-level pass would seem too deliberate. At ten thousand, he'd be high enough to be just another plane in the fairly busy airspace, but low enough to get good resolution on the digital images that he would be transmitting back to Kota Bharu.

As he approached the Malay Peninsula and began his descent, Troy could look off to the left and see the sprawl of red roofs and occasional ivory-colored skyscrapers that marked the city of Kuantan, Malaysia's ninth largest.

Turning north, he could soon make out the Sandringham base. It was larger than he expected, dwarfing the nearby village of Kemasek. He saw the black stripe of a recently paved runway. He also saw—and did a double take when he did—what looked to be a pair of F-16 fighters, just like his.

How could this be?

Harris had insisted that Sandringham airpower consisted of helicopters and executive jets.

It's a good thing we're doing this recon flight, Troy thought to himself as he imagined Harris reacting to pictures of the F-16s that were streaming back to Kota Bharu from his camera pods.

"HOW THE HELL DID THEY GET *THOSE*?" HARRIS ASKED rhetorically and angrily as Troy climbed out of the cockpit. It was almost as though he were mad at Troy for them being there—blaming the messenger for the bad news.

"Good thing we know about them," Troy said. Maintenance people were already pumping fuel into his F-16.

"We had the rest of the crews watching the feed from your pods live. They're loaded and just about ready to go."

"Just let me drop the camera pod and I'm ready to load some JDAMs myself."

"Change of plans," Harris said. "Loading bombs would take time. I want to launch the strike ASAP. I'm going to have you fly CAP for the strike package. The aircraft carrying bombs won't be able to maneuver as well as they enter the target area. They'll be at a disadvantage if they're challenged. If you come in with just your Sidewinders, you'll be ready to engage immediately."

"Sounds like a plan," Troy said. He was no stranger to air-to-air combat, and the idea of going into a dogfight without a ton or so of bombs under his wings was appealing.

"The strike pack will go in at five thousand feet and drop to one thousand for their bomb runs," Harris explained. "They'll be in two waves of three, hitting separate targets. They've already been briefed on this. You'll stay at five thousand, so you have the altitude advantage if the Sandies react and launch their fighters."

"Two against one." Troy smiled, having been assigned as the lone CAP.

"As the others exit the target area without ordnance, they'll be ready for air-to-air. Your job is just to protect them at their most vulnerable. Then the odds will be two against *seven*."

THIS TIME, THERE WAS NO LONG WAY AROUND. THE Firehawk F-16s headed straight down the coast, flying low enough to hope that ground clutter would mask their approach for at least part of the half hour it would take. Sandringham *probably* didn't anticipate a surprise attack, but then Firehawk had not anticipated the presence of F-16s at the Sandringham base. Surprises can happen, even to surprise attackers.

Troy made his return flight to the Sandringham base flying above and behind the strike aircraft, watching the sky and waiting to engage his search radar until he reached an initial point about five minutes out. If the Sandies detected search radar, they would know that a fighter aircraft was in the area.

The first wave of strike aircraft descended to the prescribed altitude as Troy lit up his radar. Watching the three aircraft going in abreast reminded him of the old days in Sudan, when he had flown a similar pattern with Jenna Munrough and Hal Coughlin.

"Bombs away."

The crackly radio sounds of the first wave attack echoed in Troy's ears.

"One 16 on the runway . . . don't see the second."

At that moment, Troy saw the other F-16 on his radar. It was airborne.

"I've been made," Troy heard someone say as he twisted his neck to get a visual on the Sandy F-16.

There!

He saw it closing on one of the first-echelon Firehawk F-16s.

A Firehawk F-16 coming in at low level, laden with bombs, didn't have the ability for evasive action. It became a huge ball of flame as its own ordnance was ignited by a Sandringham Sidewinder.

"Fox Two!" Troy shouted as he locked on to the enemy aircraft and picked off a Sidewinder of his own.

The Sandy F-16, obviously in the hands of an excellent pilot, twisted left, then right. Troy's AIM-9 made the left turn but was going too fast to make the right.

Troy climbed to stay above the other F-16, to maintain his altitude advantage as he attacked again.

With one Sidewinder left, Troy wanted to narrow the distance as much as possible. He wanted to be sure that his next shot was a kill shot.

Just as he tried to achieve a lock-on, though, the other plane sidestepped and broke the lock.

Troy bored in, eager to close in and finish the fight.

Closer.

Closer.

Whoa! What happened?

One second, he was closing on the other F-16; the next, he was watching it slip beneath him like sand through your fingers at the beach. The opposing pilot had throttled back and let Troy overshoot.

Troy banked hard. Having overshot, he was outside the other pilot's turn radius. If the other plane continued its turn, Troy knew he could possibly get back inside, but the pilot reversed his own turn as Troy turned. Again, Troy overshot him.

Troy throttled back, trying both to jockey himself back into shooting position and to prevent his opponent from getting a clean shot.

As the two aircraft scissored across the Malaysian landscape, Troy knew that if he could coax the other guy into maintaining his defensive turn, rather than reversing and turning the other way, he would have the opening that he sought. But this wasn't working. The other pilot could not be coaxed.

Again and again, Troy turned and watched the other F-16 slip away.

Gotta try something, Troy thought.

As he got behind the other aircraft, and just before the guy reversed his turn, Troy throttled back, allowing him to stem their lateral separation and turn with the other F-16.

This gave him the split second that he needed.

"Fox Two," Troy whispered.

The other F-16 banked hard to the left to avoid the missile.

This deft maneuver worked.

The missile missed by no more than a few feet from the aircraft.

However, the shock wave from the Sidewinder blowing by prevented the other pilot from reversing his turn as he had become accustomed.

Troy was very close and still in firing position as the other plane was momentarily locked in a turn and unable to execute a turn reversal.

Within a second, this situation would change, but that was then, and Troy was in the moment.

He thumbed the trigger of his M61 and watched the stream of twenty-millimeter rounds streak toward the other plane—and connect.

Troy saw a piece of the tail tear off and cartwheel upward.

Troy watched the puffs of dust and smoke as his rounds struck home and watched the hits march up the belly of the F-16, which was still locked in its leftward bank.

Everything turned into a blinding sheet of light as one of Troy's twenty-millimeter high-explosive rounds connected with the fuel tank of the other aircraft.

The whole engagement had lasted less than thirty seconds, the burst from the Vulcan cannon no more than two or three.

Troy looked around to get his bearings.

He saw the plume of black where once there had been another F-16. Beneath him, there was only jungle. There was no ocean to be seen. His rolling, running dogfight had taken him deep into the mountainous middle of Malaysia, far from Kuantan.

"Firehawk CAP here, scratch one bogie," he reported.

"This is Firehawk Leader, CAP. We're over the target. Firehawk Three didn't make it. No chute."

Part of the strike package had continued to orbit the target area looking for signs of life in the wreckage of the aircraft that was shot down by the F-16 that Troy had killed.

As he passed over the newly paved, now newly cratered, Sandringham runway, Troy could see the wreckage of the Firehawk F-16 and the other Sandy F-16. The latter had the misfortune of being ready for takeoff just as the bombers arrived. It didn't stand a chance.

When it was determined that the Firehawk pilot had not survived, the eight surviving Firehawk aircraft formed up and headed back toward Kota Bharu.

The score was Firehawk two, Sandies one. As far as the bombing was concerned, Raymond Harris had wanted to deal a blow, and a blow had been dealt.

CHAPTER 31

Marriott Courtyard, Arlington, Virginia

TROY LOENSCH OPENED ONE EYE AND GLANCED AT the red numerals staring back at him from the clock radio.

5:47.

His open eye traveled to the slit of window beneath the heavy curtain. The light was the weak, faint light of midwinter.

5:48.

Was that A.M. or P.M.?

With the faint light, it could be either.

He had arrived well after midnight. Had he slept for four or five hours—or sixteen or seventeen? He couldn't tell.

Troy staggered to the bathroom, fumbled with the

coffeemaker for a moment, gave up, and collapsed back onto the bed.

5:56.

He had arrived well after midnight, flying in on the Firehawk Gulfstream by way of Tokyo and Barking Sands in Hawaii.

It was supposed to be a moment of triumph for Troy, but either he had slept through his corporate commendation presentation or he would arrive at it hopelessly sleep deprived.

Had he still been in the U.S. Air Force, he would be receiving the Distinguished Flying Cross. As Raymond Harris had told him, Firehawk had scrambled around to come up with something appropriate to give him, something that was the corporate equivalent of a DFC.

I deserve it, he thought to himself as his mind began to awaken. *Too bad I slept through me getting awarded it.*

Troy had emerged as a hero in the war between Firehawk and Sandringham. Beginning with the F-16 he shot down on the first day, up through his blowing up both of the former Australian Navy frigates that the Sandies used to patrol the South China Sea, he had been a key part of *winning* the war against Sandringham.

8:03.

It was still light outside, and considerably brighter.

Troy had dozed off again—this time under the covers—and he felt much better after another two hours of sleep.

He made coffee, shaved, showered, and opened his suitcase—which had made it barely eighteen inches inside the door before he abandoned it last night.

He located his least-wrinkled khakis and his Firehawk Windbreaker. The ceremony wasn't until 4:00. Hopefully, by that time, gravity would have softened the wrinkles in his Firehawk blazer.

Hoping that he hadn't missed his complimentary breakfast, he located his key card and headed for the elevator.

He barely noticed the man who passed him in the hall, but he did notice the big guy with the shaven head leaning on the wall near the elevator pretending to read his complimentary copy of *USA Today*.

"Mr. Loensch, could we have a word?"

Troy took a step back as the man reached inside his sport coat.

One of the perks of not flying commercial was that Troy was always accompanied by his personal Beretta 950, an easily concealed 4.7-inch automatic that was a useful tool when it was necessary to have a little bit of .25-caliber firepower. Once in Bangkok, it had saved his life. Here in Arlington, it was Troy's equalizer to whatever was inside the man's sport coat.

"I wouldn't if I were you, Mr. Loensch," came a voice from behind him.

He felt a muzzle pressed into his spine between his shoulder blades.

Troy took his own hand away from his waistband and put both where they were easily seen.

He felt a hand relieving him first of his 950, and next of his cell phone.

The mystery inside the shaven-headed man's sport coat turned out not to be a gun, but merely a wallet.

He tipped it open to reveal a Central Intelligence Agency ID that was either for real or a facsimile that was especially believable at a distance of a dozen feet. Troy noticed that as it was displayed, the man's thumb covered the line where his name would be.

"Mr. Loensch, could we have a word?" the man repeated, nodding toward Troy's room.

"Just one?" Troy replied in a vain attempt at humor. The CIA man didn't even crack a smile.

Back inside, they insisted that Troy have a seat in one of the two straight-backed armchairs. Both of the anonymous CIA men remained standing, and the one with the shaven head did all the talking.

"A lot of people found it pretty alarming to turn on their nightly news a couple of weeks ago to find that a PMC had—to quote Raymond Harris in that infamous CNN interview—'declared war' on another PMC and they were duking it out in a Third World country using some pretty sophisticated hardware."

"I suppose maybe a lot of people did," Troy said. "I was not really in a position to be concentrating on media reaction . . . but then, you probably know where I was and what I was doing."

"You were in the midst of a war . . . essentially a gang-style turf war . . . between two extranational private armies."

"I never thought of war having 'style,'" Troy quipped. "In case you haven't noticed, PMCs are the way wars are fought now that nations no longer have a stomach for war, so they outsource it."

"And that's a good thing?"

"My opinion? It's just a 'thing,' neither good nor bad in itself." Troy shrugged. "It's just the way it is. But the United Nations and more than a hundred countries must have thought it was good, because it took all that to make PMCs a reality . . . allow them to act as international and independent outfits. Can I ask a question?"

"Okay."

"I'm taking a wild guess here that you boys didn't shove a gun in my back so that you could lecture me about what you think of PMCs, because if you had asked, I don't really care what you think . . . so tell me why you *did* shove that gun in my back."

"We need your help."

"That's a great way of asking." Troy almost laughed. "Shove a gun in a guy's back because you need his help?"

"Shoved a gun in your back because you went for yours," the other CIA man said.

"Help doing what?" Troy asked, ignoring the second agent's comment.

"Help us with a discreet investigation."

"Of who?"

"Of Firehawk in general and Raymond Harris in particular."

"You want me to spy on my own company?" This time Troy did laugh. "That's a joke. Why?"

"We suspect that Firehawk may be a danger to the security of the United States."

"You train a dog to guard your junkyard and freak out when he gets rough with other dogs?"

"Have you ever heard Raymond Harris make statements about the use of PMCs to overthrow and control countries?"

"That's not new. I can name about seven, including Malaysia at the moment, that are already controlled by one PMC or another."

"Overthrow the United States?"

Troy paused. He realized that some of the things that Harris said about the ineptitude of politicians and governments could be taken out of context. More than once, he had said that the world would be better off if Firehawk ran it, but Troy had always considered this merely a form of blustering.

"If you locked up everybody who made crude remarks about politicians, you'd be locking up half the country,"

Troy said. "You'd also probably be locking up most of the politicians."

"This is not about crude remarks. It's about a loose cannon pointing himself at this country."

"He blows off a lot of steam, but I've never heard him say anything about overthrowing the United States government," Troy said, racking his brain to recall whether this was, in fact, true. "As far as being a loose cannon, I've always found him to be the kind of commander who runs a tight ship, runs well-planned missions and—"

"Stretches the rules?"

"I suppose."

"Breaks the rules?"

"Gets the job done."

"Ends justify the means?"

At that, Troy paused.

"What are you trying to say?" Troy asked.

"That he'll step on anybody to 'get the job done.'"

"Step on who, specifically?" Troy asked.

"You say that he runs a well-planned mission?"

"I said that." Troy nodded.

"Tell me about a raid on a Sandringham facility near Kuantan."

"Which raid? There were a couple."

"The first one, the one where Harris was unaware of the presence of F-16s at the base until you yourself ran a recon."

"How do you know that?" Troy asked.

"We're the CIA," the man said, smiling for the first time. "Knowing is our business. Is what I said true?"

"Your source has it right," Troy replied. "So what? Lots of missions are flown with last-minute intel."

"Were you ever briefed on *where* those F-16s came from and who was flying them?"

"Sandringham," Troy said, acting bored.

"Do you know who was flying them?"

"It doesn't matter to me," Troy said, recalling his dinner with Aron Arnold. After that night, it really *didn't* matter. He had learned to divorce the job from his emotions.

The CIA man opened his thin briefcase and took out a folder with some photographs.

"As you have gathered by now, the CIA has been keeping an eye on Firehawk. It may interest you to know that we did reach the wreckage of that F-16 that you shot down."

"You guys went to a lot of trouble, then," Troy said, taking the photos that were handed to him. "It was pretty deep in the jungle."

At first it didn't register.

Faint recognition became solid recognition as he reached the third photo.

The images were close-ups of the cockpit of an F-16. The canopy had come off, and the pilot remained still strapped in his seat. His head was tipped at an angle that suggested a broken neck. His eyes stared lifelessly into space, his mouth was opened slightly, and dried blood covered his chin and left cheek.

The name strip on his flight suit read "H. Coughlin."

CHAPTER 32

Marriott Courtyard, Arlington, Virginia

TROY SAT IN THE LOBBY TEARING OPEN A PADDED envelope.

Inside were his cell phone and his gun, the magazine having been removed and emptied. When he and the CIA men parted company, they said that they'd leave his things at the front desk, and they had. That they'd emptied the magazine told him that they didn't *completely* trust him. That they did not take his cell phone battery told him that they didn't care who he called. They'd be listening.

The meeting that morning had not happened.

No routine camera surveillance of any part of the hotel showed the three men together. No routine camera surveillance of the lobby recorded a padded envelope being handed to a bellman, who wrote the name and room number on it in his own handwriting and handed it in to reception to hold for Mr. Loensch.

In a meeting that had not happened, Troy learned that he had killed the man with whom the story of his life had been tightly intertwined since they were both in OTS. That seemed like a very long time ago.

Had Harris known that Hal Coughlin was flying for the Sandies?

How could he?

The meeting that morning had not happened— the CIA men had said so. But they had also given him instructions for contacting them when—not if—he wished to not have a second meeting.

Jenna Munrough.

He realized that she had not crossed his mind since he had crossed paths with the CIA.

Yesterday, though, Troy had had little else on his mind, knowing he would soon be seeing her. Months ago in Las Vegas, he had taken the high road, refused her advances, and had often regretted this decision. On his last visit to the Firehawk home office, he had allowed himself to be seduced by this Ozark tigress. It was hot, wild ecstasy, but he had often regretted *this* decision. He regretted the dishonesty of what his delicious encounter meant to an unknowing Hal Coughlin, the man whose ring Jenna wore.

Then, he'd killed this man.

In less than an hour, he'd walk into the Firehawk headquarters, and he would come face-to-face with Jenna.

Did she know it was him?

What would she say?

What should he say?

How could he look into those blue eyes of hers knowing that he had killed her fiancé?

THE MAN WHO WAS SCHEDULED TO RECEIVE A CORPOrate commendation that was to be the equivalent of the Distinguished Flying Cross, the first in Firehawk history, entered the building not the same conquering hero as on his last visit, but a wary, conflicted man. This afternoon, he would play the role of conquering hero in front of Firehawk's adoring home office staff, but the man inside the shell inhabited a murky world of guilt.

There were layers upon layers of guilt that began with leaving Hal Coughlin for dead and ended with actually killing him. Amid the layers was the fact that he had decided to tell no one at Firehawk that he had been approached by the CIA. Of course, that meeting had never happened. Indeed, it *felt* like a bad dream.

Fortunately for him, it was in a crowd of people that Troy next looked into Jenna's eyes. There was an informal buffet luncheon ahead of the presentation, and Jenna was there.

She smiled broadly, but there was no hug.

"How are things?" Troy asked.

"Oh, y'know . . . so-so," Jenna replied, setting down her paper plate of potato salad. "Did you know that Hal died?"

"Oh," Troy said.

Jenna took his look of surprise that this was the first thing she said as surprise at hearing that Hal was deceased.

"Yeah, it was over in Malaysia where you were," Jenna continued. "He was working on a hush-hush project for Escurecer. They had just gotten a contract to supply an air combat component for Sandringham Partners. He went over with the first batch of F-16s. They had just arrived in country when Firehawk went to war with Sandringham."

"That must have been awkward for you, working at Firehawk and having him . . . on the other side. . . ."

"Yeah, it was." Jenna nodded sadly. "Even though we broke up before he went."

"I didn't know that."

"That's because you never read my damned e-mails," Jenna said, shaking her head. She wasn't smiling. This was not playful banter, but the despondency of an emotionally exhausted woman. The fiery Jenna he had known before had been superseded by one far more circumspect.

"Yeah . . . Hal and I broke up. It was not long after you and me . . . and no, I never told him about us. It was just one of those things. I could tell that he was losing interest . . . that the fire was gone. Now it's Hal who's gone."

Troy could see a tear forming in the eye of a woman he had never seen cry.

"Can I ask you a question?" Jenna asked, quickly dabbing at the offending eye with a paper napkin.

"Yeah . . ."

"You were flying a lot in the war, and you shot down one of the Escurecer F-16s, right?"

"Yeah . . . but we didn't know they were Escurecer. They were flying out of a Sandy base. I sure as hell didn't know that one of them was Hal . . . I feel like shit."

"You should," she said. "I know it's war, I know it's your job and all, and I know that he may have been shooting at you . . . but you still should feel like shit."

"I do," Troy said sadly.

"So did I," Jenna admitted. "I cheated on him . . . with you. Didn't think I'd feel like I did because of that . . . but I did. Then I broke up with him because I couldn't . . . emotionally . . . and then I heard he was dead . . . I'm not a crybaby . . . never been a crybaby, but y'know . . . I felt . . . and then I found out you had been. I'm just totally, y'know . . . wasted."

"I know what you mean," Troy said sympathetically.

"How?" Jenna said bitterly, as if to say that there was no way that he could possibly comprehend her regret and her guilt.

They just stared at each other.

"Congratulations on your award," she said at last, turning to walk away.

SOMEHOW, TROY MADE IT THROUGH HIS PRESENTA-TION, receiving a commendation for his part in what was simply Raymond Harris's personal war against a rival on behalf of a smuggler.

Harris spoke at length on the Firehawk program in Malaysia. Troy didn't hear the words. His mind wandered, first back to Jenna and to Hal, finally coming to rest on the words of the CIA men.

Harris really was emerging as a demagogue, his appetite only whetted by the raw-meat taste of the power that came from the omnipotent ability to declare your own wars and to fight them with the most high-tech of weapons.

Troy looked at Jenna in the audience as he accepted his award. She had been looking at him, but she glanced away when their eyes met.

Afterward, there were handshakes and pats on the back, and several people wanted their picture taken with Troy. When this tapered off, he looked around for Jenna, hoping to resume their conversation and guide it toward a more positive resolution. She was nowhere to be seen.

When he had arrived, he had parked his rental car one row back from her Porsche. When he left the building, it was gone.

Back at the hotel, he ordered a hamburger at the bar and had a couple of beers. A news-talk show came on the television, and Troy was surprised to see Raymond Harris on with a congressman from Missouri. Harris was on his familiar jag about PMCs being the future of warfare, and the congressman was gushing about how much money the government was saving.

"PMCs have proven to be excellent partners in respect to efficiency, skills, low prices, and reliability," the congressman said in his soft Midwestern drawl, looking at the talking-head moderator. "They've been able to fulfill most of the missions normally handled by regular armies, without risking political fallout."

"Initially they were just consultants," the talking head said to his guests. "But each year, they come closer to serving as fully operational armies. For many client countries, it seems that PMCs have become *essential*."

"Any time you have customers that come to rely on you as an *essential* part of the program, that's when you know that you're doing your job." Harris smiled confidently.

Troy still thought the CIA guys were wrong about Harris, but he could certainly see how they'd jumped to that conclusion.

CHAPTER 33

Headquarters, Firehawk, LLC, Herndon, Virginia

TROY WAS SHOWN INTO RAYMOND HARRIS'S LARGE top-floor office, the office that didn't remind you that he was a retired general so much as it hit you over the head with that fact. Harris was behind his big desk, next to his flagpole.

He was on the phone but waved for Troy to take a seat. As Harris finished his call, Troy's eyes roamed the room, looking at the framed photos of Harris with famous people and his collection of $\frac{1}{32}$-scale mahogany aircraft models. As his eyes came to rest on an F-16, he thought about Hal and the cruelties of war.

When the call was finished, the two men exchanged pleasantries and Harris got down to business.

"I wanted you to be among the first to know that I'm

stepping aside as Director of Air Ops here at Firehawk."
Harris smiled.

"That's sort of a bombshell," Troy said. He was
bowled over. Harris was synonymous with air operations
at Firehawk. He had run the Air Ops Division since its
inception and had watched it grow into one of the top
ten air forces in the world. "This is really astounding . . .
what next for you?"

"That's the good part." Harris grinned. "I'm staying
with Firehawk. I'm just moving to a new division."

"Which division?"

"One you've never heard of, and one I can't tell you
about . . . unless of course you accept my invitation to
come over and work with me there."

"Sounds like a desk job," Troy said. "I don't think
that's right for me. I like what I'm doing and I'm real
anxious to get back overseas and start doing it some
more," Troy said

"Well, I will tell you that this job *does* involve flying,"
Harris said.

"How much flying?"

"There'll be an opportunity for you to get into the
cockpits of some pretty extreme stuff."

"Hmmm," Troy said thoughtfully. "What does it pay?"

"As you recall the last time I offered you a job, we sat
in this room and I asked you what you were making, and
I doubled it. This time, I *know* what you're making, and
I'm offering to double it."

"Well, then I guess you have your guy," Troy said. A change of pace was always good, especially after all the anguish he'd been wrestling with since Hal died.

A doubled salary didn't hurt, either.

Troy was a little startled that Harris had already prepared the papers and nondisclosure agreements for him to sign, but only just a little. As soon as these details were attended to, he began his explanation.

"Back at the end of World War Two, when the Germans were way ahead of us on certain kinds of technology, the Army and the Army Air Forces went in to scoop up the German scientists and the stuff they were working on. You've heard of Operation Paperclip, right?"

"Of course," Troy said. "That was when the Americans got hold of Wernher von Braun, who invented the V2 ballistic missile . . . and brought him to the United States to build a whole succession of bigger and bigger rockets that led to ICBMs and to the Saturn V that took astronauts to the moon."

"Right." Harris nodded. "But Paperclip was only one of several programs of that sort. Another one run by the U.S. Air Force was called Project FALCO, for Foreign Aircraft and Logistics Capture Operations. Paperclip's bailiwick was big rockets, while FALCO's was very-high-altitude fighters. You've heard of the YF-12 and the SR-71, which came along in the sixties and flew at altitudes up to a hundred thousand feet . . . well, there were others you *never* heard of."

"Why not? That was a half century ago."

"Certain things just stay secret. In this case, HAW, the High Altitude Warfare program, was parallel to other things like the SR-71 that were *merely* top secret. HAW remained classified beyond all access partly because it *was* classified beyond all access. They had done such a good job of keeping it a secret that the biggest secret was simply that they had kept it that way."

"How does this affect Firehawk?" Troy asked. The history lesson was nice, but he was anxious for Harris to cut to the chase.

"Because the program still exists," Harris said, lowering his voice almost to a whisper, as though to underscore the secrecy. "For several decades after its heyday in the sixties, the program was underfunded and didn't really do very much, but in the last couple of years, they've really cranked it up again. It's now called HAWX for High Altitude Warfare, Experimental, because of the emphasis on really advanced systems."

"That doesn't explain how this affects us."

"It affects us because the U.S. Air Force has decided to privatize it and hand it off to a PMC," Harris said excitedly. "They're so pleased with the efficiencies of working with PMCs that they decided to let us run with it. On top of that, it's growing so big so fast that they want to keep it another step away from congressional oversight. They're afraid this increases the chance of information getting leaked."

"Where is the program located?" Troy asked.

"It's been all over. It was at Wright-Pat, then Langley, and now it's out on the Nellis Air Force Base range about a hundred miles north of Las Vegas, out by Groom Lake. Officially, it's known as the 24th Test and Evaluation Squadron."

"Mmmm," Troy purred conspiratorially. "Out by Area 51?"

"About fifty miles to the northeast," Harris replied straight-faced.

"What would I be doing exactly?"

"There are three primary missions of the 24th TES. First, just like the squadron designation says, there's testing and evaluation of experimental and secret aircraft and hardware, with an emphasis on high-altitude systems. Second, the 24th has been called on to fly live high-altitude combat or recon missions. All of these will be strictly on the 'black ops' side. You'll get to continue doing what you're doing now, it's just that nothing that you do will officially have happened."

"I understand." Troy nodded. "What about the third mission category?"

"As needs dictate, the 24th is involved in training of United States and Allied pilots, new people who come into the HAWX Program. Y'know, we might even get involved in capturing enemy technology to evaluate."

"It sounds interesting," Troy said. "I'm ready for this kind of thing. When do I start?"

"That's the spirit," Harris said, giving Troy a fatherly

glance. "Since we're all wrapped up in Malaysia, thanks in no small part to your own celebrated efforts, I'd say that you can start as soon as possible. Shall we say in ten days? That'll give you a week and two weekends to recharge your batteries. See you in the desert, Loensch."

CHAPTER 34

Glendale, California

"WISH YOU WEREN'T GOING OUT OF TOWN AGAIN SO soon," Yolanda Rodriguez complained, kicking the sheets from her naked body and sitting up in the bed. "You and me . . . like we made some real chemistry last night, huh?"

"I've missed you too, Yo," Troy said, reaching up and pulling her into his arms.

After accepting Raymond Harris's job offer, Troy had flown back to Southern California for ten days to see his parents and to fill his eyes with a change of scenery. It was only after he had been around for about five days that he phoned Yolanda. The strain of visiting his parents separately and of listening to them complain about each other had driven him to seek another change of scenery, and Yolanda was *always* easy on the eyes.

She rolled on top of him, kissing him passionately.

He was reminded yet again why he missed Yolanda so much and why he was glad he'd decided to call her.

He almost hadn't.

He hadn't seen her since he had come back from Guatemala, and then only briefly. He wasn't sure how she would react after all this time, but she happily—even excitedly—accepted a dinner suggestion.

Dinner had gone well.

They laughed, joked, and had a great time. He had forgotten how much he enjoyed just staring into her dark eyes and watching the beautiful choreography of her hand gestures as she spoke. He had forgotten how much fun it was to listen to the way she told a joke, and how he enjoyed the sound of her laughter.

After dinner, things went even better.

They made love in the car—Yolanda thrived on the naughtiness of sex in unconventional places. After that, they went to a dance club where she knew the bouncer, danced, had a few drinks, made love in the room where they kept rolls of quarters, and ended the evening at her apartment.

Her breathing grew deeper as she wrapped her legs around him and squeezed him hungrily. Troy had *really* missed Yolanda.

Though there was no hint of long-term commitment

in their relationship, they shared a genuine friendship and a very rambunctious mutual lust.

Exhausted and gasping, the two lovers lay together, holding hands, catching their breath and staring at the ceiling.

"Sure is fun, huh," she said, looking at him longingly. "Wish you'd bring your tight little ass back through town more often."

"My job, y'know. I'm on the road a lot."

"Yeah, I suppose you're right. Richard would sure be pissed big-time if I started spending a lotta time with you."

"Who's Richard?" Troy asked. There was no jealousy as there had been with Cassie's dalliance with Enrique, because there was no commitment, no presupposed boundaries with Yolanda. There was just idle curiosity.

"Richard's my boyfriend, my gringo boyfriend," Yolanda said in a matter-of-fact way. "He's a big-time banker downtown. He lives over in Bel Air."

"How'd you meet him?"

"At this big charity party. There's lots of celebrities and stuff. Richard's wife is some kind of queen of the charity party ladies."

"So Richard is married?"

"Oh yeah, and he's got some kids too, but they go to boarding school somewhere."

"Is his wife cool with you being . . . y'know . . . with Richard?"

"I don't think she knows. He says she's too busy with all her society shit."

"Is he gonna leave her and marry you?"

"How'd you know?" Yolanda asked sarcastically. "He said that he wanted to, but I know it's a line of bullshit . . . he ain't gonna leave *her*. She'd take all his money, and I sure wouldn't like that. I like things the way they are. He's got money. He buys me nice things. Jewelry and shit. Takes me places."

"Is he good in bed?" Troy smiled.

"That's none of your fucking business." She giggled, climbing on him again.

Troy imagined that it really would take several guys to fully satisfy Yolanda's boundless energy and appetite for male companionship. Once again, as often in the past eighteen hours, he did what he could to answer her compelling call.

When they had finished, Troy stood up and suggested a shower.

Yolanda literally leaped at the suggestion, but the deluge of warm water across their bodies only stirred the embers of her passion into flames yet again.

Finally, they were dressed. Troy was tying his shoes as Yolanda, dressed in tight jeans and a skimpy lilac-colored bra, rooted through her drawers looking for a particular top that she wanted to wear.

"Yo, could I ask you a question?" Troy said, his voice in a serious tone.

"Oh baby, don't tell me you're gonna pop the question, cuz I don't want to spoil what we got, babe."

"No, I wasn't, I mean I don't want to spoil what we got either. That wasn't the question."

The idea of being married to Yolanda Rodriguez had occurred to him, but only in fleeting moments of passion. To wake up as he had today held great appeal, but the thought of waking up like that every day was merely exhausting.

"I have a hypothetical question," Troy said. "I'm looking for your advice, some woman's intuition."

"Cool," she said, sitting cross-legged on the bed and looking him in the eyes with the beautiful dark eyes that always sent Troy around the bend. "Hypothetical? That's like when you make up something that represents something, like testing out some theory that you suppose is true, huh?"

Her perfect breasts looked almost better when framed by the thin, lacy bra than they did on their own.

"Yeah that's right," Troy said. "Using you and Richard as an example, what would you think if somebody . . . like the cops, for instance . . . came to you and said that Richard was mixed up in some criminal wrongdoing at the bank?"

"I'd ask them, 'What's that got to do with me?'"

"And they said it was real serious and they thought he was going to do something really bad that would affect lots of people . . . people you knew and loved . . . like your family?"

"Like if he was gonna take all the money and run off to the Bahamas, huh?"

"Yeah, something like that."

"Is somebody threatening *your* family, baby?" Yolanda asked. "If they are, I'll call my cousin, and him and his friends would kick the guy's ass."

"Nobody's threatening my family," Troy assured her. "This is kind of a work thing . . . so what if the cops asked you to spy on Richard?"

"You mean, be a snitch?"

"Yeah, sort of."

"No way I'd be a snitch for the cops, man," Yolanda explained. "You don't even rat out your *enemies* to the cops."

"Even if he was gonna run off to the Bahamas with money that belonged to your family?"

"Even if Richard was that kinda asshole, I wouldn't snitch to the cops. I'd call my cousin, y'know. I'd figure out some way to stop him so he didn't do it."

"That's sound advice, Yo."

"You must sure work with some assholes down there where you work," she said, stroking the stubble on his cheeks with her hand and beginning to breathe more heavily. "I sure wish you'd get another job and get your ass out of there if those people are like that. I sure wish you weren't going out of town again so soon, babe."

CHAPTER 35

Cactus Flat Air Force Auxiliary Field, Nevada

LANDING AT MCCARRAN AIRPORT REMINDED TROY Loensch of the last time he had been in Las Vegas. Hal Coughlin was still very much alive back then, and Jenna was far more alive. A fire had burned in her deep-blue eyes in those days, and robust eagerness and excitement about life permeated her being. The last time that he saw her, her eyes seemed vacant, drained of their vibrancy by the despondency of loss, and of guilt, a guilt for which Troy held himself responsible.

As much as he enjoyed Yolanda, the warmth of her friendship and the heat of her body, Troy felt that he had fallen in *love* with Jenna. Yet, while Yolanda was his for the asking, willingly and at any time, he imagined himself never seeing Jenna again, and it was tearing him up inside.

When he was flying with Golden West, Troy had landed often at McCarran. Each time, he had shared ramp space or airspace with one of the white Boeing 737 jetliners known only as "Janet." Unmarked except for a single red stripe on each side of their fuselage, the Janet 737s were operated by Edgerton, Germeshausen, & Grier, a longtime contractor to the government agencies operating at the Nevada Test Site and the adjacent Nellis Air Force Base Range—the place the outside world knows as Area 51.

After all the stories and tall tales about Area 51, today he had discovered that this was what the white 737s actually do. For the first time, he had not only watched a Janet taxi anonymously across the McCarran tarmac, he had boarded one.

They had flown north, he and his fellow passengers, wearing uniforms and not, making their first stop at Groom Lake, the place where the Air Force tested the SR-71 back in the sixties and numerous other "black airplanes" in the half century since. It is here, the conspiracy buffs insist, that they still have the aliens from the 1947 Roswell crash. For Troy, Groom Lake was just another airline stop. He glanced out the window at the closed hangars, finding them so disappointingly ordinary. It was rather like Dorothy discovering that the Wizard of Oz was no big deal.

The Groom Lake stop was like any commuter airline stop, quick and routine. About a dozen of the passengers who had gotten on at McCarran deplaned, and four people got on.

Troy glanced up idly, watching as the new people stowed their luggage and sat down. Suddenly, there was an unexpected flicker of recognition. It was a thin man about Troy's age with short-cropped dark hair. Who was behind this vaguely familiar face?

Aron Arnold.

Aron Arnold from Svartvand, with whom he had dueled over the Petén jungle.

As they made eye contact, Arnold nodded his recognition and took a seat across the aisle from Troy.

"Aron Arnold," he said, extending his hand. "We met down in Guatemala."

"Troy Loensch. Yes, we did meet . . . a couple of times down there. What are you doing *here*?"

"Harris invited me to get involved in a special project up in Cactus Flat . . . I'm guessing that by the fact that this plane's last stop is Cactus Flat, that you and I may be headed to the same place."

"That's probably the case," Troy said. He shouldn't have been surprised, but the irony of the easy cordiality of Aron Arnold still seemed a bit eerie. "What do you know about this program?"

"Not much. It's about experimental aircraft, but then this whole desert out here is about mystery aircraft, both black and white."

A half hour north of Groom Lake, Cactus Flat Air

Force Auxiliary Field was much the same as Groom Lake, with clusters of low, khaki-colored buildings, some closed hangars, and a long runway. The desolate landscape in which it lay was more like Sudan than it was like Mundo Maya or Kota Bharu. Everything about this part of Nevada appears brown and monotonous. The mountains have no trees and seem virtually devoid of any perceptible vegetation, except sagebrush, which is also dull brown.

It's a lot colder than Sudan, Troy thought as a blast of icy air hit him when he exited the door in the front of the cabin. It can be quite cold in the wintertime out in the high desert of central Nevada.

The other passengers, mainly engineering types carrying laptops, hurried off the plane and scurried purposefully in different directions.

"I take it by the way you're gawking around that you're the two new guys for HAWX? My name's Mike Dehnland. You must be Arnold and Loensch."

"Must be," Troy said. "I'm Loensch, he's Arnold."

Dehnland, a man in his midforties with *ex-military* written all over him, greeted them with a firm handshake and an admonition to collect their gear and follow him. He gave them a half hour to settle in before the obligatory briefing that always comes early on one's first day at a new duty station.

Troy found his quarters quite spartan, not unlike a cheap motel room, although the room was a cut or two above what he had endured in Sudan or at Kota Bharu. At least the walls seemed to be sealed up well enough to keep out the blowing dust.

The briefing room was regulation U.S. Air Force issue, although all the personnel were in civilian clothes. A Firehawk logo hung on a patch of wall where you could tell by the mismatched paint color that the shield of an Air Force unit insignia had once hung there.

"Welcome to the Flat, gentlemen, home of the 24th Test and Evaluation Squadron of the U.S. Air Force," Dehnland said, delivering what was obviously a speech he'd given to newbies before. "Until three weeks ago, the 24th was involved in the testing and evaluation of some of the most advanced high-altitude aircraft in the world. As you know, this activity has been transferred in its entirety to Firehawk, LLC. Basically, all of the facilities, operations, and most personnel remain as they were; we just wear civilian 'uniforms' to work. The 24th still exists, but only as the host unit here at Cactus Flat, *and* as the cover for what we do here."

"Almost like being in the Air Force," Troy said sarcastically.

"Almost, but not quite," Dehnland replied. "I suppose you can blame it on the president."

"Fachearon has certainly screwed things up," Arnold said, noticing a raised eyebrow from Dehnland. "Don't look at me like that . . . I voted for him."

Indeed, it seemed to many that President Albert

Bacon Fachearon had lost control of the government. Like a squirrel in the headlights of an oncoming car, he was vacillating, unsure which way to turn. The economy was in disarray, and Fachearon was unable to reassure the electorate. Around the world, America was facing challenges that went unhandled. Embassies had been burned, but Fachearon seemed confused, unable to respond.

"Seemed like a nice guy," Troy interjected. "A nice guy who's not up to the job."

"Officially, I'm still enough Air Force that I'm not gonna criticize the commander in chief," Dehnland said. "My job is with the HAWX Program. It was government . . . now it's not, but like him or not, Fachearon's still the commander in chief. Besides, it doesn't matter who's in Washington, we still have a job to do."

"That's what we came to do," Troy said. "I have no interest in politics."

"Your duties here will consist of operational flight testing of new equipment as it comes in," Dehnland said, changing the subject from politics. "All of the aircraft that reach us will have been through their initial flight test program at other remote locations and will be passed along to Cactus Flat when they are deemed ready for operations."

"Are these all prototypes?" Troy asked.

"Some are, some are not," Dehnland replied. "If a prototype got through initial flight testing with minimal tweaking, it may come here. If a prototype demonstrated a tendency to fall out of the sky during initial flight testing, DOD may decide to terminate the program or to have the manufacturer develop a completely new variant. When we get the airplanes, we know they *fly*. Our job is to determine whether they can *fight*."

"Where are the planes that we're gonna be flying?" Arnold asked.

"That's a good question," Dehnland replied. "I was just getting to that. Let's take a walk."

He led them into the first of the line of hangars that flanked the Cactus Flat taxiway. The door was secured by combination lock that made it look like a bank vault.

Inside were several aircraft of types they had never seen before.

"In most cases, these are one-of-a-kind, although occasionally they build two for operational testing," Dehnland said.

Closest to the door was a strange, lozenge-shaped airplane with acutely angled wings that Troy recognized as being similar to Boeing's top secret "Bird of Prey" stealth demonstrator that flew back in the 1990s.

From here, they stepped through another door and entered the main part of the hangar, a vast room containing a huge structure that was not immediately identifiable as an airplane. On second glance, they noticed a dozen propellers and realized that this immense object was a long, straight wing.

"This puppy is based on the aircraft that were developed for the NASA Environmental Research Aircraft and Sensor Technology program a few years back," Dehnland said proudly. "You may remember the Pathfinder and the Pathfinder Plus . . ."

"I also remember the Helios that fell into the Pacific back in 2003," Troy interjected, referring to the follow-on development of the two aircraft that Dehnland had mentioned. Like others in the family, Helios had been a solar-powered, unmanned aircraft.

"They ran into unexpected heavy turbulence and the Helios wing deformed into a persistent, high dihedral configuration," Dehnland explained, describing an airplane whose flexible wings were bent almost straight upward. "This obviously made it unstable and hard to control. It also put so much stress on the outer wing panels that the whole thing broke apart."

"I'm sure glad I wasn't the pilot," Arnold said, looking up at one end of the huge wing.

"Helios was an unmanned aerial vehicle," Dehnland reminded him.

"I know, I was talking about the guy sitting in the trailer running the thing," Arnold said. "I bet he caught all kinds of hell for losing that airplane."

"Not to mention the guy who decided they had to fly a fragile-looking thing like that in bad weather," Troy added.

"We learned a lot from that crash," Dehnland said,

nodding toward the aircraft. "Shakuru here has bene-fited a lot from the loss of Helios."

"Shakuru?" Troy asked.

"Helios was the sun god of ancient Greek mythol-ogy," Dehnland said. "Shakuru is the solar deity of the Pawnee Indians."

"I take it that Shakuru is also solar powered," Troy surmised.

"Clever deduction," Dehnland said cynically. "But unlike Helios, it carries a crew, and I bet you can deduce who they are."

"I bet we can," Arnold said, knowing that it was he and Loensch.

CHAPTER 36

Cactus Flat Air Force Auxiliary Field, Nevada

TROY LOENSCH AWOKE EARLY ON HIS FIRST DAY IN the desert. His mind seized on Jenna. Was she a missed opportunity, or had her interest in him been merely the same hot, but transitory attention that characterized his ongoing relationship with Yolanda Rodriguez?

Sleep would not return to embrace him, so Troy decided to take a run. Sunrise was still an hour away, but in the east the cloudless sky had already turned a pale salmon. Most of the stars had winked out, but some of the brightest ones still burned faintly. As he ran, Troy fixed his gaze on the horizon, where tiny Mercury, the planet that people call a morning "star," still glowed bravely.

The sun was just topping the eastern horizon as Troy

was making his way back to his quarters. He passed the hangar that Mike Dehnland had shown him yesterday, and another that was surrounded by razor wire and a guard tower. *How odd,* he thought, *to have a hangar protected in this way in the center of one of the most secure bases in the world.*

The Cactus Flat tarmac was nearly deserted, except for a woman in glasses and a baggy college sweatshirt who looked as though she too had been out for a run. Troy was about to greet her when she spoke first.

"Up early to avoid the rattlesnakes and tarantulas?" She smiled.

"Whoa, I hadn't thought of that," Troy replied.

"Cold-blooded invertebrates," she said. "In this climate, they're dormant until the sun warms them up."

"Where I've spent most of the past year," Troy said, "the bugs and snakes are up all night long."

"Where's that?"

"Tropics . . . mainly Southeast Asia, but I did short tours in Central America . . . and Zambia."

"You must be one of the Firehawk pilots who came in yesterday."

"I sure am, my name's Troy Loensch."

"My name is Elisa Meyers," she said, taking the hand he offered. "I work for Aeroworks, on the Shakuru Project."

She was a small woman, only about five foot five or so, with a warm, engaging presence. There were strands of gray in her dark hair, which she had tied back carelessly. Troy guessed her to be around forty.

"How long have you been out here dodging rattle-snakes and tarantulas?" Troy asked.

"Here? Only a couple of months, but I've been with Aeroworks for eighteen years, most of them spent at bases out in the desert . . . Yucca West . . . Groom Lake . . . and other places that officially don't have names."

"How do you like it out here?"

"I hated this place when I first came." She laughed. "But it grows on you . . . especially jogging in the desert before the sun comes up. There was a great writer once who said that the desert at dawn, in some mysterious way of its own, speaks of things eternal, a message whis-pered through the changing colors of sand and shadows of rocks, and through the air, at once fresh and seduc-tively cool."

"That's poetic," Troy said. "I spent a few months in Sudan a while back. Can't think of *any* poetry that makes that place seem appealing."

"The desert's like the moon would look if it were brown instead of gray." Elisa Meyers smiled. "*But* remember what Buzz Aldrin, the Apollo Eleven Lunar Module pilot who was the second human to walk on the moon, said of the lunar landscape after that walk; he called it desolation, magnificent desolation."

* * *

TROY SHOWERED, GOT A PLATE OF LINKS AND EGGS AT the mess hall, and arrived in Mike Dehnland's office with his coffee in a to-go cup.

"Today, you go to work," Dehnland said, looking first at Troy, then glancing at Aron Arnold, who also carried a to-go cup. "I'm going to turn you over to the Shakuru people. They'll bring you up to speed. We'll go over and I'll introduce you to Dr. Meyers; she designed the Shakuru and has been running the program."

"Dr. Meyers? Would that be Elisa Meyers?" Troy asked.

"Yeah, that's her," Dehnland confirmed. "Do you know her?"

"Just met her this morning when I was coming back from my run."

"What was she doing?"

"Coming back from a run."

"Do you know who she is?"

"She didn't say she was a doctor. Said she was with Aeroworks, on the Shakuru Project."

"Yeah, she was one of the great aviation industry whiz kids about a dozen or so years ago . . . brilliant aerodynamicist, earned her master's degree in aeronautical engineering from Caltech. Worked for NASA, got a doctorate at MIT. She was the one who first came up with the theory of a three-hundred-sixty-degree-symmetrical airframe."

"I remember," Aron Arnold said. "That was the YF-27."

"Yeah, somebody at MIT slipped a copy of her thesis to Dave Carlstrand, the electronics guy who was just then working with some venture capitalists to start Aeroworks."

"Whatever happened to the YF-27?" Troy asked.

"It was stolen by a Russian," Dehnland said. "Spectacular caper . . . got shot down over Alaska. As far as I know, they never built a second one. Dr. Meyers went on to other things."

"Including manned, solar-powered airplanes," Troy said.

"Which brings us here today," Dehnland said, gesturing for them to follow him.

She was in the Shakuru hangar, talking to some people and gesturing at a wing section as the three men approached.

"Dr. Meyers, I'd like to introduce your flight crew," Dehnland said. "This is Aron Arnold, and I guess you've met Troy Loensch."

"Yes, we've met," Dr. Meyers said, smiling at Troy. She was still wearing her oversize sweatshirt and still had her hair tied back, but without her owlish, Coke-bottle glasses, Troy could see that she had been, and was still, an attractive woman. "You didn't tell me that you were going to be working on the Shakuru Project."

"You didn't tell me you were the doctor who invented it," Troy said, shaking her hand.

"As you gentlemen can see, there is a similarity between Shakuru and the NASA ERAST aircraft, especially Helios," she began, gesturing at the aircraft.

"Yeah, we were talking about Helios yesterday," Arnold said apprehensively.

"You're thinking about the crash," she said knowingly.

"Yeah," Arnold said warily, nodding at the huge wing. "Um, I was hoping that you had figured out how to design it so it doesn't warp into a chronic high dihedral."

"We learned a lot from what NASA did wrong." Dr. Meyers chuckled. "This one's a spanloader, not built with a wing that's got a point-loaded distribution of mass on the same structure."

"So it bears the load evenly across the wing," Troy added. "Like the British Zephyr solar UAV."

"Right, and it's bigger than Helios and a lot more robust," she said. "Helios had a 247-foot wing, bigger than a C-5 or a 747, but Shakuru spans 296 feet. Helios weighed only about 1,400 pounds—it was made out of Kevlar and Styrofoam—but Shakuru weighs more than three tons, mainly in the crew support module. Helios didn't need pressurized oxygen tanks, but you will when you get up to 130,000 feet. To keep weight down, Shakuru is not equipped with ejection seats, but if you have to egress, you'll be doing so at a speed slower than what you'll find with most skydiving planes."

"That's a lot higher than Helios, isn't it?" Troy asked.

"The first two words in HAWX are 'High Altitude,'" Dr. Meyers said. "That's what we do here. That was the mandate when they created HAWX. Helios set an unofficial world record altitude at 96,863 feet, and executed sustained flight above 96,000 feet for extended periods. We're here to top that."

"But one-thirty is way over the ceiling of the SR-71, even," Troy said, excited at the prospect of setting a world altitude record.

"With solar-powered electric motors, you don't need air for combustion like you do with jets or piston engines, so there's no limit," Arnold said, emphasizing the obvious.

"And unlike rockets, which don't need air but run out of fuel in a few minutes, solar engines *never* run out of fuel," Dr. Meyers added.

"Until the sun goes down," Arnold replied.

"You just switch to your lithium sulfur battery." She smiled.

"Doesn't that add a whole lot to the weight?" Arnold said, scrutinizing the huge airplane.

"Lithium sulfur has a high energy density because of the low atomic weight of lithium."

"How high has it been flown to date?" Troy asked, thinking more and more about the idea of being part of a world record.

"It's only had three flights, just to prove it works," Dr. Meyers said. "They got it up to twenty-eight thousand, but that's all . . . so far."

"Well, let's crank this baby up." Troy smiled.

"We don't actually 'crank up' an aircraft with a top speed of ninety knots," Dr. Meyers said, as though correcting a student.

"That's . . . all?"

"I know that you boys are used to fast jets, but as I said, the mandate under HAWX is high altitude, not necessarily high *speed*."

"High altitude and high speed are not mutually exclusive," Troy interjected.

"Certainly not," Dr. Meyers agreed, nodding toward the razor wire–enclosed hangar that Troy had noticed that morning. "The HAWX Program has some of the fastest . . . but ummm . . . enough on that topic."

Troy and Aron Arnold exchanged glances. What was it about this high-speed aircraft that made her bite her tongue, about which a mere mention was saying too much?

After a change of subject, a walk-around, and a close-up look at one of the solar-powered engines, Dr. Meyers led the two pilots up the scaffolding for an inspection of the cockpit. Because the Shakuru was a massive flying wing, with essentially no fuselage, the cockpit was centered on the leading edge of the wing.

As she lit up the displays on the control panel and went through the various nuances of the operation of the aircraft, Troy noticed that the altimeter was calibrated to two hundred thousand feet.

CHAPTER 37

Cactus Flat Air Force Auxiliary Field, Nevada

"CAN'T BELIEVE WE'RE AIRBORNE," TROY SAID AS HE felt the Shakuru lift lightly from the Cactus Flat runway.

When you're used to flying Mach 1–plus jet fighters, an aircraft with a takeoff speed below that of a highway speed limit can be a bit disconcerting. So too was the turn radius. Although a highly maneuverable F-16 couldn't exactly turn on a dime, the expansive wingspan of the Shakuru meant that it took the contents of a sizable number of piggy banks to make a left turn.

"Damn, this turn is slow," Aron Arnold said.

"This is Shakuru control . . . you can't bank Shakuru like a fighter and maintain stability on a wing that size and that light." The impatient voice of Dr. Elisa Meyers crackled in the headsets of Shakuru's two crewmen. "But check your altitude."

"Shakuru flight here, we're already at fifteen thousand."

"That's what that big, oversize wing is good for, Shakuru flight."

Shakuru spiraled quickly upward. The radius of their spiral was about eight miles, but for an aircraft so slow, the rate of climb amazed the two veteran pilots.

Outside the canopy, the darkening of the sky above them was perceptible as the atmosphere thinned. They passed effortlessly through forty thousand feet, higher than most airliners routinely travel—not that there were any airliners in the controlled skies over the Nellis Air Force Base Test Range.

"This is a real astronaut view from up here," Troy said.

"Level out at eighty thousand and set a course due west," Dr. Meyers ordered.

As they emerged from the spiral, both pilots were at an altitude higher than either of them, or most pilots, had ever experienced. The sky above was black, and the curvature of the earth below was clearly visible. The Pacific Ocean could be seen in the distance, even though the California coast was more than three hundred miles away.

"I FEEL LIKE AN OLD MAN," TROY SAID TO THE CREW chief as he emerged from the Shakuru. It was nearly dark as they touched down after the long flight. "Guess I'm not used to sitting in one place for eleven hours."

"That's part of what we're evaluating in these flights," Dr. Meyers said as she approached the aircraft.

"You're evaluating joint pain?" Arnold said calmly.

"We're evaluating the exposure of long-duration flights on the human body. With its solar power, Shakuru can stay aloft for a week. Pilots have a greater fatigue factor than the aircraft."

"Weakest link?" Troy quipped.

"I didn't say that," Dr. Meyers replied.

"How was the flight?" Mike Dehnland said, arriving at the base of the ladder as Dr. Meyers began her walkaround of the big aircraft, studying each of the solar-powered engines with her halogen flashlight.

"Totally awesome," Troy said as a ground crewman began helping him out of the super-high-altitude "space suit" such as both pilots had worn for the flight. "Except for sitting in one place for half a day in this cocoon. It was a great view from up there."

"How did Shakuru handle?"

"Seems pretty slow and sluggish at first," Arnold told Dehnland. "But it sure can climb."

"That because it's light as a feather . . . comparatively . . . and all wing." Dehnland smiled. "Even in thin air up at eighty thousand, you have enough wing to keep you going."

"Very stable up there," Troy interjected. "Although I

gotta admit, I kept thinking about Helios and that wing mangling into an unstoppable dihedral."

"There's a lot of wind under the old airfoil since that happened," Dehnland said as the three men began walking toward the building where Shakuru briefings were held. "Preventing that was one of the first mandates handed to the Shakuru design team."

"Not to change the subject, but what's going on down there?" Arnold interjected, nodding in the direction of the hangar with the razor-wire perimeter. For the first time since he and Troy had been at the Flat, the doors were open, albeit just a few feet. Light was streaming out, and people were coming and going.

"Where?" Dehnland asked.

"There," Arnold said, this time pointing at the hangar.

"That building doesn't exist," he said, turning away from the mystery hangar.

"Then Raymond Harris doesn't exist," Troy added. "I see *him* down there."

"You're welcome to ask him about it, then," Dehnland said. "In the meantime, we have a Shakuru flight to debrief."

"ARE YOU ENJOYING BEAUTIFUL CACTUS FLAT?" Raymond Harris grinned as he turned from the enormous coffee urn in the Cactus Flat officers' mess. It was the first time since Troy had arrived in Nevada that the two men had come face-to-face. Harris was his usual gregarious self, but the stress lines on his face were noticeably more pronounced.

"It's excellent," Troy said sarcastically. "Can't get enough of it . . . but we had a good view from Shakuru yesterday."

"Isn't that Shakuru something?"

"Yes, sir." Troy nodded, pouring himself a cup of coffee. "It's slow on the uptake, but it sure takes you up there eventually."

"It's the near future of manned recon," Harris said. "And it's the long-term future of clandestine strike missions."

"I had no idea that it was being planned for offensive ops. I didn't see any provisions for weapons."

"Not yet, but that's where we're headed . . . eventually."

"Maybe that's why I didn't see anything about weapons in the briefing papers that Dr. Meyers handed us."

"There are briefing papers *and* there are briefing papers."

"How so?"

"It's all need-to-know, but there are a lot of things that Dr. Meyers isn't cleared on," Harris said, lowering his voice.

"I thought she *designed* Shakuru? How is it that she doesn't know . . . ?"

"There are two levels of need-to-know," Harris said, as though explaining gravity to a schoolboy. "There is the official level, the one that the government knows about—and the level that *only* Firehawk knows about."

"If the government is the customer, and Firehawk is running the HAWX Programs for the government, why are there aspects of these programs that *they* don't know about?"

"Remember why the U.S. Air Force transferred HAWX to Firehawk in the first place?" Harris asked.

"To avoid nitpicking from Congress?"

"Right. And just as there are things that the blue-suiters want obscured from the pointy heads on the Hill, there are things that Firehawk needs to keep . . . ummm . . . proprietary."

"Secrets from the government?"

"If you want to put it that way. In business, you never tell your clients everything. It makes you seem more useful if you're able to get things done that they don't know exactly *how* you got them done."

"When were you planning to tell them that Shakuru is going to be used as a strike aircraft?"

"You always have to hold some of your cards close to your vest," Harris explained. "It's a fluid world. Situations change. Remember Guatemala? Remember how we were at war with Svartvand BV one day, and sitting around the table with those guys the next? One day back then, you and Arnold were shooting at each other. Yesterday, you were flying as his copilot."

"What does that have to do with—"

"Not all the changes swing like they did in Guatemala. Sometimes your friends yesterday *aren't* your friends tomorrow."

"But you're holding back from the United States government," Troy reminded him. "You don't expect to be 'not friends' with *them*."

"The problem is that the United States government and the United States of America aren't the same thing. Ideally, the United States government has in mind the best for the United States of America. Sometimes they don't."

"I see," Troy said. His head was spinning. Maybe the two spooks from the CIA had been *right* about Harris on that awkward morning back at the Marriott Courtyard in Arlington. This was probably not a good time to change the subject to the mystery hangar.

"I figured you did," Harris said. "You're a quick study."

CHAPTER 38

Las Vegas, Nevada

NO WAY I'D BE A SNITCH FOR THE COPS, MAN.

The words of Yolanda Rodriguez echoed in his head even as Troy sat in the same bar at the Palazzo where he had been with Jenna Munrough on that night so long ago.

After two months at Cactus Flat, he had gotten a forty-eight-hour pass, and he had done as most denizens of the Flat did. He took a quick hop to Sin City on Janet for a little R&R.

Troy had stopped into this bar, of all those on the Strip, for a drink—and for old times' sake, unsure what memories of Jenna it would bring back to him.

Instead, the words spoken by Yolanda were crowding Jenna from his conscious thought.

Troy had other things on his mind as well.

After two months of listening to Harris and his cryptic comments about the U.S. government, he was ready to believe that what the CIA had told him was true.

What should he do?

No way I'd be a snitch for the cops, man.

He could hear Yolanda's pleasant but emphatic words.

What had seemed like sound advice that morning when she spoke those words seemed less and less likely to fit the circumstances. Troy found himself debating whether to cross the line and to become a snitch for the CIA.

When he was in the U.S. Air Force, he swore his allegiance to the United States and its Constitution and its government. Was his allegiance now primarily to Firehawk and to Harris?

The meeting in Arlington had not happened—the CIA men had said so. But they had also given him instructions for contacting them when—not if—he wished to not have a second meeting. Did that mean that what he was about to do was not actually happening?

Troy asked himself why, if he was never going to use it, he had kept the number the CIA stooge had given him.

Two drinks later, he decided.

The bartender looked at him as though he were nuts when he asked where to find a pay phone. When he explained that his cell phone battery was dead, the guy sent him to the last surviving bank of pay phones within a quarter mile of the hotel. His battery wasn't dead, but he decided that in anything having to do with the CIA, paranoia was just common sense.

"Nagte," the voice said.

"Who?"

"Nagte . . . who are *you*?"

"Troy Loensch."

"Where are you?"

"Is there anywhere in Vegas where we can meet . . . tomorrow?"

"Stay where you are."

TROY DID AS HE WAS TOLD. HE HUNG OUT AT THE END of the remote hallway where the pay phones were, pretending to scrutinize a piece of faux Byzantine sculpture as a handful of people came and went to and from a group of elevators down the hall.

He watched as a woman approached. She was wearing a low-cut top, a shiny leather miniskirt, and four-inch heels.

They made eye contact, and she smiled broadly.

Could this be the local CIA handler?

Things could be worse. Troy would not have minded being manhandled by her.

Giving Troy a suggestive wink, she got into the elevator and was gone.

After her, he hardly noticed two tipsy guys in Hawaiian

shirts who seemed to be lost as they argued about the
way back to their rooms.

Before he knew what was happening, he found himself between them and being shuffled through the open
door of the elevator.

Inside, neither said a word to Troy until the elevator
doors opened again on an upper floor.

"This way," one said, walking briskly down a
corridor.

Troy knew the drill.

Once inside, their tipsiness evaporated.

"You called?"

"Yeah," Troy said. "You guys got here in a hurry."

"It's our job to stay on top of things."

"I assume that you know who I am and where I
work . . . and how I got your number?" Troy asked.

"Yes," the first man said impatiently. As in Arlington,
there was one in the pair whose job it was to do all the
talking. "What do you have for us?"

"When I met your other guys, they suggested that I
keep an eye on Raymond Harris."

"Have you?"

"That's why I called."

"And?"

"Your buddies may have been right."

"How so?"

"At first, I didn't see anything astray about Harris,"
Troy explained. "As I told the other guys, Harris always

seemed like a dedicated soldier . . . loyal to the United States. They said that he was going to try to use Firehawk to overthrow the United States. I told them I thought it was just paranoid bullshit."

"You're thinking different now?"

"Maybe . . ."

"You're not sure?"

"I'm sure that he's said things about Firehawk maintaining a contingency capability within the HAWX Program . . . just in case."

"In case of what?"

"In case the government of the United States reaches a point where it no longer has the best interests of the United States—"

"Who decides when that is?"

"I guess it would be Harris?" Troy postulated.

"What steps has he made with regard to this contingency?"

"How much do you know about what we do out at Cactus Flat?"

"More than most."

"Do you know about Shakuru, the super-high-altitude, solar-powered—"

"Yes, we do," the CIA man said impatiently. "There have been press releases published."

"Did you know that he's talking about an offensive capability for Shakuru?"

"I can't see that," the man said. "It has a top speed

that wouldn't even get you a ticket out here on Highway Fifty," the CIA man said dismissively.

"But it can fly higher than any aircraft you know of that has an air-breathing engine. If anything, it's much more efficient up there with its solar cells."

"How high?"

"I've personally flown it above ninety thousand, and the altimeter is calibrated to two hundred thousand . . . not only that, it's stealthy because it's made mostly of plastic. Radar wouldn't be looking for anything above a hundred thousand feet and wouldn't notice it if they did."

"That's useful to know." The CIA man nodded.

Troy realized that he had now crossed the line. He had shared "useful" information with the CIA. He had snitched to the cops. What would Yolanda say?

"There's also a hangar out there that I've never been inside," Troy continued. "It's surrounded by wire and heavily guarded. I've been told on a couple of occasions that it doesn't exist."

"What's inside?"

"Not sure. I've never been inside. I've never had a chance to *look* in either."

"Raven?" the second CIA man asked the first.

"Have you ever heard Harris or anyone mention 'Raven'?"

"No, I don't think so," Troy said. He had no memory of such a name having been mentioned. "What's Raven?"

"It's an airplane that we don't know much about."

"What kind of an airplane?" Troy asked.

"A shooter . . . a fast shooter . . . and obviously . . . since it's in HAWX, a high flyer. That's all we know."

"I thought you said it was your job to stay on top of things," Troy said, mildly taunting the CIA guys.

"That's why we recruit people like you," the CIA man said, turning the tables back to Troy.

"What if Harris is *not* planning some sort of overthrow of the United States government?" Troy asked.

"If you believed that, you wouldn't be here with us tonight . . . would you?"

Troy took a deep breath. Why, he asked himself, had he made this decision after a few drinks?

"Guess that makes me a full-fledged snitch," he said

"If you want to believe that informing on treason makes you a snitch."

"It does, but I've made that bed," Troy said. "What do you want me to find out about what Harris is planning . . . and about this Raven aircraft?"

"Everything."

CHAPTER 39

Cactus Flat Air Force Auxiliary Field, Nevada

NO WAY I'D BE A SNITCH FOR THE COPS, MAN.

The words of Yolanda Rodriguez echoed in his head.

Troy knew, as he had told the CIA operatives, that he had made his bed. Lying in it was more difficult than he had imagined when he dropped those coins into that Las Vegas pay phone.

For nearly a month, Troy had led a double life.

His day job was enough to gratify the extreme desires of any pilot. As one of the designated test pilots for the Shakuru Program, he had flown the aircraft to an unofficial world altitude record and had made seven flights above a hundred thousand feet. His long-duration flights with Aron Arnold had exceeded twenty-four hours and had spanned the continent.

His alter ego as a snitch made him feel dirty.

Had he succeeded as a snitch, that would be one thing, but he had failed so far to find anything useful for his CIA handlers.

Aside from a report on Raymond Harris's increasingly vitriolic rants about the need to relieve the United States of its present government, he had come up with virtually nothing. He had finally seen the Raven, but only from a distance, and from the side. The dark-gray aircraft was dart-shaped, with its two vertical tail surfaces canted inward, suggesting that the aircraft was capable of speeds in excess of Mach 3.

He had met only once with the CIA since Las Vegas.

They had agreed to rendezvous at the lone bar in Paiute Wells, a dusty little Nevada town where people from Cactus Flat occasionally hung out to break the boredom of life on the base. The bar was a seedy relic from the 1950s, with a row of glass bricks in the front and Naugahyde-padded swinging doors that had small windows in the shape of spades from a deck of cards.

When Troy related the meager details that he had learned about the mysterious Raven, the CIA men had conveyed their disappointment.

"Is that all? We need more . . . and we need it soon."

When Troy asked them why they were so impatient, they implied that other information, developed from other snitches, suggested that whatever Harris and his confederates were planning, they were planning to do it sooner rather than later.

"MORE . . . MORE . . . MORE."

The words spoken to the snitch echoed in his head as he made his way to the small office that Harris used when he was at Cactus Flat. Troy knew that Harris would not be in his office today. He had just boarded his Gulf-stream and had headed out for parts unknown. Over the past couple of weeks, Harris had been away more often than he was at the Flat, a fact that tended to support the CIA supposition that something big was demanding his attention elsewhere.

The door to the office was locked, of course.

Troy had been to Harris's office a dozen times, but only when Harris was there. What he was about to do gave him the creeps. His alter ego as a snitch made him feel dirty.

Long ago, when Troy was still in high school, and still in that stage of life where pranks are part of life, he had learned the art of lock picking. Objects placed in lockers, especially gooey, messy, explosive objects, were great fun. So too was the feeling of accomplishment that came with being able to pick the heaviest padlock in order to place such ridiculous objects to ruin the day of an unsuspecting fellow student.

The office was the same as it always was—except, of course, for the absence of its usual inhabitant. As such, it was uncharacteristically quiet.

What was he looking for?

Troy really didn't know. It was one of those cases where he knew that he would know it only when he found it.

Where should he look?

That was an even bigger question. The desk was piled high with papers, folders, and memo pads. So too were most other surfaces in the room, and that didn't count the four-drawer file cabinet.

Troy realized that it would take a week to methodically search everything.

The clock on Harris's desk read 10:14.

How much time dare he spend doing this?

Even if Harris was away, someone else might have a key and come in for some reason.

Got to be out of here by 10:30, Troy decided.

How should he go about this?

He decided that he would try to imagine what Harris would do, so he lowered himself into the former general's desk chair and looked around the room.

Troy tried to imagine where, if he had something important to conceal, would he hide it in this room?

Keep it close. This would rule out anything beyond arm's length. If it's an active operation, then keep it where it can be easily accessed—but keep it out of sight.

With this in mind, Troy searched the bottom half of each stack of papers on the desk, then turned to the drawers.

The clock on the desk read 10:22.

The bottom drawers of the big, old-fashioned metal desk were crammed with folders and tablets. Pausing to read what was written on each of them was time-consuming.

The clock on the desk read 10:35.

He had already blown his schedule, and there was nothing to show for it.

Was it a wild-goose chase?

Troy sorted through the tops of the piles on the desk.

The clock on the desk read 10:48.

He had been at this for more than half an hour.

One more pass through the drawers, and then I'm done, he thought.

He started by pulling out the bottom left drawer.

What's this?

He didn't remember the blue folder with pieces of duct tape on it. He was sure it hadn't been there before.

The tape!

The first time that Troy had looked in the drawer, the blue folder had been attached to the underside of the drawer above it. Somehow, he had jiggled it loose.

This, he quickly discovered, was what he had been looking for.

Correction, this was what the CIA men had been looking for.

The first page gave a short overview of an innocuous-sounding process that was referred to as "The Transition."

If the United States reaches a point where it cannot be properly governed, read the opening paragraph, *it is the responsibility of the private sector, in the form of PMCs, to intervene . . .*

There was page after page of dry details about how an independent entity would be formed to manage and operate the government during The Transition. Most chilling was the description of how PMC military units would be activated to neutralize the U.S. armed forces. The attached tables of statistics showed how the effectiveness of the traditional armed services had declined in direct proportion to the increase in PMC capabilities.

They actually *believed* that they could pull this off?

The clock on Harris's desk read 11:17.

Troy had been at the desk for more than an hour. He had to get out of here before his luck ran out.

Having memorized as much as he could about the details of The Transition, Troy carefully retaped the blue folder to the bottom of the middle drawer.

CHAPTER 40

Cactus Flat Air Force Auxiliary Field, Nevada

"YOU'RE HAVING ALL THE FUN UP THERE IN SHAKURU, Loensch," Raymond Harris said with a grin, approaching Troy at the coffee urn.

The sun was just coming up, painting the sandstone bluffs west of Cactus Flat in the vivid colors that photographers stay up all night to capture. Harris was up awfully early for a man who had returned to the Flat after midnight.

"Not today," Troy said, returning the smile. "I don't have a flight scheduled until tomorrow. I'm going into town this morning to get some stuff at the drugstore."

In fact, he was going into Paiute Wells to attempt to make contact with the CIA.

"Your razor blades and deodorant can wait," Harris

said, sipping his coffee. "I'd like to have you demonstrate Shakuru for me. I'd like to fly as your copilot for a short flight over the desert."

When Harris said "I'd like," Troy knew that it was to be interpreted as a direct order.

An hour later, both men were in their high-altitude space suits and doing a walk-around of the Shakuru. Troy took his place in the forward of the two tandem seats, and Harris lowered himself in behind. Technicians helped the two men seal their helmets and fasten the gloves to their suits.

With a thumbs-up from Troy, the massive flying machine was wheeled through the open doorway of the hangar and onto the tarmac. It was obvious by the way Harris went through the preflight checklist that he had done his homework on the operation of the aircraft.

Troy ran up the engines, handled the takeoff, leveled out at five thousand feet, and let Harris take the controls. He was an experienced pilot, and he handled the Shakuru skillfully. Troy felt him pull back gently on the stick and resume a climbing spiral.

"The rate of climb is sure better than you'd expect," Harris observed.

"That was my reaction the first time also," Troy agreed.

"Let's take this bird up to where we can see some of the view," Harris said.

"Copilot's airplane," Troy said into the intercom,

indicating that he was letting Harris run the show. If Troy had been nervous about flying with the man less than a day after he had rifled his desk, the nervousness quickly faded.

The altimeter steadily climbed. Troy watched twenty-five thousand feet melt away, then forty-five thousand. Harris made occasional comments about the control of the Shakuru or the spectacular view. Troy felt him level out at eighty thousand feet and steady their course in a southeasterly direction.

"I had hoped to brief you on The Transition," Harris said. He said it so calmly that it took a moment for Troy to grasp what he was saying.

"I had hoped to speak with you about it, and about how I had hoped to bring you in as part of it."

"The Transition?" Troy said, feigning ignorance.

"The Transition," Harris said, his voice still calm. "I noticed that you've briefed yourself on it before I had the chance."

How?

Troy was speechless.

"I was very disappointed, Loensch. I was very disappointed to find you . . . *you* . . . of all people, going through the stuff in my office."

"Your Transition goes a bit far, doesn't it?" Troy asked.

"It goes only as far as necessary, doesn't it?"

Troy could feel Harris's eyes drilling in on him from behind as he searched his mind in vain for a reply.

"Did you decide to burglarize my office on your own?" Harris asked. "Or are you working for someone?"

"I think you're playing with fire," Troy said at last. "Who are *you* working for?"

"Firehawk. I'm working for Firehawk . . . and so, I thought, were you," Harris said, feigning sadness. "It seems as though we are at cross-purposes here. I suggest that you do the honorable thing . . . pop the canopy and leave Shakuru."

Leave Shakuru? Troy thought about it. Bailing out at eighty thousand feet while wearing his pressure suit was doable.

"I'll be on the ground before you could get back to Cactus Flat. People back there will know about your scheme before you're able to land."

"With the parachute you're wearing, you'll be on the ground much faster than you think," Harris said. Troy could hear the smirk in his voice. In his mirror, he saw only the glossy black visor of Harris's helmet.

"Well, then I guess you're stuck with me," Troy said. "Unless you want to unlatch your harness at a hundred and thirty knots and try to throw me overboard."

"I was afraid of that." Harris chuckled. "One of us has got to leave . . . I guess it will be me."

"With you gone, I can land Shakuru anywhere. I don't need to go back to the Flat."

"I'll make you a deal," Harris said. "If you tell me who you're working for, I won't disable the autopilot override."

"What?"

"If you don't tell me who you're working for, and I disable the autopilot override, you won't be able to turn. You'll be stuck at eighty thousand on a southwesterly heading until after nightfall . . . by which time you'll be several hundred miles over the Pacific."

"With the lithium sulfur batteries, I can fly this thing anywhere in the world," Troy reminded him.

"*Without* lithium sulfur batteries, you'll fall like three tons of Kevlar and plastic when the sun goes down. By that time, you'll be hundreds of miles from shore."

With that, Troy felt the pressure of the canopy separating from the aircraft and the brief lurch as Harris jumped free. Without the canopy, the drag on Shakuru made it tremble a bit, but other than that, Troy felt little change. It was suddenly ninety degrees below zero in the cockpit, but sealed inside his suit, the ambient temperature was that of an air-conditioned office.

Troy touched the stick, attempting to turn, but Harris had, in fact, configured the autopilot to maintain its heading. He tried everything he could to disengage the autopilot, but to no avail. Ahead, across the land mass of California, he could see the Pacific Ocean, gleaming blue. The sun was still high in the sky, and Shakuru plugged on, heading southwest toward Santa Barbara and oblivion.

Did he suppose that Harris would have left him with control of the aircraft if he had said he was working for the CIA? Troy thought not.

He tried to find a radio channel on which to send a distress message, but the only place that his "Mayday" was heard was in his own intercom.

With his helmet on, Troy could hear nothing of the outside world, not the whir of the solar engines, not the thunder of the slipstream blowing around the windshield and into the open canopy.

Troy tried and retried to override the autopilot.

He shouted "Mayday!" until his own ears throbbed.

As he reached the picturesque California coastline, he could see the wriggling line of sandy beaches that separated the tan and green of the hills from the blue of the ocean.

Soon, there was no longer land, only that deep-blue crescent of the curving earth and the blinding glare of the soon-to-be-setting sun.

There was nothing to do but rehearse in his mind the steps he would take to escape as the big flying wing drifted down upon the sea—deploy his flotation gear and hope for the best. Into this scenario came memories of survival school, of Hal Coughlin, and of their tortured relationship.

When your mind replays events that have come full circle, they come full circle, and you are left with the void of silence. Into the silence came the voices.

Yolanda spoke and said she told him so. If he hadn't turned snitch, he would not be heading toward a watery grave.

Jenna, who had once loathed him, but who had once craved his touch, spoke of her guilt. Having made love to Troy, she felt the guilt of cheating on Hal. Having once expressed the longing of lust toward Troy, she then expressed the revulsion borne of that guilt and the knowledge that it was Troy who had killed Hal.

Cassie Kilmer, the woman with whom he had long planned to spend the rest of his life, had abruptly closed the door on that relationship, a relationship that once had seemed inevitable.

As the sun sank to the horizon, the solar panels, starved of their sustenance, grew weak, and the engines slowed gradually to a stop. The altimeter read forty thousand feet and sinking.

As the sun sank below the horizon, Shakuru sank slowly toward the Pacific and the massive bank of clouds that now separated the aircraft from the waves. The altimeter read twenty thousand feet and sinking.

As the altimeter declined to ten thousand feet and Shakuru drifted amid the cloud tops, Troy felt a jolt, and then another, as the huge aircraft was rocked by turbulence. Within moments, Shakuru was swallowed in a cocoon of gray. Rain lashed into the open cockpit as the gyrating aircraft drifted into the heart of the storm.

Troy remembered what a little clear air turbulence had done to Helios and gave up on his imagined escape as Shakuru touched the waves. Instead of landing in the

Pacific within an aircraft that retained its aerodynamic integrity, he now expected to hit the water tangled in crumpled wreckage.

He looked out at the flapping wings with their dead engines, thankful that his soundproof cocoon spared him the sounds of snapping and tearing structural components.

The thought of dying in a plane crash occasionally crosses the mind of a pilot, but Troy had never imagined that it would be such an agonizingly slow death.

CHAPTER 41

Somewhere over the Pacific Ocean

ALL AROUND HIM, THE GRAYNESS GREW DARKER. TROY felt a chill and realized that as the power systems failed, so too did the life support system that kept his space suit at room temperature.

The ordeal of being tossed helplessly amid the storm seemed to go on for hours, though it was obviously minutes or tens of minutes. The buffeting winds kept him aloft, postponing his inevitable crash.

Eventually, it *was* hours, but by then, Troy had lost track of time. The digital clock, like all the digital instruments, had winked out as the power failed. Only the analog compass remained, shining in the darkness with its luminescent dial, but it too seemed to have failed. It read that Shakuru was headed east, when Troy knew he was going southwest.

He no longer heard Yolanda's voice, and Jenna had said all that could be said. Had he believed in God, Troy would have prayed. Had he believed in heaven, he would have expected soon to face Hal Coughlin beyond some pearly gate—or in some fiery dungeon.

Suddenly, it all went black.

The grayness did not so much fade to black but went suddenly and abruptly black.

Above him, Troy was aware of a light.

Was this heaven?

No. It was the moon.

Shakuru had been tossed free of the clouds. He could see their writhing gray forms some distance away, but for the moment he was in clear air. In the moonlight, he could see Shakuru's wings, still gyrating, but still intact.

Had he been a believer, Troy would have thanked God, first for being free of the clouds, if not of the wind, but mostly he would have thanked God for Dr. Elisa Meyers, who had designed Shakuru to stand up to what he had been going through.

Above him, Troy could see the stars in the black sky, but in the blackness below him, he saw the same.

Was this the reflection of the stars on the placid sea?

No. You can't see the reflection of stars on the ocean— certainly not from this altitude.

Boats? Were they boats?

There sure were a lot of boats. There were at least a dozen lights down there. Maybe he had a chance of being rescued?

Troy felt the sensation of Shakuru sinking lower, of the lights below growing closer.

He felt the sensation of forward momentum that you get as an aircraft descends closer to the earth.

He came closer and closer to the cluster of lights and passed over them. He looked back and watched them recede into the distance.

Beneath him now was only darkness.

THE DISCOMFORT OF FEELING LIKE HE HAD BEEN swathed in plastic wrap and placed in a microwave oven was so great that it took Troy a moment to realize that he was alive when he should not have been.

He felt a light, cool breeze on his cheek, but the rest of his body felt like it was going to explode.

He opened his eyes to a blurry, hazy world and reached up to rub the sweat and crud from them with his hands.

Gloved hands met the cracked Plexiglas of his helmet visor.

Got to get this crap off.

He tugged and struggled at the connection rings that held his gloves to his space suit with an airtight seal. The left one was easier once he had freed his right hand from its glove.

Next came the helmet. After two minutes of frantic pushing and pulling, he got it off. The feel of the cool, clear air on his sweat-soaked head and face was the most wonderful sensation imaginable.

At last, he was able to rub his eyes and massage them back to functional reality.

Troy looked at the helmet. It was badly dented and the visor was cracked, but the damned thing had saved his life. First by absorbing the impact of whatever made the dent, and second, by getting cracked. Had that not happened, Troy would have suffocated within his airtight suit.

He looked around.

Where in the hell was he?

Last night, in the darkness, he had imagined many scenarios, all involving a hard landing at sea—but he found himself on land. All around him was vegetation. He had come down in a jungle—but *where* was the jungle? It must be an island somewhere in the ocean. Maybe he had landed in Hawaii? Maybe Waikiki Beach was just over the hill?

The wings of Shakuru were snarled in limbs and foliage, but they had not splintered into a lumberyard of wreckage like those of Helios. Shakuru would never fly again, but the airframe had held up far better than Troy might have expected.

He tossed the helmet from the cockpit and heard it hit the ground some twenty feet below. Unsnapping his harness, he attempted to stand but felt excruciating pain in his leg.

AS HE HAD WAITED FOR THE MORPHINE IN HIS FIRST-aid kit to take effect, Troy had mapped out his plan for getting out of the aircraft and descending twenty feet to the ground on one leg.

As the morphine finally *did* take effect, his predicament grew more and more amusing. It was a silly irony, Troy thought, to be sitting here in an aircraft calibrated to fly as high as two hundred thousand feet, an aircraft emblazoned with the HAWX insignia, with its *HA* an acronym for *High Altitude*—yet here he was, planning the nearly impossible challenge of descending the equivalent of two flights of stairs.

Somehow, he had made it. He had made it by grabbing at a large limb and by using his football player's upper-body strength to shift himself from limb to limb like a very-slow-moving chimpanzee. He certainly could not have done this without the numbness brought to his body by the narcotic.

The last thing he remembered before he passed out was how good it felt to wriggle out of his suit and to lie on the cool ground wearing only his inner suit.

The first thing he noticed when he woke up was that the pain in his leg was back.

The second thing he noticed when he woke up was

the dirty faces of a half dozen kids. They were dark-complected and had black hair. Troy assumed they were Hawaiians.

"Aloha, kids," he said. "Could one of you guys go ask your mom if I could borrow a cell phone?"

They looked at one another as though they hadn't understood him. Two of the girls giggled, pointing to the bulge between his legs. His inner suit, which was essentially like old-fashioned long underwear, left little to the imagination.

"Cell phone?" Troy persisted. "Do you guys understand? They speak English in Hawaii . . . right?"

The kids spoke to him eagerly, but in a language he did not recognize.

"Where the hell am I?" Troy asked, knowing that there would be no answer. "Who *are* you? How far did I drift in that storm last night?"

CHAPTER 42

In a Jungle Village

THE KIDS HAD EVENTUALLY BROUGHT ADULTS, BUT NO cell phone.

The adults did, however, fashion a stretcher from a blanket and a couple of long poles, and they had taken Troy from the Shakuru crash site to their village. They had fed him, and an old man had examined Troy's leg. It was broken in two places, but the old man had secured it to splints and had given Troy some bitter-tasting tea to drink. This had seemed to ease the pain.

They were a poor people, but they were generous. They gave him food, and they gave him a shirt and an old pair of jeans to wear. Their village was little more than a camp on a hillside. The buildings were open to the air, albeit with mosquito netting, but the nights were cool, the days pleasant. With a makeshift crutch, he was at least able to access the latrine.

From the labels on the few items of packaged food that he saw, Troy surmised that he was somewhere in Latin America, but that these people spoke an incomprehensible indigenous language rather than Spanish. The storm, borne by the strong prevailing wind over the Pacific, had blown him all the way back to the continent.

Because of its low radar-observable characteristics, Shakuru had disappeared from the scopes, and a search for the aircraft over the Pacific had long since been abandoned. As Raymond Harris had hoped, Troy and Shakuru had essentially disappeared without a trace.

Except for his being immobile, Troy could not have imagined disappearing without a trace into a more idyllic place. He was the object of great curiosity for the children, and the people treated him as a sort of celebrity. He was probably the most unusual character that they had seen fall into their jungle. They appreciated his helping out a little with food preparation, and they had taken happily to his making little gadgets for the kids out of bits of wood and wire.

On his fourth or fifth day, as he realized that he was not going anywhere soon, Troy had started keeping track of the days by scratching marks on an old piece of wood with a nail that he had found. Four dozen marks later, he was finally able to stand and move around a little bit without his crutch.

Troy decided that it was time to think about rejoining the outside world, though he had grown accustomed to life in his jungle retreat. At the same time, he felt so totally disconnected from his world. He had killed a man who had once been a wingman, and he had been copilot to a man who had tried to kill him. What kind of world was that?

He had watched his parents become emotional islands, disconnected from one another—and from him. What was left for him in that world?

He had felt the icy sting of doors slammed in his face by Cassie and Jenna, the only two women whom he had ever loved. What was left for him in that world?

Could he go back to his job? Well, not after his boss had tried to kill him!

How could he return to that world?

The thought of phoning his contacts at the CIA now seemed like a cruel and ridiculous joke. Yolanda had been right.

The idea of phoning home seemed less appealing with each week that passed. Of course, there were no phones. The nearest one was probably several days' hike from this mountaintop, and the aftermath of a multiple fracture set by a stone-age shaman made a long hike seem out of the question.

An attempted bow-hunting trip with some of the guys convinced Troy that it would be a while before he would be able to walk any distance.

The weeks drifted by, and Troy thought and rethought the issue of whether to leave. He had grown familiar, though not yet intimate, with the girl who reminded him of Yolanda. It seemed only a matter of time. By the looks of the way her body curved as she moved, and the way her eyes sparkled when she smiled at him, he knew that it would be exquisite. However, his rational mind told him that it would usher in a whole new era in his status among these people, and he decided that for this, he was unprepared.

The marks on the old piece of wood had long since fallen out of pace with the actual passage of days when Troy finally said good-bye to the people who had become like a family to him. There were even some tears shed as he walked down the trail in his hand-me-down jeans and sandals for the last time.

TWO DAYS LATER, AS HE WALKED INTO THE NICARA-guan village of San Sebastian, the sound of motor vehicles was deafening. Troy wondered if he had made a mistake, and he longed for the comforting arms of the girl who reminded him of Yolanda.

He was back in civilization, with its cars, its electricity, its telephones—and its dependence on currency. Troy was flat broke. He had long since given the two hundred dollars in his survival kit to his friends in the mountains. Now he had to draw upon other survival skills.

Troy began by going into a bar and asking in his crude high school Spanish to be directed to "El Gringo." This would be interpreted as an American asking to be sent to "The American." They would—Troy hoped—assume that he actually knew this notional person known locally as "The American."

Most remote Latin American localities have one or two El Gringos, American expatriates who have drifted far from the United States in search of something or on the run from someone. Troy just wanted to find an American—any American.

San Sebastian's "El Gringo" turned out to be a mining contractor named Fred Dobbs.

"You came pretty far out in the middle of nowhere looking for a *job*," Dobbs said quizzically, when Troy explained himself as an American stranded in the outback of Nicaragua.

"Well it's a long story." Troy smiled. "My girlfriend dragged me out here on a do-gooder, tree-hugging thing, and well, y'know . . ."

"Yeah. I get the picture," Dobbs said. With his long hair and full beard, Troy indeed looked like either a tree hugger or a dope dealer, which for Dobbs were essentially the same thing. "You're stuck out here with no way back to the real world. Well, I got a gig that I could use you on. I need a gringo with no real ties to this place."

"What's the work?"

"I've got a little extraction operation going up in the mountains. Mostly low-grade nickel, but there's some of the yellow stuff. The local umm . . . authorities . . . like to have their palms crossed. They don't care about the nickel. My people working the mine up there are mainly locals. I need somebody with no connection to the locals who can go up and bring out my yellow stuff. Might take several trips . . . ought to be able to wrap it up in a couple of weeks. You want the job?"

"What's it pay?"

"I'll give you five hundred bucks and have my guy in Managua fix you up with a passport and a plane ticket to the States. Deal?"

"Deal."

CHAPTER 43

Managua, Nicaragua

IF WALKING INTO SAN SEBASTIAN TWO WEEKS AGO
had been a culture shock for Troy, then setting foot in a
real city was a culture concussion.

In the nearly five months since Shakuru had crashed
into the jungle, the world that he had blissfully ignored had
been turned upside down. For the first time since he had
disappeared from radar—literally and figuratively—Troy
had gotten his hands on an English-language newspaper
and had a chance to surf the Web at an Internet café.

To Troy, it felt as though he had been away for years,
not mere months. Political discord reigned. Al-Qinamah,
the enemy with whom Troy had battled when he had
flown with the U.S. Air Force, now reigned in Sudan—as

well as in Eritrea and Ethiopia. It was a war that he and the others had fought in vain.

In Malaysia, the government was now essentially a wholly owned subsidiary of Sandringham Partners, Ltd. It was another war that Troy had fought in vain.

In Europe, governments were collapsing. Italy was on its fourth government in less than a month. France and Portugal were both considering outsourcing most essential services to organizations modeled after the PMCs.

The United States was not immune. Washington, D.C., was in turmoil. Pundits from both poles of the political spectrum insisted that the U.S. government was out of control. Some said it was because of the PMCs. American foreign policy was in shambles because the Defense Department was now nothing more than a manager of extranational PMCs. Others insisted that the United States ought to do as Malaysia, France, and Portugal had done and essentially turn governmental operations over to the PMCs.

What stunned Troy the most was what he found when he was waiting in the office of Fred Dobbs's "guy in Managua," waiting to be fixed up with a plane ticket to the States.

The guy was in his private office with another customer, and Troy was waiting patiently on a tattered blue Naugahyde couch in the waiting room. The guy operated a travel agency of sorts, and there were posters for various regional destinations on the wall. There was one for Costa Rica with a large toucan on it and even one for the Petén rain forest.

Troy had spent part of his five hundred dollars on clean clothes, a haircut, and a cheap duffel bag. Soon he would have his ticket to Los Angeles and, hopefully, a new life in an old place.

As he waited, Troy idly began leafing through the inevitable pile of magazines that was on the low coffee table. He recognized the red border of a *Time* magazine and pulled it out.

Troy's mind did a double take at the cover photo: a head-and-shoulders shot of Raymond Harris!

Troy's mind did a triple take at the caption printed in bold letters across the cover. It identified Harris as *The Voice of Reason*.

Raymond Harris?

The Voice of Reason?

How could the man who had tried to kill him for exposing a conspiracy be remotely considered *The Voice of Reason*?

Inside, the journalists had profiled Harris, now back at Firehawk's Virginia headquarters and now the CEO of the PMC. He was described in the article as the steady hand, the man who was calmly negotiating with the polarized political factions in Washington.

President Albert Bacon Fachearon was in trouble. Overwhelmed by the job, he seemed paralyzed by indecision. Congress called for action, but Fachearon faltered.

It was Raymond Harris who had calmly spoken of outsourcing the management of the U.S. government "until the crisis period had passed."

Troy was aghast. It was all coming true. The Transition that Harris's document had described. Worst of all, the media was buying it.

Harris was the man with the calm hand—at least in comparison to other PMC CEOs, such as Layton Kynelty of Cernavoda Partners, who had been a bit more assertive about taking control. By comparison, Harris did seem like a voice of reason. According to the article, opposition to Harris, even in Congress, was depicted as strident, even a bit irrational.

Troy couldn't believe his eyes.

Just as he thought he had seen it all, Troy turned the page. There were several photographs of Harris at a memorial service. Apparently, the magazine's editors wanted to show the human, "personal" side of Raymond Harris and had sent a photographer to cover him at the funeral of a fallen colleague.

It was only when Troy recognized his own mother in one of the pictures that he realized that this was the *Troy Loensch* memorial service.

The man who had tried to kill him was comforting his mother, who thought he was dead!

That duplicitous son of a bitch!

At that moment, the door to the guy's inner office

opened. His previous customer smiled at Troy as she left clutching a ticket folder.

"Mr. Loensch, I presume," he said in Spanish-accented English. "I have your documents ready . . . please step into my office."

He smiled proudly as he handed Troy a U.S. passport with a photo Troy had taken in a drugstore kiosk the day before.

"It looks real," Troy said, suspiciously.

"It *is* real," the guy said, sounding a little disappointed that Troy would imagine him dealing in counterfeit passports. "I know a young lady at the embassy."

"I see."

"They're using nongovernmental contractors over there now," the guy explained. "It's much more efficient."

"Of course it is," Troy said.

"And here is your ticket to Los Angeles."

"Thank you," Troy said, clutching the colorful ticket folder. "But I've just been having some second thoughts."

"Second thoughts?"

"As much as I would really like to go back to L.A., there is somewhere else that I really think I need to be."

"Yes . . ."

"How hard would it be to exchange this for a ticket to Washington, D.C.?"

"Washington . . . hmmm . . ."

"How much?" Troy interrupted.

"Let's say . . . hmmm . . . a hundred dollars U.S. would take care of the exchange."

"That's a good deal . . ."

"I know a young lady at the airline." The guy smiled.

CHAPTER 44

Dulles Airport, Loudoun County, Virginia

IT WAS PERSONAL. THE LOATHING THAT TROY HAD for Raymond Harris, the loathing that seemed to grow each time Harris crossed Troy's mind, was personal—very personal.

He hung from a strap in one of the lumbering mobile lounges that carry people from the midfield concourse to the main terminal at Washington, D.C.'s principal international airport. With no checked baggage and no overhead baggage, Troy was ahead of most of his fellow passengers on the American Airlines flight from Miami. Only an energetic young guy with a suit and a laptop had made this mobile lounge. He was already on his phone, already doing business as Troy fumed.

Herndon was just a few miles away. Harris was

probably in his office on Firehawk's seventh floor, his office with the models and the flags and the framed pictures of politicians whom he now desired to put out of business.

Troy could be at Firehawk Headquarters inside a half hour—maybe as little as fifteen minutes. Getting to the seventh floor would be another matter. Nobody got to the seventh floor without an invitation. He could imagine Harris's reaction when the receptionist announced that Troy was in the lobby.

The last time Troy had walked into that lobby, he had done so as a conquering hero. Indeed, the plaque with his picture was probably still in that lobby. This time, he imagined quite a different reception. However, Troy had no intention of walking into the Firehawk lobby today, nor of allowing himself to be announced to Raymond Harris. The next time he met Harris face-to-face, he intended it to be on his own terms. How and when that would be, he had yet to figure out.

The last time Troy had walked through the Dulles main terminal, he had been headed toward the rental car section of Ground Transportation, but today, with no expense account and only about three hundred dollars in his pocket, he passed the rental car desks and took a place in line for the number 5A Metrobus.

The last time Troy had put Dulles Airport into a rearview mirror on the eastbound Hirst-Brault Expressway, he was headed for a comfortable room at the Marriott

Courtyard in Arlington. Today, he hoped they'd have a bed for him at the YMCA on Rhode Island Avenue in downtown Washington.

The last time Troy had glimpsed Firehawk Headquarters from the highway, his thoughts had turned to Jenna Munrough, and they turned that way today.

He had not seen her in the pictures of his funeral, and he wondered what she must have thought. Had she thought it an appropriate fate for the man who had shot down Hal Coughlin to die himself in an airplane crash? Had she thought about it much at all?

THE SUN WAS SETTING AS TROY CROSSED THE M Street bridge over Rock Creek Park. He had managed to get a cot at the YMCA and stashed his little duffel bag in a locker. He had time to kill, so he decided to take a walk.

Washington was not the Washington he remembered. A pall hung over the city, a pall of uncertainty. The Washington he remembered exuded a confidence, a confidence that came with knowing that all of the important institutions had lives of their own, lives that endured regardless of which party was in power, regardless of whether the president in power was up in the polls, or down in the gutter of a scandal. Today, a nervous apprehension prevailed.

The headlines in the news racks, like the chatter of the talking heads on the television screen back at the

YMCA, debated among themselves, even as Congress debated a bill that would place the executive branch under the receivership of a nonpartisan, nongovernmental commission.

Raymond Harris was on nearly every front page—he and Layton Kynelty of Cernavoda Partners. The two PMCs were now negotiating to bring in their management expertise to run the executive branch and get a handle on the myriad crises that the United States was facing around the world. It would be, in the words of the blue folder at Cactus Flat, The Transition.

Troy learned that had he indeed decided to stop off at Firehawk this morning and call on Raymond Harris, he would not have found him. Harris was on Capitol Hill, talking to Congress and offering his able services to head up the management of the executive branch. The man currently charged with that task, President Fachearon, was also testifying—across the street at the U.S. Supreme Court. He argued that, even though his approval rating had sunk to single digits, he remained the president under the Constitution. Congress had never before impeached a president so that he could be replaced by outsourced management, but as Harris insisted, there was a first time for everything.

Troy had returned from the jungle to discover that ex-generals running clandestine experimental aircraft operations had approval ratings! It mystified and infuriated Troy, but there it was. Harris had an approval rating of nearly fifty percent. In a polarized era when approval ratings rarely exceeded forty percent, that was considered very good.

Mystified and infuriated, Troy walked across the bridge toward Georgetown and turned up Thirty-first Street. He walked anonymously, with the confident anonymity of a man who could move unnoticed in a world where he was already dead. The presence of Troy Loensch in this world and on this street would raise questions, but so far, nobody knew that Troy Loensch still existed. In a moment, he would cut a razor-thin slit in this veil of anonymity.

He recognized the cobalt-blue Porsche as it made the final turn, and he recognized the woman as she stepped out to get the mail before sliding into the underground parking garage beneath her building.

"Hey, Falcon Two," he shouted as he crossed the street, wondering whether using the nickname was too cute.

Jenna spun at the sound of the voice, startled by the sound of that voice and of its choice of nickname.

Her expression was one of disbelief.

Who?

How?

"What are you . . . ?" Jenna gasped.

"You mean why am I not dead?" Troy asked as he approached close enough to see the confused expression in her eyes in the growing darkness. She looked good, Troy thought, even with her hair a little unkempt and her makeup a little bit faded, as a woman's makeup usually is at the end of a long workday. She also looked very bewildered—"seen a ghost" bewildered.

"Who are you? Are you . . . are you Troy Loensch?"

"What?" Troy smiled. "You obviously recognize me."

"Who are you? Really," she stammered.

"I took a chance that you'd be coming back to your apartment on time," Troy explained, ignoring her question. "I figured that you wouldn't be working late, since Harris is otherwise occupied up on the Hill."

"You look different, Loensch," she said, studying his face and the deep tan that he had picked up in Nicaragua. "You look like you've been on a beach for a month."

"Actually I've been in the mountains for several months . . . seems like a helluva lot longer . . . so much has happened since . . ."

"You can't be . . ."

"Is this the part where you tell me I'm supposed to be dead?"

"I was at the memorial . . ."

"Didn't see you in the pictures."

"Then you didn't see very many pictures," Jenna replied, regaining her composure. "This is the part where I ask you what the hell happened."

"And this is the part where I ask you whether you're gonna stand here with your Porsche burning through unleaded, or are you going to invite me in?"

CHAPTER 45

Thirty-first Street NW, Georgetown,
Washington, D.C.

"WANT A DRINK?" JENNA ASKED AS SHE TOSSED HER
laptop and keys on the small table in her dining nook.

"As I recall, an Ozark girl like yourself usually has a
little Wild Turkey in the cupboard."

She poured two and nodded for him to take a seat as
she flopped onto her couch and put her feet on a foot-
stool.

"Obviously y'all weren't lost at sea like we thought,"
she began. "They searched a million square miles for a
week. Never found a thing . . . where were you?"

"Storm blew in, blew the Shakuru back over land . . .
I went down on a mountaintop. Just like Noah's ark. It

was a couple of weeks before I figured out that I wasn't on an island somewhere."

"Where *were* you?"

"Nicaragua . . . but I didn't know that until about two weeks ago."

"How could . . . ?"

"I broke my leg pretty bad . . . couldn't get around . . . it still hurts."

"Couldn't you make contact with us?" Jenna asked, almost angry that he hadn't tried to phone.

"There are still places in the world without Wi-Fi access." Troy smiled. "Still places with no cell service . . . besides, I didn't have a cell phone."

"How long have you been back?"

"Got to town this morning."

"Have you been to Firehawk yet?"

"Nope."

"I need to call them and let them know that you're—" Jenna said, reaching for her purse to get her phone.

"Please don't," Troy said, his voice so stern that it surprised Jenna.

"Why?"

"Because your boss, your CEO, Raymond Harris . . . tried to kill me."

"Kill you? When? Where?"

Jenna's astonishment was almost equal to what it had been when she first confronted Troy as a "ghost."

"In Shakuru, somewhere over California."

"How . . . I thought . . . I thought he managed to escape only after Shakuru was going down and you couldn't get out."

"He sabotaged everything," Troy said. "My parachute . . . the autopilot override . . . radio. He disconnected the lithium sulfur batteries."

"Are you sure?"

"What the hell do you mean, 'am I sure?' Of course I'm sure. I was *there*," Troy said angrily. "I screamed myself crazy trying to get out a distress signal . . . I watched the damned engines shut down when the solar panels were starved of sunlight . . . I felt myself start to freeze in the damned space suit as it shut down."

"But *Harris*?"

"And I heard him calmly tell me *how* I was going to die, just before he popped the canopy—and just after he told me *why*."

"Why?" Jenna asked. "*Why* did Harris want you dead?"

"The Transition," Troy said. "Because I found the documents . . . y'know, about The Transition."

"What's that?"

"It's what's been playing out in the news back here since I've been out of touch with reality," Troy said. "He's trying to overthrow the government—him and Kynelty and their crowd."

"But this has been in the news for weeks," Jenna said. "Firehawk and Cernavoda are only two of several PMCs that have submitted proposals to Congress—"

"But Harris is trying to overthrow the government!" Troy insisted. "Can't you see that?"

"Are y'all sure you're the *real* Troy Loensch?" Jenna laughed. "The Troy Loensch that I knew wasn't this interested in politics."

"Geez, Munrough, can't you see what's going on? Why am I the only one who sees this shit? Maybe I was in the jungle too long."

"Thought you said you were in the mountains."

"It was in Central America . . . the mountains have jungles . . . but that's not the point. The point is that I go away for a few months and come back and it's like mass hypnosis back here. Everybody is going along with this. Nobody seems to see what he's doing."

"You're just being paranoid," Jenna said with a dismissive toss of her hand. "It's all politics. What the hell do y'all care about politics?"

"Maybe it's just a matter of that oath we took when we joined the U.S. Air Force . . . something about upholding the Constitution. . . . Was that all just a big pile of crap? I came *here* to see *you*, rather than going to see anybody else, because I thought *you* of all people would be able to see through this, see what Harris and Kynelty are doing for what it is."

"Look, Loensch, the politicians are fighting this out

in rooms up there on Capitol Hill . . . it ain't guns in the streets."

"Is that what it's gonna take for you to see? Guns in the streets? Look at *me* . . . you're lookin' at the dude who was damned near the first casualty of this fuckin' revolution that Harris has up his slimy little sleeve."

"What exactly was in these 'documents' you found that you say he tried to kill you over?"

"That *I say*?" Troy asked angrily. "This was very, *very* damned unambiguous. He tried to *kill me*."

"Okay . . . I believe you," Jenna said, backing her tone off a few notches from the accusatory. She could feel the Wild Turkey starting to flutter its wings in her head and imagined that the same was true with Troy. "Just start from the beginning . . . tell me what you found . . . actually start with telling me *how* y'all found these documents."

"I found them in his office—his office at Cactus Flat."

"What were you doing in his office?"

"I broke in to look for—"

"You *broke into* Harris's office?"

"Yeah," Troy said in a tone that implied, *Of course*.

"Shit, Loensch, if you'd broke into *my* office, I'd be pretty pissed, too. Why the hell did you do a thing like that?"

"Because the CIA asked me to," Troy admitted sheepishly.

"The C-I-friggin'-A?" Jenna said, rolling her eyes

in disbelief. "I *guess* you're paranoid, if you're seeing the CIA."

"You think I've gone around the bend?" Troy asked angrily.

"You're serious?" Jenna asked. "The CIA . . . Really? The CIA *really* asked you to spy on Raymond Harris?"

"They really asked me to spy on Raymond Harris."

"*Why?*"

"They came to me at the Marriott last time I was in town. They wanted to know whether Harris had ever said anything about PMCs being used to overthrow and control countries."

"We've all heard him talk about that." Jenna nodded. "That's just Harris being Harris."

"I agree. That's what I told them. I said I could name a half dozen countries that are *already* run by a PMC. But then they said that they suspected Harris wanted to overthrow the United States."

"What kind of proof did they have?" Jenna asked suspiciously.

"None."

"Great." She laughed. "So y'all agreed to spy on him, even though your CIA pals didn't have any proof."

"No. Not then. I told 'em that a lot of people say things about politicians, and that what they were saying was paranoid bullshit."

"Sure sounds like it to me." Jenna nodded.

"So they left, and I didn't think about it much until

a few weeks or so after I got out to Cactus Flat. Harris showed up and started talking about exactly what they said he was going to do."

"That's when you decided to break into his office?"

"No, I had another meeting with the spooks in Vegas."

"Then you decided to break into his office?"

"Yeah."

"Okay . . . so now we're back to the place where you were gonna tell me what you found."

"There was a blue folder that talked about something called The Transition, presumably because it's about a transition from an elected government to an outsourced management like they're doing right now."

"It's not something they're doing in secret," Jenna said. "It's not something that's being done in the dead of night. This is just about as fall-into-broad-daylight as you can get."

"I'm no student of history, but I think I remember that this is how Hitler got in," Troy said. "The German government got into such a fix that they just brought him in, and the people were okay with it."

"And they sure got 'it,'" Jenna said. "But I can't see Harris—"

"This blue folder went on to say that if the politicians didn't give the PMCs what they wanted, they'd be ready to take it by force."

"How could they?"

"Think about it, Munrough," Troy insisted. "The PMCs have all the guns now. The armed forces outsourced so much that they hardly have any assets. They're just management agencies. The generals are nothing but paper-pushers running PMC contracts. When the PMCs take over the government, the PMCs will be running the PMC contracts. This country won't have armed services anymore."

"The PMCs pay a lot better," Jenna reminded him. "It's better for the folks doing the work."

"This is not a joke," Troy insisted. "The PMCs could take over . . . they could *walk over* the United States armed services. Kynelty's Cernavoda has more, and *newer* APCs and main battle tanks than the U.S. Army. We both know that Firehawk is better equipped than the Air Force."

"Yeah," Jenna agreed. "I know that most of the F-22s and F-16s have been transferred to Firehawk squadrons, and there's that new plane that was being tested by the HAWX Program out in Nevada. You must know about that one."

"Raven. I heard that it's called Raven, but I didn't have anything to do with it. It was kept under wraps. I'm surprised that you've heard about it. Most people at Cactus Flat didn't even know about it. What *have* you heard?"

"Not much." Jenna shrugged. "Just the usual prattle around the watercoolers at Firehawk. I heard it was very fast . . . And I heard that they brought a demonstrator in to Andrews Air Force Base last week."

"That can't be good," Troy said.

"There's a fine line between paranoia and—"

"This *ain't* paranoia," Troy insisted.

"What do your CIA spook friends think of Harris trying to kill you?"

"I haven't told them."

"What? Why not?"

"I've been back in the United States for less than eight hours . . . I wanted to see you first."

"I'm touched." Jenna smiled.

CHAPTER 46

K Street, Washington, D.C.

"HI," THE VOICE SAID CHEERFULLY. "I CAN'T COME TO the phone, but please leave your name and number and the time you called, and I'll get back to you."

Eight times in four days, Troy had found a pay phone and had made a call. Eight times in four days, Troy had listened to the message and hung up without leaving one of his own.

Where was Nagte, or whatever his name was?

If the CIA was so damned anxious to be contacted, why didn't they do a better job of manning their phones?

If he could have, he would have done as he had with Jenna Munrough. If he had known *where* Nagte was, or any of the other, nameless CIA spooks, he would have staked them out and contacted them face-to-face.

Troy had left Jenna's apartment with a distinct sense that she still considered him a paranoid nutcase, interpreting the noble intentions of Raymond Harris as a sinister scheme.

She had agreed to tell no one of their meeting, and he trusted that she would not—at least most of him trusted that she would not.

She had not, however, invited him to stay the night. When he had gone to see her, at least part of him had been yearning for that, but the frostiness of their previous meeting still remained as a barrier to the renewal of the sparks that once had flown between them. Hal Coughlin was still the unseen but strongly felt third presence in the room whenever Troy and Jenna were together.

Today, however, Troy was not in the room with Jenna. He was in a crowded elevator in an office building on Washington's "Lobbyist Gulch."

Hardly anyone noticed Troy—not that people do anything but conspicuously ignore one another in crowded elevators—but he could tell that they all were noticing what he was carrying. It was nearly lunchtime, and he was carrying two large, steaming pizzas with extra meat *and* extra cheese.

Once, the U.S. Air Force had trusted him with eight figures' worth of high-tech airplane. Today—his second on the job—Mr. Mahmud had trusted him to deliver two large pizzas.

There are actually many places in Washington, D.C.,

or any major city, where someone who doesn't want to share his true identity can find a job. Such was the case with Troy when he realized that his money was running short, and he saw the HELP WANTED sign in Mr. Mahmud's window. It was a small place with just three tables, but being in the proximity of K Street, it did an enormous takeout business. The only question Mahmud asked was, "When can you start?"

Troy wondered if he had made the right decision to come to Washington. If he had chosen to keep the Los Angeles ticket, would things be any different? He would still be dead—unless he wanted Harris to know that he wasn't. At least his parents had access to his bank account—they had inherited it—and he wouldn't have to be delivering pizzas.

He made the decision to come to Washington because he was obsessed with confronting and stopping Harris, but he had no plan.

How?

When?

Where?

Troy wished that he had gone to the Capitol on the day when Harris was testifying before Congress. He could have just walked up to him in front of a dozen television cameras.

He could see the headlines, and he could imagine the creepers on the news channel screens.

Firehawk Hero Confronts Firehawk Boss.

Did Firehawk CEO Attempt to Murder Firehawk Hero?

Would they even bother to figure out who Troy was before Firehawk security hustled him away?

Unidentified Pizza Man Assaults the Great Raymond Harris.

Would they even *notice* Troy before Firehawk security hustled him away?

Journalists Ignore Another Nutcase.

The lobbyists who'd ordered the two large pizzas were discussing the PMC takeover of the government as Troy arrived. While he was making change, he overheard them talking excitedly about the business opportunities that would present themselves. There were so many rules and restrictions involved in the red tape of lobbying government agencies. Now that they would be lobbying private companies for essentially the same business, it would be much easier. They were excited and in a buoyant mood. Troy walked away with a twenty-dollar tip.

"THAT DUDE HARRIS, HE'S GONNA KICK SOME ASS tomorrow," Vicente observed a few days later, as he rolled pizza dough with his eyes glued to the television set that was bolted to the wall high above the counter.

"You think so?" Troy asked.

It was a slow time of day, just before the lunchtime rush, and the two men were taking care of their prep work.

"Yeah, man."

Like Troy, Vicente had a past that he didn't talk about, but Mr. Mahmud didn't care. He paid them in cash, and he paid them pretty well. They made pizzas, and they made them pretty well. Who would have thought that a guy from Sinaloa who probably had felony warrants in his name on both sides of the border would take such an interest in American politics.

"I hope he does, man," Vicente continued in accented English. "This dude Fachearon ain't got no cojones, man. I like this dude Harris."

"You think he's gonna kick Fachearon's ass?"

"Don't you?" Vicente asked. "That's what they're all saying on TV, y'know."

"Where did you get your interest in American politics?" Troy asked.

"It used to be so boring, man. I been here eight years . . . first time I've seen all this excitement, man. Back in Sinaloa, you get somebody like Fachearon who can't do nothing . . . he's in deep shit. Even if he don't wanna be gone, he's gone, man. This is cool, man. This Harris is cool. What he's doin' to Fachearon, man, is cool. I like to watch it. Up here . . . really boring . . . until now."

"So you like Harris?"

"Fachearon's a weak man. Everybody can see that. America needs a strong man. You need a strong man to show the world who's boss. Everybody says he's the man."

News and political gossip are the lifeblood of Washington, D.C. The flow of such chatter was the sustenance that underpinned the politicians, the journalists, the pundits, the news junkies, and the anonymous guys who made the pizzas that kept them going. Each day, Troy saw this lifeblood grow more and more bizarre as President Albert Bacon Fachearon fought an uphill battle against the rising tide of the PMCs. For Troy, the most bizarre thing about it all was that nobody else seemed to find it strange that Congress was on the verge of privatizing the executive branch. Some opposed it on its merits, but none on the sheer peculiarity of the concept.

Congress was doing what it does best. It held hearings while its members were taped doing sound bites and appeared on morning talk shows. What Congress had *not* done—at least not yet—was take a vote.

An impatient Raymond Harris complained, telling an interviewer that in the private sector, decisions were made quickly—especially important decisions like this. The pundits quickly did what they do best, criticizing Congress for dithering. Like Harris, with whom they had become captivated, the journalists waited impatiently for Congress to take a vote.

Troy opened a big plastic bag of mozzarella cheese and glanced up at the television. He was almost getting used to seeing Raymond Harris's name on the screen.

News Alert: Harris to Appear, read the screaming yellow and red headline.

The talking head was standing in front of the Capitol quoting Harris, who had just said it was time for decisive action, and explaining that Harris would be back on the Hill tomorrow, advocating a vote.

"So will I," Troy said, looking at the screen.

"Huh?" Vicente asked.

"I gotta tell Mr. Mahmud that I'm gonna be late tomorrow," Troy said. "I've got something to do in the morning."

CHAPTER 47

U.S. Capitol, Washington, D.C.

"WHAT'S GOING ON?" TROY ASKED A MAN STANDING near the barricade.

He had gotten an early start Friday morning on his hike to the Hill. He knew that Raymond Harris was scheduled to testify at 9:00 A.M., but he wanted to be sure that he was on hand when the Firehawk CEO's limo arrived. What he found was an unusual flurry of activity as one black Town Car after another sped up to the Capitol steps to disgorge passengers.

"I heard they called Congress into session this morning for a vote on this PMC deal," the man said. "All the senators and congressmen are showing up."

"Nobody wants to be absent for *this* vote," interjected a woman who was standing nearby. "It's about time if you ask me. They've been sitting on this thing for weeks. It's like General Harris says . . . they've gotta get off their duffs and make a decision already."

"Is Harris coming up today?" Troy asked. "They said on the news yesterday that he was supposed to testify."

"All the committee hearings were canceled," said a Capitol policeman who was standing near the crowd barricade. "Everybody's going to be in their chambers for the House vote and then maybe a Senate vote this afternoon."

Feeling defeated, Troy turned away from the barricade and headed down the hill on Pennsylvania Avenue toward the pizza parlor. He would be there well before the lunch rush. The vote in favor of turning the executive branch over to Harris and the PMCs was widely reported as a foregone conclusion. The analysis by every news channel showed that the opposition just didn't have the votes to block the tidal wave of inevitability.

Things were busier than usual at Mr. Mahmud's that day. A lot of people were making a bit of a party out of watching the live television pictures from Capitol Hill.

"Didn't expect to see you 'til this afternoon," the proprietor said as Troy arrived.

"I got done earlier than I thought," Troy said. "So I thought I'd come in."

"Good thing you did," Mr. Mahmud said. "I need help here at the take-out counter."

Troy was glad that it was busy. It took his mind off his

distress over a missed opportunity to confront Harris. After today, if there actually was a vote, Harris would be unlikely to show up in public. Unlike politicians, CEOs didn't have to show up to smile at voters.

He watched the television out of the corner of his eye as congressmen were going on the record from the floor with last-minute statements. He couldn't hear the audio, but the creepers kept him abreast of the essentials.

At last, it finally came time for the vote. The people seated at the few small tables craned their necks to watch, and Mr. Mahmud turned up the volume. Most of the people ordered a second soft drink.

The roll call began, and within moments, the Executive Branch Management Bill, the bill to put the executive branch in the hands of a consortium of PMCs headed by the Firehawk CEO, had a lopsided majority in favor.

Then, a strange thing happened.

The vote in the House of Representatives started to swing the other way. When it was over, the bill passed, but by a razor-thin margin of 221 to 214.

The hush that had fallen over the room ended as the pizza parlor pundits at the tables began discussing and rationalizing the unanticipated results of the long-awaited vote.

Troy heard Vicente say something about Harris kicking Fachearon's ass—his favorite analysis of the situation—and they heard reports that the bill was being hand-delivered to the Senate chamber.

Troy took some consolation in knowing that Raymond Harris was not resting easy at this moment. He was probably sweating bullets and making calls to every senator who owed him a favor. The CEO who had been above the fray was having to get his hands dirty in the trenches of politics.

As the lunch crowd thinned out, Troy went out on a couple of nearby deliveries. People in the offices seemed just as absorbed in the Senate debate as were the people in the pizza parlor during the House debate earlier in the day. Lobbyists whose clients had big government contracts were concerned about keeping them. Those who represented people with smaller slices of the government spending pie saw it only as an opportunity to be exploited.

At times like these, Troy remembered the words that had been spoken to him long ago when Harris was explaining why the Zapatistas were anxious to keep the Chiapas pot growers in business.

"It's complicated," Harris had said. "But if you follow the money, it all makes sense."

Troy wondered how much money had been spent to skew the vote in the House that morning—and how much Harris was spending right now.

The Senate vote was in progress as Troy walked through the building lobby after his last delivery. A group of people had paused in front of the television above the reception desk, but Troy couldn't bring himself to watch. It was too painful. He just hoped the senators would give Harris a close enough margin so that he'd have to sweat it out as he had in the House vote.

When he got back to the pizza parlor, everyone was just staring at the television screen. Vicente, who always had plenty to say, was speechless. So too were the four customers. It was so quiet that one woman stepped outside to make a phone call.

The Senate had voted.

The Executive Branch Management Bill had lost, 59 to 41.

Harris had lost, and President Albert Bacon Fachearon would continue to run the executive branch as the voters had elected him to do.

The pundits, none of whom had predicted this outcome, were now spinning the news so as not to appear totally out to lunch.

Troy just smiled and breathed a sigh of relief.

"WE'RE GONNA HAVE TO STOP MEETING LIKE THIS," Jenna Munrough said, glancing up from her mail. As had been the case earlier in the week, she saw Troy Loensch walking across Thirty-first Street. "You could have called."

"I happened to be in the neighborhood." He shrugged.

"Speaking of which, I tried your cell number and it was disconnected. I need your new number."

"I'm dead, y'know," Troy said. "Dead men don't have cell phones. I don't have a cell phone or much of anything else. All my worldly possessions were at Cactus Flat. Guess maybe they were shipped to my mother's place in California."

"Where have you been?" Jenna asked.

"Around. Trying to figure out a way to confront Harris."

"Y'all must have been pleased by the 'Senators' Surprise' this afternoon."

"Is that what they're calling it?" Troy smiled. "I bet there was some gnashing of teeth over at Firehawk today."

"I wasn't there."

"Where were you?"

"Capitol Hill," Jenna explained. "The administrative liaison people were up there helping out the congressional liaison people. They wanted a maximum lobbying effort."

"So you were lobbying congress for a 'yes' vote?"

"That's my job."

"You must have been pleased with the vote in the House."

"Not really," Jenna said. "Not personally . . . not after I started thinking about what you said the other night. Not after I started listening to a lot of what was coming in from the constituents."

"What do you mean?"

"Around Washington, it seems like everybody is ready to run Fachearon out of town . . . all the talking heads anyway. When I was in those congressional offices, the staffers were showing the e-mails that their bosses were getting from back home. You're on the side of the majority, Loensch."

"That's good to know," Troy said, feeling vindicated. "What do *you* think of the way it turned out today up there?"

"Relieved. Glad it's over."

"Thought you said it's your job to *not* be glad of how it turned out?"

"My job isn't hurt." Jenna shrugged. "The government still needs to spend money on PMCs. It really doesn't have an army of its own anymore."

"What's wrong?" Troy asked, noticing that Jenna suddenly had a concerned expression and was looking at something out of the corner of her eye.

"Nothing. . . . Listen, not to change the subject, but I think it might be a good idea for us to go inside."

"Thanks for the invite." Troy smiled.

"We shouldn't be standing out here . . . shouldn't be seen together."

INSIDE, JENNA KICKED OFF HER HALLS-OF-CONGRESS three-inch heels and went straight for the Wild Turkey, pouring one for Troy without asking.

"You're worried about Harris catching you with the late Troy Loensch," he said, touching her glass with his.

"That would put a little hurt in my job situation," she said. "You've got *me* paranoid now."

"Put a little hurt in my *life* situation," Troy said. "He put his cards on the table that day when he left me at eighty thousand feet in an uncontrollable airplane. I'm sure he could come up with some ideas for Jenna Munrough's accidental demise."

"Y'all still want to confront him?" Jenna asked.

"Yeah. I want to see him explain what happened up there that day. I want to see him explain what happened in front of some television cameras."

"You'll probably have your chance next week. Now that this thing has failed, he and Kynelty will be back on the Hill lobbying for a resubmission of the bill."

"How likely is it that Congress will do that?"

"My opinion? Not very. I saw what people were saying in those e-mails. Even if they were going to take it up again, it wouldn't be any time soon. Matter of months. Maybe not even in this session."

"But you think Harris is gonna be up there again *next week*?"

"You know him. He doesn't like to take no for an answer."

"Will you be going up with him?"

"Probably not," Jenna said. "He'll just be trying to

meet with the House leadership. The congressional liaison people will set it up. . . . Will *you* be there?"

"Probably. I gotta do this thing."

"Be careful," Jenna cautioned.

"Thank you for your concern."

"I care about you," Jenna admitted.

"That's sweet of you." Troy smiled.

"I'm *serious*," Jenna insisted. "I really do care about you."

"I thought that after . . . y'know . . . after that . . . after Hal got killed . . ."

"You thought I blamed you for killing Hal?"

"I *did* kill Hal," Troy admitted. "I didn't know it was Hal . . . but that doesn't mean that I didn't do it."

"I understand that . . . intellectually," Jenna said. "But it was hard to look at y'all . . . knowing."

"I understand," Troy said, casting his gaze downward.

"Mainly, I was pissed off at *me*," Jenna said.

"At yourself?"

"I slept with you while I was engaged to Hal. I hid his ring in my damned purse and made hot, sweaty lust with you all night. And that was after trying to seduce you one time before that."

"That you did." Troy nodded.

"I'm pissed at myself because Hal loved me and he was basically the sweetest, most caring man I ever met . . ."

"Why are you pissed at *you* for that?"

"Because ever since that night in Eritrea, I've wanted your body, Loensch. I loved Hal and he loved me, but I wanted *you*. He was sweet and thoughtful . . . you're an arrogant asshole . . . but you are just *so* good in bed."

"Well . . ." Troy started to say as Jenna took his glass from his hand, set it on an end table, and pushed him down on the sofa.

Having unbuttoned her blouse, she pounced on him, kissing him madly and pressing her body against his.

CHAPTER 48

Thirty-first Street NW, Georgetown,
Washington, D.C.

"WHAT TIME IS IT?" TROY ASKED, AS HE AWOKE TO the slippery, pleasant sensation of the naked body of Jenna Munrough being pressed against his.

"I don't care. It's Saturday," Jenna said, lifting her head slightly. Her tone underscored the fact that she was annoyed at the interruption to her ongoing search for physical gratification.

Outside the window, the blackness of the night had been superseded by the faint, cold, metallic gray light of dawn.

Troy could still detect traces of Jenna's perfume amid the smell of sweat and the savory aromas of their bodily fluids. It had been a wild and passionate night, and Jenna craved that it continue.

It continued. Rather, it resumed after a half dozen hours of deep and invigorating sleep. It resumed, and it continued as the first rays of daylight pushed the night aside.

"I don't want it to end." Jenna gasped, out of breath, as she rolled off Troy and flopped onto the bed.

But at last, it ended. The desire was willing, but the bodies were exhausted.

For a time, they just lay there, Jenna squeezing Troy's hand.

Finally, she staggered to her feet, visited the bathroom, slipped on her robe, and went into the kitchen.

Troy rolled off the bed as he heard the rattling sounds of Jenna beginning to fuss with the coffeemaker.

"That was good." He smiled as he came into the kitchen.

"That was *very* good," she said, looking longingly at his tired, naked body. "It was everything that I've been yearning for all these months. Y'all may not always be a nice man, Loensch, but you're *good*."

Troy thought of saying, "*Nice* guys finish last," but he didn't want to bring up the finish of Hal Coughlin's life and career. Hal had been a nice guy.

As they sipped their coffee, Jenna idly reached for the television remote and clicked it on.

Neither of them was prepared for what they saw.

A line of armored personnel carriers bearing the logo

of Layton Kynelty's Cernavoda Partners were lined up along Constitution Avenue adjacent to the Capitol building. The text at the bottom of the screen read *Breaking News.*

Jenna looked at Troy. They were both speechless.

The picture changed to a view of the White House as seen from Pennsylvania Avenue. The fact that this block, the famous 1600 block, is closed to traffic had not deterred two M1A4 tanks with the Cernavoda logo on their turrets. Near the north portico of the White House, a group of men in black combat gear were speaking with a uniformed Secret Service man in shirtsleeves.

The picture changed again, this time to an earnest young newscaster doing a field report from Lafayette Square across the street.

"We repeat," she said nervously. "Raymond Harris of Firehawk and Layton Kynelty of Cernavoda Partners are at the White House and are said to be conferring with the vice president at this moment. We have no confirmation of the location of the president, but there are unsubstantiated rumors that he is at Camp David . . . back to you at our Washington studio."

"It's The Transition," Troy said somberly. It was as he had read about it in that blue folder back at Cactus Flat.

The picture changed to a head shot of a familiar cable channel newscaster. The absence of a necktie made him look a trifle unkempt, but all that more earnest.

"For those of you just joining us, we have breaking

news here in the nation's capital," he said anxiously. "Washington has awakened to unfolding events of momentous consequence. Just before dawn this morning, senators received an urgent personal call from the vice president, who convened an emergency session of the Senate at seven-ten this morning. The senators arrived to find that all of Capitol Hill had been secured by armored units of Cernavoda Partners."

The picture in the background changed to one of the Cernavoda vehicles surrounding the Capitol. The man took a drink of water and continued.

"The first item of business on the agenda at this emergency session was the reconsideration of the Executive Branch Management Bill, which the Senate had defeated yesterday. When the session was called to order, the eighty-eight senators who were present voted unanimously to pass the bill."

"Those SOBs!" Jenna spat out angrily. "They had a gun to their heads . . ."

"The Transition," Troy repeated.

"We have received word that in the past few minutes, the House of Representatives has been called into session to pass articles of impeachment against President Fachearon," the talking head continued. "The second item of business in the Senate was to pass a bill ordering him removed from office immediately after the impeachment . . . pending the trial in the Senate. The Senate took the further, unprecedented step of authorizing duly constituted authorities to use deadly force against the pres . . . um . . . I suppose, soon-to-be *former* president."

"I told you so," Troy said.

"I know you did," Jenna replied. "I guess I never imagined that it would come to this. . . ."

"We just have word in to our studio that President Fachearon will be making a statement from Camp David . . . momentarily . . . Please stand by while we try to bring this to you."

There was some fluttering of video images and Fachearon appeared on the screen. He look tired but composed. He wore a jacket and tie, presenting the same image as he had for other televised speeches during his troubled term.

"My fellow Americans, I come to you at a perilous moment in our nation's history," Fachearon began. "What has been happening in the nation's capital this morning is nothing short of a coup d'état, an attempt by malevolent parties to overthrow the legally constituted government of the United States. Yesterday, the Senate voted to deny attempts by the PMCs Cernavoda and Firehawk to take control of the executive branch through legislation. Today, under threat from tanks and armed thugs, the Senate was compelled to reverse a decision that had been freely arrived at. No decision of this kind, reached under such duress, should be allowed to stand. I am speaking to you today to assure you that I *will resist* these actions with all of the power that I still have at my disposal. I call on all Americans to join me in resisting and defeating this grave threat against our liberty. May God bless the United States of America."

The screen went fuzzy momentarily and the cable newscaster was back.

"That was the president . . . um . . . Mr. Fachearon, speaking from Camp David. . . . We understand that Raymond Harris will be speaking from the White House."

The next face they saw on the screen was the familiar visage of Raymond Harris. He exuded firm self-assurance, but he looked tired. Maybe it was just the way the wide-screen television stretched things, but it looked as though he had gained weight.

"My fellow Americans," Harris said confidently. "Our nation has reached a crossroads in its history. Of that, there can be no doubt. It is a time for action, it is a time for strength. Until about seven o'clock Eastern Time this morning, our country was an oligarchy. Our nation was in the hands of a man whose approval rating had languished below six percent for more than a year. More than ninety percent of the American people were being ruled by an elite cadre of *six percent*. This morning, the Senate, like the House of Representatives yesterday, bravely acted to pull the plug on the oligarchy."

Harris smiled a "getting to the good part" smile and continued.

"Congress, *your* Congress, *your* representatives, have handed Mr. Kynelty and myself a tremendous responsibility. It is a responsibility that we shoulder as a sacred trust. We will not let you down. With that responsibility comes many challenges. The first and foremost challenge that we face is to remove the outlaw who claims authority that he does not have, who exercises power despite the will of Congress. We have word that Mr. Fachearon and his supporters have barricaded themselves at the Camp David compound and intend to resist all attempts to dislodge them. This is, my fellow Americans, not an insignificant nuisance, but a major threat to the security of the United States . . . Fachearon has his finger on the trigger of America's nuclear arsenal."

"This is gonna be bad," Jenna said, glancing at Troy.

"This could be *real* bad." Troy nodded.

"Fear not, my fellow Americans," Harris continued. "We shall not shrink from our newly bestowed mantle of responsibility. *I* shall not shrink from this newly bestowed mantle of responsibility. I intend to *personally* ensure that Mr. Fachearon and his six percent will not stand in the way of our nation's future."

With that, the screen faded and chattering talking heads appeared.

"What did he mean by that?" Troy asked.

In the other room, Jenna's cell phone was chirping.

"This is Jenna," she said. "Hi, Lucy . . . yeah . . . I saw it. . . . Yeah . . . lot to digest for sure . . . Harris is like that. . . . For sure . . . he'd be an oligarch himself if he had half a chance. . . . Yeah . . . I guess he *does* have half a chance now. . . . Well, he *said* he was going to do it personally. . . . No, Lucy . . . I won't tell. . . . Y'all are *kidding* me . . . no shit? . . . You can't be serious. . . . Where? . . . When? . . . Can you stop him? . . . Can y'all slow him down? . . . I'll think of something. . . . I dunno, Lucy . . . I'll think of something. Just slow him down."

Jenna tossed the cell phone on the counter and gave Troy a bewildered glance.

"What the hell was that about?" Troy asked, having heard only Jenna's side of the conversation.

"Harris," Jenna said, beginning to pace. "That was Lucy . . . she's in special projects. She was with Harris this morning as this whole thing was going down."

"Wild. What's going on?"

"Harris . . . It's Harris. The son of a bitch has got a tactical nuke loaded on the Raven aircraft . . . he's gonna fucking *nuke* Fachearon."

CHAPTER 49

"THANK YOU FOR COMING," ALBERT BACON FAC-hearon said sarcastically. "And yes, it *is* rather awkward to receive an emissary from Firehawk on a day such as this. I had presumed that you were bringing an apology and a memorandum of capitulation from Layton Kynelty or Raymond Harris, but apparently not. You can tell them that nothing less than these will be acceptable. You may stay for lunch if you wish, but after that, please make your way back to Washington and convey my sincere dissatisfaction to those 'gentlemen.'"

With that, Fachearon turned and strode away, leaving his visitor standing in the foyer of Laurel Lodge.

Aron Arnold might have been impressed by the gold-leaved eagles, the flags, and the trappings of American presidential pomp and power. His father, who had grown up in a United States that valued patriotism, a nation where loyalty to flag and to country matter, would have been. Aron Arnold was not. As he was growing into a man in the featureless suburbs around Orlando, it was a world in which flag-waving was an irrelevant anachronism.

He had joined the U.S. Air Force because he wanted to fly. He had grown up playing video games, and he wanted to do it for real. He had been good at the game console and proved himself good in real cockpits as well. His total and all-consuming attention to being the best at doing what he did, combined with his detached and easygoing temperament, made him an ideal candidate when Svartvand BV was recruiting pilots—and killers. Aron Arnold was the ideal PMC man, with loyalty only to his employer of the moment, not to the flag beneath which he had been born.

When Svartvand was acquired by Firehawk, Arnold had no nostalgia for Svartvand, just as he had no particular loyalty to flag or country. For Arnold, it was never personal. When he had met Troy Loensch on the night that Svartvand had merged with Firehawk, he had detected a trace of uneasiness. Sure, they had been fighting to the death early that same day, and that was a serious irony—but it wasn't personal. At least it had not been personal for Aron.

He had felt that same uneasiness from Troy Loensch when they met again at Cactus Flat. Arnold was impressed by how Loensch had allowed his professionalism as a pilot trump any bad feelings he had for a man who had tried to kill him in air combat, but on the ground, they had stayed apart. There had been no rounds of boozing at the officers' club that ended with slaps on the back and vows of "no hard feelings."

When Loensch had been killed in the Shakuru crash, there had been wailing and gnashing of teeth at Cactus Flat. A lot of people had been saddened by his death, as people are often saddened by deaths of co-workers. Dr. Elisa Meyers had expressed much anguish for the loss of her Shakuru but had shed a tear for the man as well. Aron Arnold shed no tears. He had no feelings of empathy. It was a job, and Loensch had simply not come back.

Like Dr. Meyers, Arnold was sad to see the Shakuru Program come to an abrupt end, but the broader HAWX Program remained. Within HAWX there would be many possibilities. Raymond Harris had even intimated that there would be a place for him in the cockpit of the Raven—and that prospect came with great excitement for Aron Arnold.

When Harris was named CEO of Firehawk, Arnold was brought back to the corporate headquarters in Herndon with the promise of "big things" within the HAWX Program.

Arnold had no distinct loyalty to Harris, nor to Firehawk, but rather to his job. Like the knights errant of the Middle Ages, or mercenaries throughout time, his master was the task at hand.

Today's task, amid the pastoral beauty of the Catoctin Mountains, had been to persuade Fachearon to submit to Firehawk authority as demanded by Congress.

Today, Arnold had failed, just as he had failed on that day over the Petén jungle to bring down Troy's F-16. It was Arnold's belief that in the long run, Troy Loensch *had* gone down to a watery grave in the vast Pacific. It was Arnold's belief that in due time, Fachearon *would* go down, down to obscurity as a footnote to a turning point in American history.

CHAPTER 50

Reagan National Airport, Arlington, Virginia

"THIS IS A FIREHAWK-AUTHORIZED OPERATION," JENNA
said sternly—and she could be *very* stern when the moment demanded sternness—as she flashed the Firehawk
ID card with its high level of security authorization.

"I don't know," stammered the guard at Reagan
National's government hangar. "I wasn't given any
advance notif—"

From the airport, they could look across the Potomac
and see the dome of the Capitol building. "In case you
aren't aware, this city is in crisis mode this morning,"
Jenna said angrily. "Not everyone is getting advance
notification of everything. In fact, damned few people are."

"I'm still not—"

"Do you want me to put you on Raymond Harris's personal shit list?" Jenna asked.

"No—"

"Do you know what will happen to you for impeding a Firehawk operation at this time?"

"Well—"

"Trust me, you have better things to do with your life than to be sitting around in a cell waiting to be executed for treason," Jenna asserted.

"Okay," the guard said, glancing again at Jenna's ID.

"Thank you," she said impatiently.

"What about him?" the guard said, nodding at Troy.

"He's with me," Jenna said, pushing the guard aside.

"Nothing works on a day like this like a Firehawk ID," Troy quipped as they entered the hangar.

"Wish *you* had brought your Firehawk ID," Jenna said.

"I left it in the jungle." He shrugged.

Parked before them were a pair of Virginia Air National Guard F-16s. When the PMCs had taken over for the armed forces, the assets of the National Guard, which were under state control, were not included.

Shortly after she had hung up from Lucy's phone call, Jenna had a brainstorm.

Troy's first reaction was one of "We gotta *stop* that bastard!"

Neither he nor Jenna had any idea how.

According to Lucy, Raymond Harris was already

headed for the car that would take him Andrews Air Force Base. She had promised that she'd try to delay Harris, but they all knew he could not be stopped.

That was when Jenna had her brainstorm. She remembered that the Air Guard kept F-16s on strip alert at Reagan National. After September 2001, every state on the eastern seaboard kept at least a few interceptors primed, even though more than a decade had passed without their having been called into action against a serious threat.

Amazingly, Troy and Jenna caught a taxi on nearby M Street—one of the cabs that were avoiding the disarray downtown. The driver crossed the Potomac on the Key Bridge, bypassing all the congestion around the White House, and made it to the airport from Georgetown in fifteen minutes.

They knew that it would take Harris at least a half hour to get to Andrews Air Force Base, where the Raven was parked. They also knew that he'd be in no rush. He was out to attack a fixed target at Camp David—one that was not going anywhere.

Troy and Jenna found flight gear and helmets in the hangar and suited up. Being on strip alert, both aircraft were fueled and ready to go, so the two concentrated on making sure that the AIM-9 Sidewinder air-to-air missiles were live and armed, and that the M61 cannons each had a magazine full of ammo.

"First time I've been in an F-16 since Sudan," Jenna said longingly as she started up the stairs.

"Just like riding a bicycle," Troy said. "It all comes right back to you. Let's take it low level to Andrews and try to get him on the ground."

"Roger that," Jenna agreed. "From what I've heard about the Raven, I sure would rather take it out on the ground than have to fight it in the air."

The Air Guard personnel dutifully pushed open the doors as they powered up their General Electric F110 turbofans, and Troy gave Jenna a thumbs-up to taxi out ahead of him.

"Ladies first," he said over the radio.

Jenna just replied with her middle finger and released her brake.

Seeing the two Air Guard fighters leave their hangar, the air traffic controllers in the Reagan National tower dutifully followed procedure, ordering a ramp hold on all commercial takeoffs and instructing all incoming flights to remain in the pattern. The Air Guard always went to the head of the line.

With both runways available, Troy and Jenna took off simultaneously. They kept their altitude to a thousand feet, low enough not to stand out on radar, but high enough to avoid transmission lines and power poles in the congested area around Washington.

They deliberately avoided overflying the city itself, not wanting to have the hundreds of news crews down there speculating about what these two F-16s were doing and alerting whatever air assets Firehawk might have flying this morning.

The flight time to Andrews from Reagan National is measured in minutes, so Troy and Jenna were confident that they could catch Harris.

Their confidence was misplaced.

"Falcon Three, target is on the main runway," Jenna said urgently as they got their first visual on the dart-shaped Raven.

"Go for it, Falcon Two," Troy said as Jenna dove toward the runway.

The dark-gray aircraft was already on its takeoff roll as Jenna took her F-16 to two hundred feet.

It was racing down the runway at seventy-five knots, then a hundred knots, as Jenna overtook it at much higher speed.

She lined the aircraft up in the ring on her head-up sight and thumbed the trigger of the M61 Gatling gun.

Nothing.

The Raven continued to roll.

A hundred and fifty knots.

She thumbed again as the Raven reached takeoff speed.

Still nothing.

"Falcon Three, my guns are jammed!" Jenna shouted, banking hard to the left. "Go for it!"

Troy was on the deck, just behind Jenna as she rolled left.

He had a clear, unobstructed view of the Raven as Harris achieved takeoff speed and lifted off the runway.

He thumbed his trigger and watched a stream of twenty-millimeter cannon shells pour toward the Raven.

Harris banked hard right just as Troy flew past him.

"I still have a visual on him," Jenna said calmly. "I'm turning to give pursuit."

"Don't lose him," Troy said as he slowed his F-16 to come around. "He's invisible on radar."

"Roger that. I've got him northbound over Greenbelt, flying very low."

RAYMOND HARRIS HAD NOT TURNED TO FIGHT. HE WAS single-minded about his mission. It was a strike mission, and he had a high-value target that he must strike.

Albert Bacon Fachearon sat at Camp David defying the authority that had been given to Harris by Congress.

Articles of impeachment had been passed.

Duly constituted authorities had been authorized to use deadly force to remove him.

Raymond Harris was the duly constituted authority.

Albert Bacon Fachearon must go. Deadly force must be used.

Somewhere at the Camp David complex, Fachearon was hiding.

Raymond Harris did not know exactly where, but he did not care.

He might be at the large, hotel-sized Laurel Lodge, or in the comfortable presidential quarters at Aspen Lodge—or he might be skulking in the theoretically bombproof bunkers beneath.

Raymond Harris didn't care.

With a twenty-kiloton nuclear weapon coming down upon his head, Albert Bacon Fachearon would not survive.

CHAPTER 51

Camp David, Frederick County, Maryland

"ARE YOU WORRIED ABOUT YOUR JOB?" ARON ARNOLD asked the young U.S. Navy petty officer who was escorting him. Officially, Camp David is a landlocked Navy base, Naval Support Facility Thurmont, so the uniformed staffers are mainly from that branch of the service.

"No, sir," Tiffanie Talleigh replied nervously, her hand unconsciously brushing the holster that contained her M9 sidearm. When this slender, average-looking man with short-cropped hair had driven up to the main gate in a Firehawk Lexus an hour ago and had explained his purpose, she had been assigned to follow him wherever he went at the facility. Had conditions not been in such turmoil, had Camp David not been so thoroughly understaffed because of the crisis, there would have been a whole platoon of Marines escorting Arnold, but today, it was just Petty Officer Tiffanie Talleigh.

"Are you nervous that you're on the wrong side of history?" Tiffanie asked.

It had been too early for lunch when Albert Bacon Fachearon had invited Arnold to remain, but he had seen nothing wrong with stopping in at the post commissary for a cup of coffee. He was in no hurry to get back to the mess in Washington.

"I don't see this change of direction in history as having 'sides.' I think that it's just what it is," Arnold said as they walked beneath the dogwood trees. It was a cold day, and the gloomy, gray clouds added to an atmosphere of despair that seemed to hang over the people whom they passed.

"Like the president said, it's a coup," she replied. "These guys . . . Kynelty and Harris . . . like they overthrew the government!"

"I don't really want to get into a debate with you." Arnold smiled. "But I could remind you that this is the will of Congress, which I believe is elected?"

"They passed that bill this morning with *tanks* on the streets outside."

"Even if that mattered, what about the House of Representatives *yesterday*?" Arnold said in a *gotcha* tone.

The young petty officer had no reply, just a stern, angry glance at Arnold.

"Where are you from?" Arnold asked.

"Why is that important?"

"Just making conversation."

"Logan, Utah . . . and yes, sir, I'm LDS . . . Mormon."

"Then you answer to a higher authority than that flag over there?" Arnold observed, nodding at one of the camp's many flagpoles.

"What are you saying?"

"I'm saying that authority—and allegiance—are relative."

"What authority do you answer to—the authority of Firehawk?"

"I'm just a pilot."

"What are you doing *here*?"

"My job."

"Harris must be running short of staff if he's sending pilots to do a diplomat's job," Tiffanie said, apparently pleased with herself for getting a verbal dagger through a chink in Arnold's suave armor.

"Touché." Arnold laughed. He liked her spunk.

"Do you really believe that the American people are going to tolerate Harris and Kynelty running the government?"

"Like I said . . . Congress already does."

"What happens to you if this thing unravels?"

"I'll get another job." Arnold shrugged. "What happens to you if it *doesn't*?"

"It *will*, sir," she said, her tone uncertain. "It *has* to. This has never happened before."

"That means that it can't happen *now?*" Arnold asked.

As they reached the commissary, they heard the sound of a low-flying jet aircraft. Both Aron Arnold and the young petty officer craned their necks, searching the sky for a sight of the plane, but the sound died away.

CHAPTER 52

The Skies over Northern Maryland

"FALCON THREE, THE BOGIE IS CHANGING DIRECTION," Jenna said, the trace of relief in her voice reacting to the fact that Harris was heading away from Camp David.

"Roger that, Falcon Two," Troy confirmed. "But he's coming at you."

As a HAWX Program bird, the Raven was very capable of extreme-high-altitude ops, but Raymond Harris had been flying extremely *low* to evade his two pursuers. The Raven may have been capable of speeds in excess of Mach 3, but to use that capability would have hampered Harris's ability to put his B61 nuclear weapon on target, so he was also flying well under Mach 1.

"He's trying to gain altitude," Troy shouted as Harris suddenly began climbing. "Let's keep him low!"

"Roger that," Jenna replied.

Had Harris been carrying a conventional weapon, a low-level pass would have been just what the doctor ordered for a perfect strike on the target, but with a nuke, a low-level pass meant that the Raven would have been incinerated along with the victim. The fact that Harris seemed to want to climb indicated that the weapon had not been fused with a delay mechanism.

For Troy and Jenna, their job was to keep Harris low and away from the Catoctin Mountain retreat until they could line up a kill shot.

Getting that kill shot was easier said than done. Only Troy had the use of his gun, and the heat-seeking infrared targeting capability of their AIM-9 Sidewinders worked only so long as there was heat to detect. The Raven, like most recent jet fighters, such as the F-22 Raptor, had suppression systems that physically masked the heat signature of the engines.

Initially, Harris had flown out of Andrews Air Force Base on a north-by-northwest heading that would have taken him more or less straight to Camp David. Had it not been for the two F-16s, he would have come in at about nine thousand feet, released the guided B61, and used the Raven's extreme vertical-acceleration capability to exit the target area without getting cooked.

His plans upset, Harris banked right, heading eastward over the Baltimore metro area, trying to gain altitude while shaking off the two F-16s.

"He's climbing," Jenna said angrily.

"Take a shot," Troy said. "Get on his ass and take a shot."

"Okay . . . but if I miss, the Sidewinder comes crashing into Baltimore. If I don't, the Raven burns a hole in the city. He knows that . . . that's why he's flying this way . . . buying time . . . buying altitude . . . figuring I won't shoot."

She accelerated, trying to overtake the Raven, get close and minimize the possibility of a bad shot.

As Harris raced over downtown Baltimore and the broad mouth of the Patapsco River, Jenna closed to within half a mile.

"Closer . . . dammit . . . closer."

In the split second that she pondered just thumbing off a Sidewinder anyhow, Harris jinked hard to the right.

If his plan had been to turn south and continue over populated areas, he missed that by a split second. Suddenly, he and Jenna were over Chesapeake Bay, and Troy was there as well. Coming in at a different angle, he had nearly managed to cut Harris off in his turn.

In that turn, the Raven slowed slightly, and Troy could see the boiling yellow back end of the Raven's two engines.

This is as good a shot as I'm going to get, Troy thought to himself, and a Sidewinder ripped off his wingtip.

It seemed like slow motion as the contrail corkscrewed toward the Raven.

Far below, boaters and fishermen on Chesapeake Bay watched the scene above with great amazement. The three jet fighters had been climbing, but were still relatively low, so the noise was earsplitting—just like at an air show.

They watched as the fast jets raced across the sky and as the faster missile snaked its way from one jet toward another.

In that twinkling of an eye that their eyes had to witness the scene, they were aware that this was not an air show—this was life-or-death.

The dart-shaped jet turned just as the contrail reached it, and the trajectories of the two objects diverged.

As quickly as the whole scene in the sky had materialized, the jets were all gone, into the distance and over the horizon.

The contrail remained. With its forward momentum slowed considerably, it arced downward toward the waves of Chesapeake Bay.

For observers who had expected a *bang* when the thing hit the water, there was only a disappointing splash, a column of white water, and then nothing.

CHAPTER 53

The Skies over Chesapeake Bay

"WHO *ARE* YOU?" RAYMOND HARRIS GROWLED.

Nobody answered. Nobody was listening.

He was flying radio silent, answering to no one, because he was Raymond Harris, who answered to no one.

He had climbed into the Raven for a twenty-minute strike mission, planning to be back at the White House by midafternoon, reporting the results. He would tell a world waiting with baited breath that Albert Bacon Fachearon was no more. The weapon chosen to dispense with Fachearon, deliberately chosen by Raymond Harris, would get the attention of everyone and underscore the fact that he and Kynelty meant business.

Soon the Fachearon era would be in ashes—literally. The Transition would have occurred.

In the grand plan of The Transition, the United States would move forward as it was meant to move forward—smoothly, expeditiously, and under the steady, guiding hand of Raymond Harris.

But the plans changed.

The last thing that Harris could have imagined as he began his takeoff roll was tracers racing past his cockpit.

"Who *are* you?" Raymond Harris howled.

Out of nowhere, someone was shooting at him.

Harris, who had flown combat missions going back to the second Gulf War, considered himself a fighter pilot of the first order—even if he was a bit rusty.

Was he *really* all that rusty?

He had certainly proven himself when he neatly side-stepped that bastard in the F-16 who was shooting at him when he took off.

"Who *are* you?" Raymond Harris barked.

Where had this F-16 come from?

Wait, there were *two*.

"Who *are* you?" Raymond Harris snarled.

Where had they come from?

Somebody was trying to interfere. Had Fachearon somehow called in the U.S. Air Force to aid him? Even so, how had they managed to catch up to the Raven so fast? Just a few seconds sooner and this fabulous product of the HAWX Program would have been smoldering crud on the Andrews Air Force Base runway. It was a miss, Harris breathed thankfully, but it was a near miss.

Harris had intended to continue the mission as planned, but with F-16s diving all around him like crows attacking a hawk, he couldn't fly his mission profile, the "low-high-higher" profile that would keep him from winding up as a radioactive ember.

"Shake them . . . gotta shake them," Harris muttered as he turned hard to the right and dashed across Baltimore.

"Shit," was all Harris could mutter as he found himself over Chesapeake Bay presenting a clear shot to his pursuers.

"Shit," Harris repeated as he heard the *ping* of a radar lock-on and saw that one of his pursuers *took* that shot.

But the Raven performed. Thanks to its heat-shielding characteristics, the AIM-9 lost its lock-on like a blind man in a crowded room. Nevertheless, being shot at raised Harris's ire considerably.

"You wanna fight, bastards?" Harris shouted, again out of the hearing range of anyone.

Harris was also armed but had chosen evasion as a defensive tactic—until now.

Like the older F-22 Raptor, the Raven carried all of its armament within an internal weapons bay to preserve the clean lines and stealth characteristics of the aircraft. Like the Raptor, the Raven was capable of carrying six

AIM-120F Advanced Medium-Range Air-to-Air Missiles. They were the latest variant of the weapons acronymed as AMRAAMs but known to aircrews informally as Slammers. However, with the B61 weapon installed in the Raven's central weapons bay, all but two of the Slammers had been removed that morning. At the time, Harris gave no thought to having to use them. Now he was glad to have them.

Heading south over Chesapeake Bay, he was putting five miles between himself and Camp David every second, so he yanked back on the stick and threw the Raven into a climbing right turn that took him over Maryland's Western Shore.

He had given up wondering who was in those two F-16s. He just wanted them dead, and he knew that the Raven plus its Slammers was more than a match for F-16s and Sidewinders.

Harris lit up the datalink guidance system for the AMRAAMs as he came out of the turn, acquiring a target almost immediately. He didn't especially care which one—there were two targets and he had two AMRAAMs. He could see on his radar that one of the two F-16s had greatly overshot him and only one now stood in his way.

One of the Raven's weapons bay doors popped open.

The F-16 pilot was smart, beginning to jam the Slammer's radar lock-on instantly. However, Harris had an ally in the form of the missile's home-on-jamming capability.

As soon as the AMRAAM detected an attempt to jam its radar homing system, it switched from active homing to passive.

Harris fired.

The AMRAAM left the rail homing not on the F-16 itself, but on the F-16's own radar-jamming signal.

Having fired, and having left the destruction of the other aircraft in the capable, albeit inhuman, hands of the missile, Harris banked left and headed north by northwest.

"Have to get back on target," he muttered to himself.

With one F-16 going down in flames, and another too far away to catch him now, it was time to resume his primary mission. He could deal with the second F-16 while its pilot gawked at the mushroom cloud over the Catoctins.

Suddenly, there was a pinging in the Raven's cockpit.

What?

Harris had been made. He had been acquired in a missile lock-on.

Who?

On his scope, there was the unmistakable image of two aircraft pursuing him.

How?

The Slammer must have been slammed!

Harris knew that just about the only way to achieve a lock-on against the stealthy Raven was from directly behind. Essentially, the F-16 was looking up his ass, up the high-Fahrenheit tailpipes of his afterburning engines.

Once again, Harris threw the Raven off course to save his ass.

Harris knew that under the circumstances, just about the only way to *break* the F-16's lock-on against the Raven was to get out from in front of the F-16.

Once again, Harris found himself flying *away* from Camp David.

CHAPTER 54

Camp David, Frederick County, Maryland

"CARE TO SIT DOWN?" ARON ARNOLD ASKED THE YOUNG
petty officer. "I'm not going to bite you."

"No, sir," Tiffanie Talleigh replied. "Rather not, sir."

Arnold sat at a table near the window of the commissary sipping his coffee. His escort remained standing—nervously—at a discreet distance. Perhaps he wouldn't bite, she thought, but a man associated with the overthrow of the government that she was sworn to protect was certainly dangerous.

"How do you expect this whole thing to play out today?" Arnold asked in a making-conversation tone.

"Can't say, sir. Wouldn't speculate."

"Above your pay grade?" Arnold smiled.

"Couldn't say, sir, I just don't know."

"It's above *my* pay grade too," he admitted. "You're a lot like me in a lotta ways."

"How so?"

"Like we were talking on the walk over here . . . we're just a couple of people doing our jobs and following orders . . . right?"

"Can't speak for you," she said suspiciously. "Why are you here?"

"You know why I'm here, Petty Officer Talleigh. You've been with me every step of the way since I walked through that gate. You drove me to Laurel Lodge in your vehicle . . . you listened to what I told Fachearon . . ."

"I mean, like what are *you* doing here?"

"You mean, me personally?"

"You said you were a pilot. Why did they send a pilot to drive up into the mountains in a Lexus?"

"Why did they send a twentysomething petty officer to guard a guy whom they see as a traitor?"

He watched her blush slightly. She was obviously on the long side of thirtysomething, but nobody ever lost ground underestimating the age of a woman over thirty.

"They have confidence in my ability to do a job," Tiffanie replied.

"There you are." Arnold nodded as he took another sip of coffee. "That was, I assume, why I was sent on this little errand this morning. Like we were saying . . . we're both doing our jobs."

"What do you hope to gain by this?"

"Gain?" Arnold asked. "By coming up here? I was sent here to ask Fachearon to give it up and get with the program."

"I meant, like what do *you* expect to gain by being involved in this 'program' as you call it?"

"I keep telling you . . . it's my *job* . . . I'm paid to do what Firehawk needs me to do. It's nothing more than that. I'm a very straightforward person."

Tiffanie Talleigh just shook her head.

"I think we'd better go, sir," she said assertively. Her resuming the use of the formal term indicated to Arnold that their chat was over. "The president indicated that you could stay for lunch; are you staying for lunch, or not?"

"I guess not," Arnold said. "Not that it hasn't been a fun conversation. Maybe I should check in with him again—y'know, give him one more chance to reconsider."

"I don't think so," Tiffanie said tentatively. "The president's orders were explicit. You were to stay for lunch, then leave. Since you're not staying for lunch—"

"What if he *did* want to reconsider the Firehawk proposal?" Arnold. "You'd be the one who made the call that stood in the way . . . made it *not* happen."

"But he said—"

"But he could change his mind."

"I don't know," Tiffanie said, furrowing her brow.

"What can it hurt?" Arnold insisted. "He'd just tell

me to get the hell out of Camp David and never come back—"

"I believe that he already said that."

"What if?"

"I'll check," she said.

"Petty Officer Talleigh for the chief of staff's desk," she said, keying her two-way radio. "I'm with the subject . . . and he has a question . . . over."

"This is the chief of staff's office, Petty Officer," crackled the reply. "What is the question?"

"He wants to know whether the president will reconsider his proposal, over."

"What the . . . he what?"

"He wants to know whether the president will reconsider his proposal."

There was a long, crackling pause before the man who worked for Fachearon's chief of staff responded.

"Petty Officer Talleigh?"

"Roger."

"They tell me to tell you to tell him that the president is absolutely not interested in reconsidering, but he has something to tell the Firehawk man . . . so bring him back up to Laurel."

"Aye-aye, sir. Petty Officer Talleigh, out."

"The president will speak with you," she said. "But don't hold your breath about talking him into anything."

"Yeah . . . I heard." Arnold nodded.

They exchanged no words on the walk back to Laurel

Lodge. They had exhausted their topics of conversation. There was nothing more to be said. The mood was as dark and gloomy as the weather.

For Albert Bacon Fachearon, though, there was one more thing.

"Mr. Arnold," he said, meeting Raymond Harris's emissary on the doorstep. "Tell Raymond Harris . . . tell him emphatically . . . that I will not relinquish the presidency unless or until there is a trial. Under the Constitution, an impeached president can't be removed until convicted in a Senate trial . . . a fact obviously lost on Raymond Harris."

Fachearon was angry. Fachearon was taking it personally. Fachearon could feel his systolic blood pressure surging toward two hundred.

"Suit yourself," Aron Arnold said calmly, not taking it personally. "I'm here because I'm ordered . . . and apparently the senators and congressmen gave my boss the authority to issue that order."

"It will suit me to do as I have said I will do," Fachearon replied, unnerved that Aron Arnold betrayed no emotion, while he could feel the pressure of the blood throbbing in his neck.

"I will convey this information to the appropriate parties." Arnold nodded calmly.

Overhead, they heard the distant thunder of jet engines, and all eyes turned skyward. The clouds were low, and there was nothing to be seen. The sound soon died way.

* * *

AS ARON ARNOLD BADE TIFFANIE TALLEIGH GOOD-BYE, he could sense her breathing a sigh of relief.

His Lexus remained as he had left it, the lone vehicle in the visitor parking lot outside the Camp David main gate. As he opened the door, he took out his cell phone. He decided that it would be a good idea to check in.

He dialed, pressed the send button, and put the phone to his ear.

Nothing.

What?

How could he have a dead battery?

He looked at the phone. Everything about it looked normal.

He turned it over and slid out the battery. Maybe some dirt had gotten on the contacts.

Then he saw it.

Someone had inserted a GK356a4 high-power, miniaturized homing transmitter.

When could this have happened?

The only time that he had taken his phone out of his pocket since he set foot at Camp David was when it went through the metal detector when he had arrived. None of the guards had touched it.

When was the last time that it had been out of his sight?

Then he remembered.

It had been in his jacket pocket that morning at the White House. In turn, he had left his jacket on the back of a chair in a conference room while he went to the bathroom.

Who?

Damn. *Shit. Fuck.*

A half mile down the mountain road, Aron Arnold stopped the Lexus, got out, and tossed the cell phone as far as he could into the thick brush.

CHAPTER 55

The Skies over Northern Maryland

"FALCON THREE, DO YOU HAVE A SHOT?" JENNA asked.

"Gotta get a lock-on," Troy said, gritting his teeth.

By this time, Raymond Harris knew he was up against someone good. He had tried to run, single-mindedly trying to get back on his trajectory to the target.

However, to do this was to put his vulnerable hindquarters into the eyes of the F-16's Sidewinders. Each time, he heard the ping of a lock-on. Each time, he was able to maneuver out of the way, but with each maneuver, he was off course for his target.

The Raven and the F-16 twisted and turned across the sky as Troy tried to achieve lock-on and as Harris tried both to prevent this and to push the Raven itself into a shooting position.

They had gotten into the dogfight maneuver that dogfighters call a scissors, a series of repeated turn reversals in which the aircraft being chased tries both to stay out of the line of fire *and* twist itself in such a way as to cause the pursuer to overshoot. The idea is that the hunted suddenly becomes the hunter.

Harris groaned and cursed.

The HAWX Program had designed the Raven to be as maneuverable as it was fast, but with seven hundred pounds of nuclear bomb in its central weapons bay, the Raven was not as agile as it might have been otherwise.

Troy thumbed off a burst of twenty-millimeter rounds as the Raven crossed his pipper.

They went wild, but at least Harris knew he was there.

Aha!

For a split second, Harris stopped maneuvering.

It is a natural impulse when you are taking fire to stop moving, and Harris had succumbed.

It is a natural impulse, when you see your quarry pause, to take a shot, and Troy succumbed.

The Sidewinder got its lock-on and streaked forward.

The distance was short—probably less than half a mile.

It is a natural impulse when you catch yourself pausing in a pursuit to move quickly to compensate for a moment of inaction, and Harris moved quickly.

He banked hard to the left.

Troy watched the Sidewinder arc left.

Harris scissored to the right.

The Sidewinder was going too fast to turn so quickly, and it missed him by barely a few feet.

It is a natural impulse when you are chasing your prey to push yourself to catch up. So it was with Troy.

However, he moved too fast, and he slid past the Raven.

He had overshot his prey.

The hunted was suddenly the hunter.

The pinging came, and Troy reacted.

He was in a left turn already, so he rolled hard left.

To evade a heat-seeking missile, you have to obscure the heat source. This was far more difficult for the F-16 than for the Raven. The F-16 does not have the advantage, like the Raven, of the heat signature of its exhaust duct being shielded. Therefore, evasive action must be *very* evasive.

Troy banked into a roll, rolled into a dive, and dove into a diving turn—all in an effort to outmaneuver the missile from which he could not hide.

JENNA HAD KEPT PACE AS SHE WATCHED TROY CHAS-ING the Raven across the sky in a fast-paced pursuit, flying above and behind the two aircraft as they raced through Maryland airspace.

They were above the clouds, with no view of the ground, so Jenna had no bearings on how close or how far they were in relation to Camp David. They may have failed in their efforts to keep Harris too low to fly his strike mission—they were now above fifteen thousand feet—but at least they were keeping him from his primary mission.

Jenna watched the two aircraft scissoring across the sky, silently urging Troy to take a shot and knowing that he was the type to take it the moment he could.

However, suddenly, it was the F-16 that was in the lead.

The hunter was the hunted.

As she watched Harris launch an AMRAAM, and as she saw Troy roll out and dive, Jenna seized the initiative and swung in behind Harris.

She could sense by the way that he rolled his wedge-shaped aircraft that Harris heard the pinging of her lock-on.

She fired.

Another hunter had become the hunted.

THREE WARPLANES.

Two missiles.

Crowded skies.

Dangerous skies.

Harris's AIM-120 Slammer was gaining on a desperate Troy Loensch, while the electronic brain of Jenna's

AIM-9 Sidewinder sought to maintain its lock-on to Raymond Harris and the Raven.

Troy had one chance, and that was to use the Slammer's speed against it. He would allow it to follow him into a turn, then turn abruptly in the opposite direction, knowing—or at least *hoping*—that its speed would restrict it from so tight a turn.

Troy rolled into a hard left, and prepared to turn right.

That was when he saw it.

Just a quarter of a mile away, and on the same heading as Troy, was a US Airways Airbus A321-200, on approach to Baltimore-Washington Airport with about 170 passengers aboard.

Crowded skies.

Dangerous skies.

As Troy turned, the AMRAAM lost its lock-on for a split second—a desired effect.

As it is programmed to do, the AMRAAM sought to reacquire the broken lock-on.

It did.

However, the lock-on was not now to the F-16's F110 turbofan, but to the larger, hotter CFM56-5 turbofan engine hanging beneath the starboard wing of the US Airways jetliner—very much *not* an effect that Troy had desired.

* * *

JENNA WATCHED HER OWN SIDEWINDER CHASE THE Raven, knowing that she had denied Raymond Harris the luxury of watching his AMRAAM chase Troy's F-16.

She did not notice the Airbus A321-200 until she glanced away from Harris for a second to watch the AMRAAM's contrail coiling across the sky toward Troy.

She saw Troy's F-16 slip out of the trajectory of the AMRAAM and the trajectories of the two separate. It was not until that moment that she saw the red and blue tail of the jetliner.

The crew on the flight deck may have seen the AMRAAM, although it was approaching from behind. They certainly had seen it on their radarscopes, and they were probably calling a mayday to the Baltimore tower.

They banked the aircraft slightly but were unable to muster serious evasive action.

Jenna saw the white contrail streak into the engine and watched helplessly as the right wing dissolved in a dirty orange fireball.

The force of the blast tossed the one-winged jetliner into a roll, and soon it was tumbling uncontrollably across the sky. Pity the passengers who had not been knocked unconscious by their being thrown into a five-G spin.

CHAPTER 56

The Skies over Northern Maryland

RAYMOND HARRIS WAS STARTLED, EVEN SADDENED, by the sight of the jetliner—slammed by his own Slammer—cartwheeling across the sky. For the man who was prepared to drop a nuclear weapon on the president of the United States, it was a rather paradoxical reaction.

Was it that the sight of 170 innocent people dying a frightening death was more real than the abstract notion of a thermonuclear blast?

It didn't take long for him to snap out of it and to place his mind back in the moment.

How many missiles had been fired?

He had dodged three. That left just one missile left between the two F-16s.

He had fired two. As the Raven carried no gun, he was depleted of defensive armament—but the F-16s need not know that.

Where were they now?

He saw one—and then the other F-16.

The nearest one, flying about two thousand feet beneath him, had bare wingtips. It was unarmed.

JENNA HAD LITTLE TIME TO PROCESS THE SIGHT OF the aluminum coffin with its 170 screaming souls before it disappeared into a cloud.

Meanwhile, her own Sidewinder had missed hitting anything. The unstoppable Raven was still in the air. Damn those people at HAWX who had invented this machine.

She had no way of knowing that the pinging she heard, that of the Raven locking on to her F-16, was a lock-on with missiles that did not exist.

"Falcon Two, this is Falcon Three. I got your back."

Maybe Falcon Three could distract Harris long enough for Jenna to escape.

As Jenna dove toward the clouds, preparing to evade the imaginary AMRAAM, Troy was diving from above to try to save her.

Troy expected to see the contrail of an AMRAAM at any moment as he accelerated toward the Raven.

Suddenly, he saw nothing. First Jenna, then Harris, fell into the boiling cumulus.

On his radarscope, they were just tumbling green specks, like a pair of fireflies on methedrine.

HARRIS PUSHED HIS CHARADE AS HE PUSHED THE fleeing F-16—down, down, down.

One moment, they were falling through the clouds, the next they were beneath them. At last, having reached nine thousand feet, he broke off his pursuit and checked his GPS coordinates. Somewhere out there, and he could now see *exactly where*, was Camp David.

Aron Arnold should have arrived by now. He had gone to Camp David, briefed with orders to *stall*. Harris had instructed him to linger as long as necessary to give Albert Bacon Fachearon *two*—not just one—opportunities to consider Harris's demand for capitulation. Arnold would also have arrived bearing a GK356a4 high-power, miniaturized homing transmitter—although the presence of this gadget had not been part of his briefing.

Raymond Harris had no idea where Fachearon was within the Camp David complex, but he did not care. The blast radius of the B61's active ingredients was considerable—but best of all, the weapon would be directed to its target by the GK356a4 transmitter that was ideally

standing within a few feet or a few yards of Albert Bacon
Fachearon.

"FALCON THREE, HE'S BROKEN OFF HIS ATTACK ON
me," Jenna said. "He's broken off and is heading toward
the target."

"Got him," Troy promised hopefully, willing it to
be true.

He lit his afterburner and felt the F-16 lurch as it went
supersonic.

At nine thousand feet, the two planes raced toward the
crest of the Catoctin Mountains. Had they crossed the
path of any other jetliner in the crowded northern Maryland skies, it would have been catastrophic—but quick.

Troy could not afford to think about such a thing.
Closing to within missile range was the only thing on
his mind—it had to be.

Troy knew that the Raven was fast—probably capable
of something north of Mach 3—but he knew that Harris
couldn't deliver a payload from an internal weapons bay
at that speed. He would probably have to slow to below
Mach 1. Troy still had one Sidewinder and one chance to
catch the Raven before Harris got to Camp David.

HARRIS WAS RUNNING HARD AND FAST. HE HAD PICKED
up the GK356a4 and was homing in on it.

It was a matter of minutes.

He glanced at his radarscope as he throttled back for his bomb run.

Damn. There was an F-16 still on his tail. It was many miles back, but still coming. It had to be the one that still had a live Sidewinder. Harris made a fast, educated guess that whoever the pilot was, he would wait to fire until he was at a no-miss distance.

Harris figured that he had time to reach his release point.

Once the B61 was away, he could ratchet up the Raven's throttle and outrun any F-16. He could even wring enough speed out of the Raven to outdistance the Mach 2.5 Sidewinder.

But that was then; Harris was still in a now that meant covering fifty miles of Maryland countryside at subsonic speeds with his weapons bay door open.

As he urged the Raven forward, he heard the pinging of a lock-on.

IN HIS F-16, TROY SAW THE RAVEN SLOW AND KNEW that this was it—the bomb run.

Could he catch Harris and take a no-miss shot?

Never mind. Lock on now!

The Sidewinder had an effective range of around ten miles. He was almost there. He could ride the lock-on all the way.

Raymond Harris, meanwhile, still had an advantage. His maneuverability options increased proportionally to his slower speed. Because he had only one vulnerable spot—straight back—any evasive action, no matter how slight, was potentially effective. He could remain on course, weaving slightly, and still interrupt the F-16's lock-on.

Troy watched his lock-on stop and start, flicker and hiccup, like a bad connection on his iPod jack.

There was nothing he could do but put the pedal to the metal and get closer to the Raven.

Seven miles separated the two aircraft.

Inside the Raven, Harris dodged between trying to interrupt and evade the pinging and maintaining his own lock-on to the GK356a4 at Camp David.

Six miles.

Rocking and rolling, Harris raced onward as the F-16 gained on him. He counted the seconds before he could arm the B61 for his strike against Albert Bacon Fachearon—and all that for which he stood.

Five miles.

When? Troy sweated the decision to shoot.

Four miles.

Okay, this is it.

"Missiles hot," he announced.

Jenna was barely two miles away, also on afterburner and following Troy into battle.

"Roger, Falcon Three, you are a go with missiles hot."

Three miles.

Okay, dammit, this is it.

"Fox Two!" Troy shouted.

CHAPTER 57

The Skies over Northern Maryland

IN THE COCKPIT OF THE RAVEN, RAYMOND HARRIS battled to evade the F-16 lock-on, while also fighting to keep his own weapon homed in on its target.

Each time the pinging stopped, it bounced back a moment later.

When the pinging stopped and stayed stopped, he couldn't believe his luck.

Was there something wrong with the system?

He glanced at his mirror. There was no coiling contrail back there. The F-16's Sidewinder was a dud.

Harris couldn't believe his luck.

There was no contrail, but there *was* the F-16.

The bastard must be coming at nearly Mach 2.

Suddenly, Harris felt the turbulence of the aircraft

roaring past him. The blast of air nearly caused him to lose control.

The bastard was on top of him, then a short distance away.

He was matching his speed to the Raven.

What was the bastard trying to do?

Harris considered evasive action, but he was seconds from the release point.

The F-16 was so close that he could read the specs stenciled on the tail.

The F-16 was so close that he imagined feeling the heat of its engine.

The F-16 was so close that he felt its wing touch the forward fuselage of the Raven.

This was the last thing that Raymond Harris ever felt, for in the next infinitesimal slice of time, the two aircraft became one, an enormous ball of wreckage.

Imagine two dozen tons of scrap metal hurtling through the air at several hundred miles per hour, a mile and a half above a verdant, wooded hillside.

Fragments, many fragments, of scrap metal spun off the main ball of wreckage and began plunging earthward.

Within that ball of wreckage, the remnants of what had been a human being were pulverized and shredded by the slicing and dicing of a thousand knifelike shards.

High above, Troy watched the burning wreckage tumble, lose momentum, and fall. He hung from the straps of his parachute, having punched out of that mass of scrap metal at the moment that it had ceased to be two separate airplanes. When his second Sidewinder—his second hand-me-down Virginia Air National Guard Sidewinder—had failed, Troy decided to ram the Raven and hope for the best.

Watching it fall, from his silent perch in the sky, the wreckage seemed so unreal, so far away in both time and space. Yet Troy knew that within it were the remnants of a nuclear weapon whose fireball would very much encompass him in both time and space—if it had been armed.

Had Harris armed the weapon?

He knew that all of this was happening close to Camp David, but he didn't know exactly how near.

Had Harris armed the weapon?

JENNA HAD WATCHED THE COLLISION AND HAD SEEN the fireball plummet downward.

She had heard Troy call his "Fox Two" and had seen nothing happen. She knew what he had decided to do, and she had breathed a sigh of relief at the sight of the single parachute.

She shared Troy's thoughts about the potential nuclear incineration and orbited the scene cautiously.

Like Troy, she knew that if the weapon had been armed, any second could be the end.

Conversely, they both knew that an unarmed weapon was virtually harmless. Like the black boxes on airliners, they were designed to withstand enormous concussions without breaking apart. There had been a whole series of events during the Cold War, known as Broken Arrow incidents, in which aircraft carrying nukes had crashed and the unarmed weapons had *not* exploded. There is always the danger of a radiation leak, but only remotely of an explosion.

With each passing moment, both Troy and Jenna breathed easier.

As she flew close and saw the dangling figure wave to her, Jenna felt enormous relief.

However, her relief was short-lived.

What next?

Had this been the pivotal closing scene in a movie, she would return to her base, welcomed by the open arms of her compatriots.

This was not a movie. Jenna had no base, and her only comrade was floating to a landing in the Catoctin Mountains.

What could she do?

Where would she land the surviving one of a pair of stolen F-16s? How could she land in a country now ruled by Firehawk after she and her comrade had just killed Raymond Harris?

* * *

LANDING AMID THE PINES IN THE DOGWOOD BRUSH was challenging, but Troy managed to avoid getting his parachute snarled in a tree. He was scratched and bleeding, but they were superficial wounds. All his moving parts moved as they were supposed to move. His bad leg ached, but he recalled the old adage stating that any landing you walk away from is a good landing.

He was also reminded of that day so long ago when he and Jenna had both come down in the inhospitable Denakil Desert. The impulse then, as now—as on that mountain back in the Colville National Forest with Hal Coughlin—was to evade.

He sat on the hillside beneath darkening clouds, listening to an impulse.

Today had been a progression of impulsive acts, unencumbered by contemplation. It began in the dark of night with the impulsive need to have Jenna's body and to succumb to her impulsive need for his. That morning—it seemed so long ago now—they had awakened to their mutual impulse to stop Raymond Harris, to fight Raymond Harris, and to kill Raymond Harris.

Troy had landed in these woods, reacting on an impulse born on those Colville woods.

Evade.

Evading capture was an impulse, but with it also came a moment for contemplation.

Who was he evading? What was he evading?

First there was the impending rainstorm that felt as though it could start any moment.

Next, however, Troy contemplated *who* he was trying to evade.

The man who had tried to kill him, and who had tried to kill Albert Bacon Fachearon, was no more, but this death did not change the fact that Firehawk and Cernavoda still ruled the United States. What had happened here had bought Fachearon some time. It had probably bought him his life, but it had not bought him back his job.

The death of Raymond Harris had not stopped The Transition.

Removing Harris had done no lasting harm to the cabal of Firehawk and Cernavoda, and certainly not to Layton Kynelty, who would now emerge stronger than ever from Harris's shadow. If anything, Troy had saved Firehawk and Cernavoda the embarrassment of having to justify a nuclear strike within the United States.

As the first cold drops of rain began pattering on the dogwood leaves, Troy headed for the cover of some trees. The forest was thicker over there, and he could probably stay relatively dry as he made his way off this mountain.

He had yet to decide where exactly he was headed. The only thing on his mind at this moment was self-preservation—the impulse to get as far from the crash site as possible.

CHAPTER 58

Morgan County, West Virginia

STATE TROOPER RALPH OVERGEIST HAD BEEN FOL-
lowing the news all day on his radio as he cruised up
State Route 29. He kept the news channel on low—he
didn't want it to interfere with his hearing calls on his
two-way radio—but he did keep it *on*.

How could he not?

Washington, D.C., was in a heck of a pickle this morning. There were tanks on the streets and an arrest warrant out for the president. Ralph didn't care too much
for Albert Bacon Fachearon. He had not voted for the
man, but it sure seemed that an arrest warrant was a bit
over the top.

He hadn't thought too much about the PMCs taking
over the federal government. It did not directly affect

him. He figured it would be a long, long time before anybody decided to let them take over the West Virginia Highway Patrol.

Hampshire County and Morgan County, which were Ralph's beat, had been real quiet, quieter than normal, today. Of course, it was a Saturday, and he figured most folks were home watching the fireworks in Washington on television.

Ralph Overgeist was a few miles north of Slanesville when he rounded a bend and saw a woman walking alongside the road. She had long, unkempt blond hair and ill-fitting clothes. The boots she was wearing looked a few sizes too big. Of course, mountain people didn't dress all fancy like folks in the cities, like over in Martinsburg.

It seemed a bit out of the ordinary to see her just walking down Highway 29 out here in the middle of nowhere. A lot of people walked everywhere they went in this part of West Virginia, but still, something didn't seem right.

"Good morning, ma'am," he said, pulling over and rolling down his window. "Is everything all right?"

"Thank y'all for stopping." She smiled. "Everything's just fine . . . but since you're asking, I was wondering if I could get a lift?"

"Where you going?" Ralph asked. He couldn't quite place her drawl, but she definitely wasn't a city girl.

"Somewhere that I could catch a Greyhound . . . I'm trying to get back to D.C."

"What are you doing way out here without a vehicle?"

"It's a long story . . . I guess you could say that I was chasin' after a fella."

"He *left* you out here?"

"No . . . actually, he didn't even know I was following him. I'm over him now though. He's *long* gone."

THERE WAS LITTLE TO DO FOR TWO HOURS AT THE Greyhound depot in Martinsburg other than to watch people or watch the television set that was mounted to the wall. Since most of the people were doing little other than watching television, Jenna wound up watching it as well.

She sat there in the uncomfortable Day-Glo pink fiberglass seat, wearing the clothes that she had stolen from a clothesline as she was hiking out of the woods where her parachute had brought her down.

She sat there watching history unfold on the television—or at least today's crossroads chapter of American history. It was a blizzard of alerts, updates, and breaking news. Reports of Raymond Harris's death were confirmed. He had died in the crash of a highly advanced aircraft that Firehawk was testing. Many people had seen other aircraft in the area, and some had reported missiles being fired. There was speculation that rogue elements within the U.S. Air Force had killed Harris.

What kind of a world was it, Jenna wondered, where those who had killed the man who had helped engineer a coup were considered rogue?

There was no mention of a nuclear device, nor would there be. The viewers would never get to know about this, but apparently Albert Bacon Fachearon *had* heard.

If not, he had at least gotten the message. One of the breaking news items confirmed that he had tendered his resignation and was negotiating his return to his home state in exchange for a pledge of no public statements.

She thought of Troy Loensch and how preposterous his tale of The Transition had once seemed: his tale of PMCs overthrowing the government.

She also thought about how her relationship with him had evolved. For the first couple of years she had known him, she had found his asshole behavior nauseating, but revulsion had turned to tolerance, and tolerance had turned to her deciding that he was not so bad after all. This realization had opened the door to lust, and the realization that—whatever his faults, and there were many—he was *very* not-so-bad in bed. As she had told him to his face, Troy might not always be a nice man, but he *was* good.

She had been wondering all day whether he had gotten down in one piece, but she assumed that he had. She had been wondering all day whether she would see him again, and she hoped that she would. She wasn't ready to allow herself to *fall* in love with this man whom once she had hated, but she was ready to *make* love again.

Jenna bought a bag of chips from the vending machine and stepped outside. The rain that had been falling earlier had stopped, and the sun was fighting to break through the clouds. She had never been in Martinsburg before, but it looked as though people were coming and going more or less as people in any small American city might do. There were SUVs with kids in car seats, and a plumber's pickup with copper pipes gleaming in his overhead rack. The U.S. government had been taken over by forces whom Jenna knew to be forces of darkness, but somebody was still spending a Saturday remodeling a bathroom.

She wondered how many of these people passing by the Greyhound depot had voted for Fachearon. What did they think of what had happened? Not much, apparently. Like Jenna, like most people, they had other things on their minds today.

Back inside, fewer people were watching the television. One group had boarded their bus, bound for Harrisburg. Others, like Jenna, had gone to visit the bank of vending machines. A few had simply dozed off.

Jenna's bus finally arrived, so she missed Layton Kynelty's address to the nation from the White House. She could imagine what he might have said. He probably paid tribute to Raymond Harris, who had been his co-conspirator in this bizarre fantasy that the world seemed to accept as a matter of course. He probably said a great deal about national unity.

She was glad that she had missed it.

An hour out of Martinsburg, Jenna Munrough was fast asleep.

CHAPTER 59

Headquarters, Firehawk, LLC, Herndon, Virginia

"THEY WERE USING FIREHAWK ID CARDS," JENNA'S colleague told her. "But nobody recalls any of the names. It was chaos over there at the airport on Saturday. It was chaos everywhere. There were at least five of them. One of them was a woman, but she drove away with the others in a van when the two guys took the F-16s."

"They just let them get away with it?" Jenna asked, silently noting how wrong the rumors of her own encounter at Reagan National Airport had become. As much as she deplored the inherent sexism in the rumor's distortion of fact, she was glad to discover that the imaginary woman had not been one of the pilots.

"Somehow they got their hands on Firehawk ID, and

on Saturday, *nobody* was questioning Firehawk ID . . . *anywhere*."

Even after this exchange on Sunday, Jenna's decision to go in to the Firehawk offices on Monday morning was made with great trepidation. It need not have been. The media had consulted with itself and had decided to stick with the theory of rogue Air Force pilots— *male* rogues—and once decided, the theory took on an unshakable life of its own.

The Justice Department, the NTSB, and even the U.S. Air Force itself launched investigations—but they sought only people who fit the profile decided upon in this theory with a life of its own.

It was strange to walk through the lobby, with its stylized aluminum rendition of the company logo, a bird's head surrounded by flames, and to hear the buzz of conversation about the death of Raymond Harris.

"Ms. Munrough."

Jenna spun around at the sound of the receptionist calling her name. She was still a bit on edge, still expecting to be busted at any moment.

"Yes?"

"Ms. Munrough, you're wanted at a briefing in the seventh-floor conference room . . . um . . . they asked me to tell all the top management that there's a nine o'clock meeting up there this morning."

"Thanks," Jenna said, breathing a sigh of relief. A

meeting. Even at Firehawk, home office life was a succession of meetings. The bureaucracy must go on. The king is dead—long live the bureaucracy.

She checked the time on her cell phone. She could get a cup of coffee to go and still make the meeting.

As Jenna rounded the corner going into the coffee room, she found herself face-to-face with Lucy, her friend from special projects who had alerted her to the nuclear weapon.

Lucy flashed a glance that asked, *Did you have anything to do with Harris getting killed?*

Jenna replied with one that asked, *Are you kidding? Of course not. Did you?*

Lucy just shook her head, nervous to be accused by Jenna's expression.

"Did they find the thing?" Jenna asked under her breath.

"Yeah," Lucy said nervously as she poured her coffee. "How was your weekend?"

"Fine," Jenna lied for the benefit of a couple of people who came into the coffee room. "I just hung out . . . did some laundry . . . watched a lot of television. How about you?"

"I was down at the White House on Saturday. Avoided the television, myself."

"I know what you mean," Jenna said, taking her coffee and heading toward the elevator that would take her to the rarefied atmosphere of the celebrated seventh floor.

The conference room was filled with all the top home office people, the department heads, and some of the people from Raymond Harris's staff. She recognized Aron Arnold, the pilot whom Harris had recently brought in from Cactus Flat as sort of a fair-haired boy.

Jenna knew Arnold's history with Troy Loensch, though he had little to say about him. She knew of their inauspicious first meeting, but that they had flown together with the HAWX Program.

The mood in the room was one of expectation. With Harris out of the picture, everyone was curious to know what the board of directors might have in mind for Firehawk's future.

This question was answered moments after Jenna set her cup on the table and slung her purse strap over the back of her chair.

An unassuming, middle-aged Hispanic man entered through the door at the opposite corner of the room.

"I'm José Turcios." He smiled. "But most people call me Joe."

With that, he went on to explain that he had been with Firehawk for nearly a dozen years, running special projects and field operations around the world.

"I'm honored to tell you," he continued, "to tell you that the board has named me to succeed Raymond Harris as CEO of Firehawk. They are big shoes to fill and I'm just a size ten."

He paused for the few chuckles that came in reaction to his poor attempt at levity, and continued.

Conspicuously absent in Joe Turcios's comments was the increasingly vitriolic diatribe about the evils of ineffective government that everyone had grown used to hearing from Raymond Harris. Maybe it was that Turcios just had a different style, or perhaps it was simply that the events of the past seventy-two hours simply spoke for themselves.

"The future at Firehawk is promising, and it will obviously be a busy one," Turcios added. "Now that Firehawk and our PMC partners at Cernavoda have the added responsibility of managing the executive branch of the federal government, there will be plenty to keep us busy . . . but I don't want to allow that to detract from our core business of conducting air operations."

For many of the people in the room, who had aviation backgrounds, this was a welcome comment. Even though most were indeed part of the home office bureaucracy, few wanted to think of themselves as bureaucrats.

"With this in mind, I'd like to officially announce that we are going to expand and add additional resources to HAWX, our High Altitude Warfare, Experimental, Program. The future belongs to those who own the technology of the future, and I intend for this to be Firehawk. With that in mind, I'd like to introduce the new head of the HAWX Program. Some of you have met Aron Arnold. He's new to the home office but not to Firehawk. . . ."

As the meeting broke up, Jenna noticed Arnold coming toward her.

"I don't believe we've been formally introduced, Ms. Munrough," he said, extending his hand.

"Might as well call me Jenna. I've seen you around. You're in from Cactus Flat, I hear."

"Yeah, I was there until the general invited me to join him back here a couple of weeks ago . . . and you can call me Aron."

"So, I guess you'll be headed back out to Cactus Flat, Aron?"

"I'm not much of a home office guy." Arnold shrugged. "By the way, I had a chance to fly with Troy Loensch out there. I hear that you were in his Air Force unit over in Sudan?"

"Yeah. I flew with him over there. That's where we first met Harris."

"Too bad about what happened to Loensch," Arnold said. Jenna couldn't detect whether he was being sympathetic or just making conversation.

"Too bad for sure," Jenna replied. She detected no trace of emotion, but then, Arnold struck her as an emotionless individual.

"Helluva way to die . . . lost at sea and all. I was out there at Cactus Flat when the word came in that he had gone down," Arnold said. "We crewed together on a few Shakuru flights before it happened. . . . Actually, that's one thing I wanted to talk to you about."

"What's that?"

"How long has it been since you've been in the cockpit of a high-performance aircraft?" Arnold asked.

Jenna felt herself jump slightly.

What was he asking? What was Raymond Harris's fair-haired boy asking? Did he know? Did he expect her to answer that just two days ago she was in a cockpit shooting Sidewinders at Raymond Harris?

"It's been a while," she answered noncommittally. "Why?"

"Because from what I've heard . . . and seen in your resume, you're the kind of pilot we need at HAWX. I'd like to ask you to consider transferring from Herndon to the HAWX Program."

"Y'all are inviting me to come out to the desert and fly high-altitude stuff?"

"Exactly. I'll talk to Turcios and we'll work it out. Are you interested?"

"Tell me more," Jenna said, unslinging her purse and setting it down on the conference room table.

"We have a lot of new stuff coming on line out there," Arnold said. "I figured you wouldn't mind trading a desk chair for an ejection seat."

"What the hell," Jenna said thoughtfully. "I think this probably *would* be a good time for me to be getting out of Washington for a while."

CHAPTER 60

**Thirty-first Street NW, Georgetown,
Washington, D.C.**

LIMPING SLIGHTLY, TROY MADE HIS WAY UP THE
tree-lined street as the sun hung low in the western sky.
The pain in his leg from the injuries he had suffered on
that mountaintop in Nicaragua was exacerbated by the
hard landing in the Catoctins, but it wasn't as bad today
as it had been on Sunday.

He probably should have cooled out for another
couple of days, bunking anonymously at the YMCA and
slinging pizza dough anonymously at Mr. Mahmud's—
but he was anxious to see Jenna Munrough. He convinced himself that it was to assure himself that she was
all right, that she had survived, but he knew that he

longed to feel her touch. He admitted to himself that he was in love with Jenna.

It was a different kind of love than he had felt for Cassie. Back then, it was a simpler schoolboy-schoolgirl sort of love—after all, they *were* in school, in that insulated and insular world where things are so much less complex. With Jenna, it was a relationship founded on mutual respect. Long before they liked one another, they grew to have a professional respect for each other as pilots. Gradually, respect had grown into friendship, a kind of laughing, joking, disarmed friendship.

From friendship, there followed a mutual lust that had become a component of this friendship. Watching Jenna scream past in her F-16 as he floated earthward in his parachute harness, Troy had felt a powerful surge of longing. Strangely—for him—he longed not so much for his own survival, but for hers. He imagined that this was the moment when a religious person would have said a prayer. Troy longed for them both to get through this ordeal, and to be together. As he crashed into the dogwoods and bundled up his parachute, he thought of their last quiet moment together, that last calm moment before the phone call that catapulted them into the skies over the Washington metro area. He was surprised to find his mind riveted, not on the thrill of sex, but on the way that her soft, smooth shoulder rose and fell rhythmically as she slept. He remembered having watched that for a long, long time. He remembered the two tiny moles behind her shoulder and how he had found himself almost hypnotized by the sound of her breathing.

"I love you, Jenna," Troy had said out loud as he made his way down the mountain. He had said it so effortlessly, and he said it often, hoping beyond all hope that he would have a chance to say it to her in person.

"I love you, Jenna," he shouted, startling some birds whose squawks seemed to torment the man who had thought he'd experienced love before, but who had discovered vastly new dimensions to this emotion.

AS HAD JENNA, TROY READ THE PAPERS, WATCHED the television, and decided that the world truly believed Harris's assailants to be U.S. Air Force pilots. Nevertheless, like Jenna, Troy feared that their escapade in the Maryland skies would not go unpunished in a world in which Firehawk ruled, and in which Troy and Jenna had conspired to kill Firehawk's shining star.

Troy had absorbed the television news voraciously, carefully watching for an item about a dead woman in a parachute hanging from a tree somewhere, or of a Firehawk employee arrested for conspiracy. No such story had appeared, and finally, on the Monday after the infamous Saturday, Troy left work before the dinner rush so that he could be at Jenna's condo complex, waiting and watching for the Porsche.

Troy walked through Georgetown anonymously, as

he had on his previous visits. He walked, not as a moth to a candle, but with the confident anonymity of a man who was already dead.

"Loensch," came a familiar voice, seemingly out of nowhere.

Troy was barely aware of the sound of a car window coming down.

A familiar voice. A familiar face.

"What are *you* doing here?" Troy asked angrily. "Where the fuck have you been for the past week when I've been trying to phone you?"

"Things have been in motion."

"No shit," Troy affirmed. "Where were you when Harris tried to kill me? And how did you find me *here*?"

"I didn't know that Harris tried to kill you, but it looks like he won't get another chance."

"I saw on TV that it was some Air Force pilot that they couldn't find," Troy said.

"We saw you and Munrough running out of here pretty fast on Saturday morning," the CIA man said, half smiling. "It was almost like you were in a hurry to get to the airport."

"If you guys are so good at knowing things like that, how is it that you weren't able to stop this thing on Saturday . . . or are you working for Kynelty now?"

"We're the good guys, Loensch."

"There are guys, and there are guys," Troy said. "I'm not so sure I believe in good guys and bad guys anymore."

"On one level that's true, but there's always more than meets the eye."

"*Who* are you guys, Nagte?" Troy asked. "Who are you, *really*?"

"You've seen our company ID."

"I've heard that your 'company' has been a wholly owned subsidiary of Firehawk and Cernavoda since Saturday morning," Troy retorted.

"They swallowed some pretty large fish when they swallowed the executive branch on Saturday. I don't think that they'll ever fully digest them, and I predict a spate of indigestion when the euphoria of that meal fades."

"What do you want with *me*?" Troy asked. "You wanted Harris compromised, and he's about as compromised as he can be. I'd say that the job you asked me to do is finished."

"I think the job is only just beginning."

"I'm through," Troy insisted. "I've got to go . . . gotta check on a friend."

"She came through it in good shape," the enigmatic CIA man said. "Just want you to know that she's okay. Back on the job today, in fact."

"At Firehawk . . . at Herndon?"

"I'm sure that you'll hear all about it."

"I'm sure. Now, if you'll excuse me, I'm out of here, and I hope you guys can carry on without me."

"This thing isn't over, Loensch," Nagte said somberly. "It isn't over by any stretch of the imagination."

Unleash the FEROCIOUS SKILLS of
RENEGADE AGENT, Sam Fisher
TOM CLANCY'S
SPLINTER
CELL
CONVICTION™
You've read the book,
NOW PLAY THE
GAME!
COMING MARCH 2010
www.splintercell.com
RATING PENDING
RP
CONTENT RATED BY
ESRB
May contain content inappropriate for children. Visit www.esrb.org for rating information.
© 2009 Ubisoft Entertainment. All Rights Reserved. Splinter Cell, Splinter Cell Conviction, Sam Fisher, the Soldier Icon, Ubisoft, Ubi.com and the Ubisoft logo are trademarks of Ubisoft Entertainment in the U.S. and/or other countries.
UBISOFT

M560OA0809

Tom Clancy's
SPLINTER CELL®

WRITTEN BY DAVID MICHAELS

penguin.com

M223AS0809